Sleepless in Southampton

The Hellion Club, Book Four

by Chasity Bowlin

Dragonblade Publishing, Inc. is an imprint of Kathryn Le Veque Novels, Inc.
P.O. Box 7968
La Verne CA 91750
ceo@dragonbladepublishing.com

Produced in the United States of America

First Edition July 2021
Print Edition

ARE YOU SIGNED UP FOR DRAGONBLADE'S BLOG?

You'll get the latest news and information on exclusive giveaways, exclusive excerpts, coming releases, sales, free books, cover reveals and more.

Check out our complete list of authors, too!

No spam, no junk. That's a promise!

Sign Up Here

www.dragonbladepublishing.com

Dearest Reader;

Thank you for your support of a small press. At Dragonblade Publishing, we strive to bring you the highest quality Historical Romance from the some of the best authors in the business. Without your support, there is no 'us', so we sincerely hope you adore these stories and find some new favorite authors along the way.

Happy Reading!

CEO, Dragonblade Publishing

Additional Dragonblade books by
Author Chasity Bowlin

The Lyon's Den Connected World
Fall of the Lyon

The Hellion Club Series
A Rogue to Remember
Barefoot in Hyde Park
What Happens in Piccadilly
Sleepless in Southampton
When an Earl Loves a Governess
The Duke's Magnificent Obsession
The Governess Diaries

The Lost Lords Series
The Lost Lord of Castle Black
The Vanishing of Lord Vale
The Missing Marquess of Althorn
The Resurrection of Lady Ramsleigh
The Mystery of Miss Mason
The Awakening of Lord Ambrose
A Midnight Clear (A Novella)
Hyacinth

Prologue

LORD HENRY MEREDITH, Viscount Marchwood, stared at the broken wheel of his carriage and uttered a mild curse. They were not even fully out of London yet. He could still see the heavy cloud of soot that marked the city behind them as it hovered just above the tree line. Not that he'd had any great desire to go to London anyway. He detested being in town and was far more content at his country estate. But alas, prior to his jaunt to Hampshire, he'd been summoned by his cousin who was having some issues with his eldest progeny and gambling. In fact, his younger cousin had been sent down from University and rather than returning to the family fold, had fled to Hampshire himself.

Recalling the conversation with his cousin, Horace, and Horace's pleading look as he'd stated, *"But you're going to Southampton anyway. Surely it won't be too much of a bother to have a word with him, will it?"*

It would, actually. But as always, Henry felt he didn't have the luxury of saying no. He never refused them anything and that was part of his frustration now. He had a limited amount of time and a new task added to his schedule.

Glancing at the coachman who appeared far less concerned about the matter than he should, Henry demanded, "I asked you to have that wheel replaced a week ago. Not just repaired—again—but replaced." Was it his lot in life to be so "nice" that even his own servants had no fear of reprisal for blatantly disobeying his edicts? Of course, it was hardly an edict when he always phrased it as a request.

"Aye, m'lord. But it were so expensive to replace when patching it would do," the driver protested in his heavy brogue.

Henry blinked at the man in disbelief. Was he truly so lacking in spine that even his servants felt disobeying direct instructions was without consequence? "Clearly just patching it did not do. If it had, I wouldn't be standing on the side of the road four miles out of London."

The coachman had the grace to look somewhat sheepish. "I can have a new one made and have it on by the morning."

Henry sighed. It wouldn't work. He'd promised his aunt that he would be in Southampton by the following day. There was much to do in advance of his uncle's birthday. After all, the Duke of Thornhill's fiftieth birthday was not an occasion to be missed. The entire family was gathering at the seaside to spend several weeks together at the family's estate there. Southampton had become their gathering place of choice given poor Philippa's deteriorating condition. The resort town with access to many spas and sites for sea bathing made it a good destination for them. The less strenuous and active social whirl, as compared to Brighton and Bath—or heaven forbid, London—made it perfect for them. Of course, it wasn't just his uncle's birthday which made time of the essence. There was the other matter for his cousin.

If he was to catch the boy still at the Duke of Wellington Inn in Southampton, he'd need to move quickly. Indeed, if someone didn't step in and take the reins, young Julian could find himself in a world of trouble. Julian was getting into a great deal of trouble and a great deal of debt that his branch of the family had no means of correcting.

Still, it wasn't entirely duty and obligation. The notion of gathering with his family in its entirety, when he spent so much time alone, was something he'd been anticipating for a while. He enjoyed his aunt's and uncle's company, so long as they weren't throwing potential brides in his path. And spending time with his cousin was always a welcome respite from estate management and endless rows of columns that had to be added and subtracted and balanced. Henry had long suspected that he wasn't cut out to be a gentleman of leisure. He'd have much preferred working in the fields to working on an account book. Being locked in a study all day poring over documents was not the life he wanted for himself.

He couldn't say precisely where it came from, but a feeling of restlessness had been slowly creeping over him. It was a feeling of being unsettled by the sameness of his days, a need to escape his ever growing sense of ennui and the resentment his position as heir apparent had sparked inside him. Perhaps having his seemingly well-ordered travel plans interrupted was a blessing in disguise.

"Burton, how long has it been since I've done something irresponsible?" Henry asked.

"Far as I know, you've never done anything irresponsible, so I couldn't rightly say, my lord," the coachman replied, his tone cautious as if perhaps he thought his employer was ready for Bedlam.

"Neither could I," Henry mused. "In fact, for the last several years, I've done nothing that wasn't related to managing my own estate or preparing for the heavy workload of managing those my uncle will leave in my care."

"Yes, my lord." Now the coachman was simply humoring him, agreeing with whatever he said in order to not get sacked.

He could be angry or frustrated. He could fire his longtime coachman or castigate the man right there in the middle of the road. But ultimately, Henry decided to go a different route—a route that might, even if just for a day, give him a chance to alter that sameness which was weighing so heavily on him. If one chose to look at it in a more favorable light, he was being presented with an opportunity. "There's an inn a mile or so up ahead where the public stage stops, isn't there?" Henry asked.

The coachman nodded, but his expression had gone from slightly wary to entirely skeptical and perhaps even scandalized. "Aye, my lord. But a gentleman such as you on a public stage is hardly—"

Henry walked away abruptly. His motions were brisk, purposeful and quite decisive as he opened one of the small trunks strapped to the back of the carriage. After rifling through it for a moment, he emerged victorious having found what he was looking for. An older coat with a frayed cuff and a waistcoat that was more plain and of slightly less luxurious materials were clutched in his hands. By adjusting his wardrobe, he could alter his position in the eyes of others quite easily. Rather than a wealthy viscount who was heir to a duke, he might now be taken for a second or even third son, perhaps a clerk or even a would-be cleric. In short, he could be someone else, at least for a day.

Without even checking to be certain anyone was about, he switched them out there on the roadside and then reappeared. "Now, I'll blend with my fellow travelers."

The coachman looked dubious. "My lord, I think it's a very bad idea. There's all sorts on the public coach—"

"Get that wheel replaced, Burton, then return to Haverton Abbey. I'll hire a coach when I return," Henry instructed one last time and then began marching down the road. He needed to get there in time to get on the next coach to Southampton. Besides, it was an adventure. He needed an adventure. He needed something in his life that was not expected, that was not determined by others, and that would allow him to forget that he was not only a viscount, but the heir apparent to a dukedom with vast wealth and properties to be maintained. In short, he was running away from his life, albeit temporarily. And it felt marvelous.

"YOU'RE CERTAIN ABOUT this?"

Miss Sophia Upchurch, or Sophie as she preferred, checked her valise once more, making certain that it was properly fastened. "I'm quite certain," she replied.

Miss Euphemia Darrow sighed heavily. "You are the youngest of my pupils to set out on her own, Sophie. I know you're tired of hearing it, but I'm very worried. You are only just eighteen, after all. And while many of the other girls were of a similar age to you, they were—well, they knew much more of the world than you do. I fear I have sheltered you too much."

Sophie let out her own sigh. She'd been with Effie since she was so young she couldn't recall where or whom she'd been with before. She'd been left on Effie's door like a foundling with a hefty sum of money to cover her care and education and a note that promised more would be forthcoming so long as she remained there. It was an old and familiar story to her, but she was still very grateful to Effie for taking her in when the Darrow School had never been intended for children as young as she had been at that time. It was so much more than a school. It was her home and its occupants were her family. "Effie, I will be fine. Why, I'll be there long before nightfall even. Besides, you've met Lady Parkhurst. She's very respectable!"

"And utterly horrid," Effie replied with a grim expression. She reached over and adjusted the collar of Sophie's pelisse. "I don't have favorites, Sophie. It would be terrible of me to do so. In truth, I love all of my girls. Every one of you that has crossed that threshold has become my family, like my own daughters, and I simply adore you all. But you are very special to me. You were such a tiny thing when you first came that perhaps my feelings toward you do tend to be much more maternal than for some of the other girls."

"I love you, Effie. And yes, for all intents and purposes, you are my mother and I could not have asked for better," Sophie admitted. "But I can't simply hide behind your skirts forever. I have to start making my way in the world. The more birds that fly from your nest, the more room there will be for new ones who need you, too. Also, it is terribly unfair to the other girls that they should have to become independent while you continue to support me! Not to mention that this is an excellent opportunity."

Effie nodded. "I could at least see you all the way to Southampton. There is no need to take the public coach!"

Sophie bit the inside of her cheek to keep from laughing. "Yes, because all servants are delivered to their employer's doorstep in a fashionable barouche! No, Effie. I will take the public coach as befits my station and you will stop worrying. It's one day's travel time along a route that is well trafficked and quite safe. I shall be at Lady Parkhurst's before nightfall and ready to begin my duties."

Effie threw her hands up as she stepped back. There were tears in her eyes. "Fine. You're right. I know that you are and that I'm worrying needlessly. You are a very good girl and a very smart and capable one. I have taught you well and prepared you for every eventuality that I could foresee. But it's the ones which I could not foresee—those leave me utterly petrified. Be careful. Promise me that you will."

"I will," Sophie promised.

"And if Lady Parkhurst is too difficult, you will come home," Effie stated. "There are other positions. You need not be miserable and bullied by her."

"She surely will not be so bad," Sophie protested. Actually, she could possibly. During their one meeting the woman had been sour and contrary. But she'd also been amusing, though that amusement might wear thin after a while as it had tended to be rather mean-spirited in nature. "I can do this, Effie. I'm ready."

As if on cue, the coach pulled in then and the bustling activity of the busy inn suddenly doubled. It became so noisy that not a word could be heard between them. So they both said a silent goodbye, punctuated with a long hug as Sophie climbed into the coach with the assistance of the driver and settled herself on one of the ill-sprung seats. A glance through the grimy window showed Effie still standing in the inn yard watching, her face etched with worry, as the coach pulled away.

I will not fail, Sophie vowed to herself. *I will not be cowed and I will not come running back to cling to Effie's apron strings.*

Chapter One

THE PUBLIC COACH was not at all what she'd expected. One hour into the journey and that was abundantly clear. Admittedly, Sophie's existence had been fairly sheltered. Even living all of her life in London and witnessing some of the more unfortunate aspects of poverty and vice from afar, she had not quite been prepared for it in such close proximity. The woman beside her reeked of gin. The man on the opposite seat leered at her despite his ecclesiastical garb and the Bible that remained in his hand at all times.

She'd been trying desperately to concentrate on the book she'd brought to read but the jostling of the coach with its worn springs and lumpy seats had made it nearly impossible. Glancing up, she once again caught the vicar staring at her in a way that made her terribly uncomfortable. Hunching her shoulders forward, she wanted nothing more than to disappear into the seat. Unfortunately, that allowed her already drunken seat mate to list sideways until Sophie found herself crushed beneath the woman's not insignificant heft.

"Blue ruin," the vicar uttered in a stage whisper. It was accompanied with a very inappropriate wink.

Sophie didn't reply. She simply tried to prop the woman's nearly limp form up as best as possible. Thankfully, the coach began to slow, easing into the yard of a busy inn presumably to pick up more passengers as they were far from full. The change in pace awakened her fellow traveler who turned and glared at Sophie as if she were somehow the offending party.

"I got my eye on you!" the woman warned, jabbing a very round and stubby finger near Sophie's face just as the coach rocked to a jarring halt. "I'll not be robbed by some whey-faced trollop!" With that, the woman and the vicar both left the coach and made for the inn.

Uncertain whether to be more offended by being called whey-faced or a trollop, Sophie contented herself with disembarking from the vehicle and strolling about the inn yard for a moment. Mindful of her surroundings and careful to stay well in sight of the building, she did so just long enough to stretch her legs. When she returned to the coach, she faced a quandary. She could resume her previous seat and have that alarmingly aggressive and increasingly intoxicated woman as her neighbor for the duration or she could take her chances with the vicar and his winks and wandering eyes. She was very concerned that perhaps more than his eyes might wander if she were to be in such proximity to him.

At that moment, the coach door swung open and a large shadow filled the doorway. It then gave way to the large frame of a gentleman climbing inside the small vehicle. Sophie glanced only at his clothing, noting that it appeared to be clean and of good quality if somewhat worn. He looked far more appropriate than her other traveling companions, though given that one of those companions was actually a vicar, the irony of it was not lost on her.

"Is this seat taken?" he said, pointing to the spot next to the vicar's recently emptied seat.

"No. It's vacant," she replied. Then inspiration struck. "But—" Sophie stopped. It was terribly inappropriate. It might also cause quite a row, but did she have a better option? No. She did not.

"But?" he queried.

"Well, I don't suppose you would consider sharing this seat with me? It's just the woman sitting here is a bit of drinker and perhaps a bit of a brawler, as well and... the vicar who is occupying that seat... well, I'd prefer not to sit with him if I have any other options," she finished lamely. "I think perhaps he is not well-suited to being part of the clergy. The best word I can think of to describe him is... lecherous. You must think me quite horrid!"

Other than a raised eyebrow, he said nothing. Instead, he simply moved to take the seat next to hers and settled in.

Sophie sighed. "Thank you so very much. I know it's a terrible imposition, but I'm very grateful!" She turned to face him fully and then realized that she might have made a terrible error in judgment. When he'd first entered the carriage, she'd simply made an assumption based on the value of his clothing that he was a gentleman. But his face had been concealed by the shadows of the carriage and she'd had no notion of what he actually looked like. Now, seated and with the sunlight pouring in, she could see that he was terribly handsome. With chiseled features and kind brown eyes, his hair was dark as well, though perhaps with gold streaks woven into the rich brown strands. He looked like a man who enjoyed the outdoors, a man who would ride and hunt and shoot. He also looked very much like a man who could turn a girl's head. And she was a girl who could not afford to have her head turned.

"It's no imposition at all," he answered. "Having a pretty girl ask me to sit beside her is the best part of my day thus far. I have good company and get to fancy myself a chivalrous hero in the process."

Sophie felt herself blushing, the heat of it rising in her cheeks. Without conscious thought, she ducked her head, tucking an errant curl back into her bonnet and then glanced up at him through lowered lashes. "Thank you again."

"For sitting beside you?"

Sophie's blush deepened. "For that, yes... and for the compliment."

"You are very welcome for both," he replied. "I realize it isn't exactly the done thing, but I feel, under the circumstances—my heroics in choosing to brave the wrath of my fellow travelers by taking up this particular perch—I should at least have the benefit of knowing your name."

"Miss Sophia Upchurch," Sophie answered, hating that her voice sounded slightly breathless and tremulous. "And your name, sir?"

⋙⋘

IT WASN'T IN his nature to lie. And in truth, it wasn't a lie. It simply wasn't the entirety of the truth. "Henry Meredith," he answered, omitting his title. Impetuous, unplanned, and yet he didn't regret it. No sooner had he stated that than he felt as if a weight had been lifted from him. It felt good to just be Henry, not to be Marchwood. Not to be the heir apparent to the Duke of Thornhill. For that moment, sitting on a public stage with a very pretty girl who clearly only smiled at him because she liked him and was grateful that he might have spared her the discomfort of an unpleasant neighbor. She had no knowledge of and therefore no interest in his title or his prospects. For the first time in a very long time, he didn't have to question whether or not it was his wealth, his position or his well-mapped future that prompted the pretty smile of a woman who'd caught his eye.

Caught his eye. Henry tamped down that particular line of thought. It sounded as if he were considering her for a potential bride. He wasn't in the market for one of those, and if he were to bring home some young woman he met on a public coach, regardless of how proper she appeared in her prim pelisse and traveling gown, his aunt and uncle would have apoplexy. Well, actually they would probably only be grateful he'd decided to seriously pursue a woman. Of course, if he wanted a bride, no one's opinion but his own would or should matter. But he wasn't looking for marriage. Not yet. He was much too

11

young. No. He would just enjoy a brief flirtation with her and then they would go their separate ways. After all, he'd uttered that half-truth and damned himself with it. He could never pursue anything further with her, even if he desired to, not without coming clean.

"Tell me, Miss Upchurch, are you traveling to Brighton?" He posed the question as much as a distraction from his own spiraling thoughts as a way of getting to know her better.

"No, only as far as Southampton. I've obtained a position as a companion to an elderly lady there," she answered softly.

That complicated things. She would be in Southampton. He would be in Southampton. She would be a companion to a woman of some means. Which meant they could potentially cross paths again.

The other travelers returned to the coach then, a somewhat wea-selly-looking vicar climbing in first followed by a woman who appeared to be foxed already though it wasn't even eleven in the morning yet. Her ruddy cheeks and the broken veins in her rather bulbous nose indicated that it was a fairly common occurrence. Still, rough and possibly disreputable as they were, they were welcome because it again pulled him back from spiraling thoughts that might have him confessing his title—the very thing he was running from—to her.

"You're in my seat!" the woman snapped, leveling a menacing glare at Miss Upchurch.

"Are there assigned seats on a public conveyance?" Henry asked. "If so, it must be a fairly recent policy." There was no such policy in place and they all knew it. In most cases, it was simply a matter of being nice and minding ones manners that kept order on public transportation. But given that the pretty and very sweet girl sitting beside him appeared to be genuinely and reasonably anxious of the woman, his bad manners were warranted.

"Not a policy," she sneered mockingly. "But I was sitting there 'fore we stopped!"

"Well, you may sit on the other side of the coach now," Henry replied. "There are ample seats available, fortunately."

The woman grumbled again, but seeing that he wouldn't be cowed, she made her way to the other seat and settled in, glowering at him the whole while. If he had achieved nothing else, he had at least managed to shift her ire from Miss Upchurch to himself. Henry simply smiled.

"Are you going on to Brighton, Mr. Meredith?" Miss Upchurch asked softly. The question was clearly an effort to defuse the tension amongst the coach's inhabitants.

Henry turned to her and spoke softly. "No. As a matter of fact, I will also be ending my journey in Southampton. I'm going to visit family there. Nothing so exciting as your journey... embarking on a new position in a new city. You're quite brave, Miss Upchurch, to take on such challenges."

The drunken woman across the way let out a snort and rolled her eyes. Henry cast a baleful stare in her direction while Miss Upchurch simply laughed nervously and played with the ties to her bonnet, wrapping the ribbon about her fingers.

"I'm not certain how challenging my position as a companion will truly be... though, I think my employer is referred to as something of an eccentric," Miss Upchurch answered sheepishly. "Still, it will be an adventure, I hope."

The twinkle in her pretty eyes as she said it, the slight dimple in her cheek and the way the sunlight burnished the red-gold curls just visible beneath her bonnet—Henry was completely charmed by her. When she smiled, her nose crinkled just a bit, animating the smattering of freckles there. Not the traditional beauty, but a beauty nonetheless, he thought. *What if he did want to see her again? What if braving her temper by confessing the concealment of his identity wasn't such a terrible idea?* "And who is this eccentric woman? I have some degree of familiarity with Southampton's higher society."

"Her name is Lady Parkhurst. Do you know her?" Miss Upchurch asked.

He did know her. She was a close acquaintance to his aunt and uncle, unfortunately. Which meant that his identity would likely be discovered whether he confessed it or not. "Not well, I'm afraid. Mostly by reputation." It wasn't a lie, he reasoned. No one knew Lady Parkhurst well. The woman was more prickly than a hedgehog and made it a point not to be well known to anyone save for her circle of gossipy harpies. He did have a moment of pity for poor Miss Up-church, though. Lady Parkhurst was not at all an easy person to deal with.

"Oh," she said, somewhat let down. "I thought perhaps you might be able to offer some insight into her personality and how I might best proceed with her. This is actually my first position since graduating from the Darrow School." The admission was offered in a hushed tone, as if she were somewhat embarrassed by her lack of work experience.

Henry kept his expression neutral but the Darrow School was known to him. It was known to everyone. While not exactly scandalous by nature, the origins of many of the school's students were steeped in scandal and secrets of the most salacious nature. Euphemia Darrow, a by-blow herself, had taken the sizable fortune her father had settled on her and used it to establish a school where she could care for and train fellow illegitimate daughters of the nobility so that they could provide for themselves through respectable employment. There were many conversations that occurred at parties and clubs about which of the students of the Darrow School had been sired by which lord. In fact, he was fairly certain there were bets on the books at both White's and Boodle's regarding whether or not specific gentlemen were paying tuition there.

"The Darrow School? It's quite infamous, I do believe," he commented. A glance across the way showed the drunken woman to be sleeping, or more likely simply passed out. The lecherous vicar, however, was all ears.

"I suppose it is," she agreed. "Though I can't imagine why people would find it so very interesting. It's just a school, after all. Not so different than any other despite the somewhat unusual parentage of its pupils."

He didn't argue the point. He couldn't help but wonder if her opinion was a reflection of her own insecurity about its notoriety or if it reflected instead her naïveté about where it was that she'd spent her life and received her education. In her plain dress and plainer bonnet, it was clear to him that Miss Darrow had schooled her students on how to blend into the wallpaper and not be noticed. It was, he supposed, a way of protecting oneself as a woman alone in the world. "How old were you when you became a student there?"

"Oh, I've always been there," Miss Upchurch answered. "I cannot recall a time when I was elsewhere. Alas, I was too young to be a true pupil when I first arrived there, but Effie—Miss Darrow—has been most excellent to me over the years. She has treated me more like a daughter than a student."

"So you have no family?" he asked. It brought the sting of guilt. He was complaining about his own, hiding from them, in truth. And for the day at least, pretending they did not exist. And yet the young woman beside him was alone entirely.

"None that I am aware of," Miss Upchurch answered. "I was left at the Darrow School as a foundling. I was quite fortunate that Effie— Miss Darrow—was sympathetic to my plight rather than sending me to a workhouse or an orphanage as so many might have. But Effie is all that is kind and generous. I should hope one day that I might manage to be just like her."

She said it rather plainly, as if she weren't discussing something that was completely heartbreaking. To be abandoned and alone, to be dependent on the love and care of strangers as an innocent child—it was something he couldn't quite imagine. Yet she had lived it, and seemed not the least bit jaded by the experience. There was no hardness or bitterness in her and he found himself quite taken with her for that. He found himself quite taken with her for any number of reasons.

"I'm sorry for that, Miss Upchurch, and for bringing up something that must surely be painful for you," he offered in sincere apology. The last thing he'd ever want to do is cause such a bright and beautiful young woman any pain. *So, tell her who you are. Stop lying to her.*

"Honestly, I can't recall anything but Effie," she admitted with a soft laugh and a shrug. "And one could not ask for a kinder or more caring person to rear them. I have no regrets about how my life has turned out. I feel very, very blessed. Do not trouble yourself on that account, Mr. Meredith. I am quite content with what I have been granted in life." Her reassurance was accompanied with a sweet and winsome smile.

He was simply astounded by her and what appeared to be her truly astonishing resilience. "What a remarkable person you are, Miss Upchurch, to have so much positivity… no doubt your generous spirit is a testament to the kindness of your Miss Darrow."

There was another pretty blush and Henry then turned the conversation toward more pleasant things and things more pertinent to her current situation. "What do you know of Southampton, Miss Upchurch? And what are your interests that I might offer some insight as to activities there you will enjoy?"

"I have never seen the sea before," she admitted with a twinkle in her eyes. "Naturally, I know that what I'm seeing at Southampton is more of an estuary but, still, I'm quite curious about the natural beauty of the seashore and about the opportunities for sea bathing!"

And so for the remainder of their journey, Henry acted as a sort of tour guide, regaling her with information about Southampton and the many delights it could offer. It occurred to him during their journey that she and Philippa were of an age. He regretted that they would not have the opportunity to meet and become friends for he could only think that Miss Sophia Upchurch would be an excellent influence for his very isolated young cousin.

Chapter Two

"WHAT DO YOU mean *dead*?"

"I mean just that, Miss. Dead. Dead as a doornail. Ashes to ashes and all that bit," the small rather puckish man offered with a slightly elfin grin. As he did so, he raised an apple to his chest and attempted to polish it on his shirt. It appeared that he deposited more dirt than he removed. Standing in the elegant doorway of Lady Parkhurst's townhome, he looked remarkably out of place. Which begged the question, who had hired such a man? Surely it had not been the very discriminating Lady Parkhurst!

Sophie stared at him for a moment longer, willing the words to make sense. She'd been hired by a dead woman. Well, no. She'd been hired by a woman who had subsequently died. But the particulars of that did nothing to improve her current situation. She was miles and miles from London on the promise of a position that apparently no longer existed. There was not a soul in Southampton she could call on to ask for assistance. *And she'd told Effie she would be fine.*

"But I've come all this way. She hired me to be her companion!" Sophie protested, as much to the fates as to the poorly chosen caretaker in front of her. She'd braved the public coach, though really it had not been the ordeal she'd imagined it might be thanks to Mr. Meredith and his delightful company. Still, her nerves about it had been quite real and quite distressing.

"Well, won't be much in need for company now will she? Nor, dare I say, would you have wanted to join her where she's gone off to!" The little man cackled at that, thought about it for a moment, became even more amused at his own witticism and then cackled harder. When he'd managed to stop slapping his knee in amusement and his laughter had died away to a sort of wheezing, gasping rattle of a cough, he added, "Wicked old bird, she was. No one'll be missing her. I reckon you dodged it, all right. Shame you've come all this way for nothing though."

It wasn't a shame. It was a catastrophe. A calamitous confluence of events that she might one day laugh about, but not this day. Nor likely any of the days that would immediately follow. This was the sort of very costly and very difficult situation that it would take years to appreciate the absurdity of, if ever. Shaking her head, Sophie began mentally calculating exactly how many coins she had remaining in her reticule. Would she even be able to pay the fare to get her back to London? To buy food while she waited for the public coach? A glance at the darkening sky was only a confirmation of yet more difficulties. It would be night soon and she was alone.

"Of course, I suppose there's other types of work for a girl like you," he offered suggestively. "Bit plain, but you'll do."

"I'm a lady's companion. Or a governess. Those are the only positions that I would ever consent to," Sophie stated firmly. She didn't fully grasp what the man was implying but it was very clear to her that he was implying something.

"Can't be a companion to a dead woman," he remarked. Then, once again finding himself humorous, he cackled loudly. "Well, you can if you like, I guess! Might as well be a dead woman I'm cuddling up with my wife!"

"I'm sorry, but what are you talking about?" Sophie demanded.

"You can hear, can't you?" the man asked. "Wouldn't be much of a companion if you were deaf! She's gone off to meet her maker, love, whether that be above or below. No work for you here now! Not the sort you're interested in no ways."

Sophie just stared at him. "But... I'll need transportation back to London."

"I need a miracle to cure my aching back and for my wife to be struck mute. We all needs things, Miss. Don't rightly mean we'll get them," he chortled, clearly amused by his own low witticisms.

"Surely you can at least provide transport given the nature of the situation? I traveled here on good faith expecting a paid position," she reasoned, but softened her blunt words with a smile, hoping to appeal to his higher sensibilities. *Assuming he had them.*

"No can do, Miss. Wish I could help, but it's done for. Carriage she used has already been sold off on orders of the executioner of her estate."

"Executor," Sophie corrected automatically.

"What I said," the man snapped, his puckish face now appearing quite belligerent as he crossed his arms over his chest and glowered at her.

"What am I to do? Perhaps you could reach out the executor of her estate and ask for assistance on my behalf?" she suggested.

"I could ask a hundred times and a hundred times that blighter'd say no. You're on your own here, Miss. No transportation to be provided, I'm afraid! Next stage leaves in the morning and you'll have to wait at the inn with the rest of the travelers!"

In the morning. After she, an unmarried woman whose livelihood depended on her ability to maintain a sterling reputation, spent the night at an inn without any sort of chaperone. "Sir, you must understand, I came here to be employed as a companion, but I am not the sort of young woman who would simply sit overnight in the common room of an inn. I'm a graduate of the Darrow School!"

At that, his expression hardened. "Well, you ain't exactly the sort that can afford to do otherwise, now are you? The inn, Miss, or the street. Choice be yours."

"Those are my only options?"

Apparently he wasn't completely without sympathy, despite his earlier suggestions about what other positions she might be suited to. "The inn is your only option. Girl like you can't be on the street. It can be a rough town here if you're not careful. Take a right at the corner and keep walking until you see the church. The inn is just beyond it!"

With that, the elegantly carved door was closed in Sophie's face with a resounding thud. If she were given to fits of hysterics or flights of fancy, she could imagine that it was the very sound of all future doors closing in her face when it was discovered that her reputation was not above reproach. All of Effie's dire warnings about how important it was to always maintain the appearance of being a lady in public, even if they were only governesses and companions, all came rushing back in a veritable cacophony in her mind. She'd promised Effie she was ready, promised her that she could make her way alone in the world. Now she would have to return home, to the Darrow School, with her tail tucked like a whipped dog. And that was on the presumption that she could even get home!

Sophie sniffed, her eyes suspiciously damp. But she wouldn't cry. Crying was pointless. It only wasted time and energy and left her with an aching head, a splotchy face and a red nose. Instead, she'd focus on doing what was required to get herself safely back to London with as little impropriety as possible.

No one knows you. Just because your name is Sophia Upchurch doesn't mean you have to tell anyone it is. Women and men alike have certainly assumed identities for less honorable purposes than simply preserving their reputations. Use your head, Sophie.

It was as if Effie herself were speaking to Sophia. She could hear the dry and slightly amused tone of the other woman's voice almost as if they were having an actual conversation rather than her own fevered imaginings leading her down a rosy path.

"I will be Miss Sophia Darlington," she decided, whispering the new moniker aloud as if to make it more real. "No. Mrs. Sophia Darlington. A widow. NO! Not a widow. People might ask what he died of and then what would I say? No. He's working in the city and I'm traveling to London to join him. Yes! I can make do. I can get through this without ruining my reputation and my employment prospects," she declared, talking to herself. If the little man on the other side of the door had heard her, there was no indication of it. Just as well. Glancing down at the bags stacked by her feet, Sophie gave a weary sigh. It was only two valises but they'd be terribly heavy to carry for a long way. Still, she could hardly leave them on the doorstep.

Baggage in hand, Sophie turned and climbed carefully down the steps, following the man's very vague directions on how to get back to the inn. She had very little in the way of funds, having been extravagant and hiring a hack to bring her from the coaching inn to Lady Parkhurst's home. It would be a miracle if she had enough to see her back to London, and that was if she didn't eat or drink anything between now and then. But she had no position. The letters of reference that had been written for her, one from Effie and one from Lady Broadmore, for whom she'd worked for a short time in town, filling in for another of Effie's students, were locked away amongst Lady Parkhurst's things, or heaven forbid, simply discarded as unimportant by the executor that had handled her estate. She had no references, no position, limited funds, and no prospects.

As if to punctuate the dire nature of her current circumstances, at that very moment, the heavens opened and a rain began to fall. It was cold enough to make her doubt that it was June. It splashed against the paving stones with such force that it seemed almost as if it were raining up and down at the same time. Surely such a rain could only fall in the midst of a harsh winter?

Sophie sighed, hitched her bags a bit higher, noting that the longer she carried them the heavier they felt, and marched on. As she did so, the street narrowed. The houses took on a less affluent appearance. The stone exteriors were no longer shiny and new, but stained with age and soot. There was an occasional gap in the shutters and bits of refuse on the street. Had she gone the wrong way? She must have gotten turned around leaving Lady Parkhurst's and gone the opposite direction she should have.

"It will be all right," she told herself, as she turned about and headed back the way she had come. "It is difficult now, but in two days' time, I will be back in my comfortable room at the Darrow School and Effie will know exactly what to do."

And then a tiny form barreled into her, sending Sophie and her bags crashing to the wet paving stones as her arms pinwheeled about her. She was too off-center, her balance beyond precarious, and Sophie went down hard, her backside connecting with the hard edge of the stone stairs of the house behind her and her head smacking against an iron railing.

Before she could even catalog her injuries or take stock of her damaged property, the child who had bumped into her reached down, snatched up her fallen reticule and made off with it. The little beast moved so quickly she had no hope of catching him. Or her. She honestly didn't even know if it was a boy or girl. What she did know was that it was a disaster... a complete and utter disaster.

Half. Half her funds were in the reticule. The other half had been hidden in one of her valises which had thankfully been left behind. Still, it would not be enough to see her safely back to London. It wouldn't get her anywhere. What on earth was she to do?

HENRY WAS SIPPING an ale, still waiting for his cousin to arrive. He'd been assured by his cousin that Julian would be at the Duke of Wellington Inn. Horace had even shown him the last letter from the boy with that as his direction and every indication in the letter that he would be there for some time to come. Why the task of putting the boy on the straight and narrow had fallen to him when he was only a few years Julian's senior was anyone's guess. Though truthfully, Henry had been inheriting tasks and being volunteered for the duties no one else in the family wanted for years. And those tasks were many. That particular branch of the family were two things—incredibly stupid and incredibly fertile. They managed to produce one generation after another of utter imbeciles who courted disaster and ruin at every turn and each generation was significantly more numerous than the last.

Julian had inherited a rather particular brand of stupidity. He'd bet on anything. Literally, anything. And always, it was met with disastrous and expensive results. The boy was on the verge of ruin. He'd already squandered his allowance and was living off credit from friends.

A glance at his watch produced a sigh from Henry. He could not wait much longer. There was no sign of Julian. And there was every possibility that Julian was not there at all. If the boy thought he was in trouble, he might have tried to conceal his true location to avoid consequences. His cousin needed to take himself straight to London, beg his father's forgiveness and pray that he could get back into University before his future was utterly ruined. But that required Julian to do the thing he was already struggling with—behaving responsibly.

The truth, of course, was that his current mood had very little to do with his would-be wastrel cousin or his other problematic relations. It had far more to do with the lovely young woman he'd met on the public coach that morning. A woman that, by his own albeit unintentional design, he could never see again. He had lied to her. He had presented her with a, not necessarily fabricated but certainly heavily edited, false identity.

He had, by the time the coach had reached its stop in Southampton, elected to tell her the truth and beg her forgiveness. He'd wanted to arrange to call on her. But in the bustle and turmoil with debarking and boarding of other passengers, just as the mail coach pulled in, he'd lost sight of her. He'd searched the common rooms and discovered, much to his dismay, that Miss Upchurch was nowhere to be found. She'd hired a hack and taken herself off to the home of her employer, as it should be. Still, he regretted not having a chance to set things right before she left. It would only make it even more impossible if their paths crossed again.

Perhaps, he thought, he could write to her at Lady Parkhurst's and confess the truth of his identity. How on earth was he to explain it all? *Oh, by the way, I lied to you from the moment of our first introduction.* It hardly boded well for any future interactions. Of course, the option remained to continue embellishing the truth and he could compound one lie with others. He could tell her that he'd only recently come into the title and was not yet accustomed to using it. But the more lies told multiplied the risk of discovery, not to mention that it simply didn't sit well with him, so that was not a favorable option. His lark had turned into something quite complicated.

"Damn it all," he muttered to himself. She was the first girl he'd met since he'd come into the title who held any interest for him. And perhaps it was because he knew her shy, flirtatious smiles had been directed at the man and not the impending dukedom, but he found himself wishing fervently that he might see that smile again. He would have to find some way to repair the damage he'd inadvertently wreaked and find some way to further his acquaintance with Miss Upchurch. Based on things he had heard from her during their journey, he knew that his deception would not be easily forgiven. She was a forthright person to whom subterfuge was clearly foreign.

Determined to take some sort of action, whatever it might be, Henry was preparing to leave, had even gone so far as to get up from his seat and gather his coat and hat when the door opened. He couldn't say what it was that prompted him to turn and look, to see who it was that had invaded the small inn at that moment. Some last minute hope, perhaps, that Julian hadn't been fabricating everything he'd written to his father to avoid the consequences of his actions, but that was unlikely.

It's because you are looking for her. The little voice whispering in his mind was more honest than he cared to admit. From the moment he'd parted ways with Miss Upchurch, he had been looking for her. Every second in her company had been a stolen bit of joy. Their short journey had been too brief for his liking and he'd have loved nothing more than to spend another few hours in her company. Or days. Or perhaps even weeks.

And it appeared his wish was to be granted, at least on some level. Standing in the doorway, disheveled and dirty, it appeared that in the course of seeking out her employer, Lady Parkhurst, she'd encountered some of Southampton's more unsavory elements. It wasn't the same as London, but it was a port town and there were always risks. Worried for her, Henry's heart was pounding in his chest as his gaze swept over her, searching for injury.

"Miss Upchurch," he called, rushing forward to relieve her of her bags. "You are injured!"

She looked at him, a mixture of relief and embarrassment on her face and a hint of tears in her pretty blue eyes. "Oh, Mr. Meredith, how happy I am to see you. I have taken a rather nasty fall but I am not really hurt... unless one considers the serious blow to my pride that is about to occur. I'm so grateful you are here, sir!"

"What happened?" he asked as he ushered her toward the table he'd just recently vacated. There was a small bit of blood on her forehead, more of a scrape than a cut, and her gloves were scuffed and dirty from the pavement no doubt.

"I've come all this way for nothing," she whispered, her voice quavering. As she uttered it, her lower lip trembled slightly.

It was heartbreaking to see the positive and vivacious girl he'd met on the stage be brought so very low. "Surely it can't be all that bad? Tell me. Perhaps we can, between the two of us, identify a solution to your problems."

"Lady Parkhurst is dead," she stated. "I have no position."

Relieved that it wasn't something worse, he smiled encouragingly. "Well, that isn't so terrible."

She blinked at him in confusion. "Of course it is! I've left London and my friends and my school and come all this way, and for nothing. She's dead. I have no position. And my letters of recommendation have likely been tossed into the rubbish bin by whoever is executing her estate!"

"Well, that is worse," he agreed. "But it is not an insurmountable setback. We can rectify this. I vow it."

Her face crumpled then and tears rolled freely down her cheeks. "And now, I've been robbed and I do not even have the coin required to get back to London with any hint of respectability. Should I manage to get back to London safely, if word of this reaches any prospective employer they will refuse me on the spot!"

It was bad. It was very bad, but it wasn't insurmountable. "There are other positions," he offered, attempting to be cheerful. It was difficult in the face of her utter setdown.

"But not without references which are amongst Lady Parkhurst's belongings and now completely inaccessible to me. I'll never obtain any sort of respectable position without proper references and with such limited experience. Certainly, Effie will write another letter for me, but it's just—I told her I was ready, you see? I told her that I was perfectly capable of making it in the world on my own. And if this debacle of a journey has shown me one thing with any certainty, I am not. I'm a terrible failure at being an independent woman of the world."

He could help her. It would cost him greatly, Henry thought, but he could make all of her problems simply go away. He could get her a position, but not without disclosing the truth to her. He was not simply Mr. Meredith, but Viscount Marchwood, heir to the Duke of Thornhill. Would she hate him for it? Would she think him some sort of cad for lying to her? Would she ever trust anything he said to her again afterward? He'd been contemplating how best to tell her the truth, if he should tell her the truth, and it appeared that decision had been taken entirely out of his hands.

He looked at her again and saw the fear and desperation she felt. Did it really matter in the end how it affected him? He couldn't let her face the kind of ruin she mentioned. He certainly couldn't leave her alone and without any sort of guidance or protection in a strange city. Her opinion aside, that truly would make him a cad.

"What would you say if I told you that I can offer you a very respectable solution to your problem?" Henry asked.

"I would say you are a miracle worker, Mr. Meredith," she answered tearfully.

Henry signaled to the innkeeper. "A meal please, for me and the young lady... and a pot of tea."

"Aye, my lord," the innkeeper answer back.

"Oh, you should correct him! He would be so embarrassed to address you incorrectly, but I imagine it will only be worse if allowed to continue," Miss Upchurch said.

"He's quite correct in his form of address, Miss Upchurch... I was not entirely honest with you when I introduced myself on the coach," Henry admitted.

She frowned, her pretty lips turning down slightly at the corners and a hint of confusion shining in her eyes. "Then you are not Mr. Meredith?"

"I am Henry Meredith," he answered. "But I am not simply Mr. Henry Meredith. I am Lord Henry Meredith, as a matter of fact. Viscount Marchwood at your service, Miss Upchurch."

"Viscount?" she asked, her eyes wide and her lower lip trembling. "You are a viscount and—why on earth would you hide such a thing?"

"Have you never wanted to be someone else, Miss Upchurch? Even if just for a day?"

"I am, at best, the discarded bastard of a wealthy man whose name I do not even know. If not that, just a child abandoned by those who couldn't be bothered to care for it," she said. "I have wanted to be someone different every day of my life, but I have never lied about it or hidden it from someone intentionally. Though, to be perfectly honest, I was considering using a false name here at the inn to preserve my reputation."

"So you do understand?"

She was shaking her head. "No. Not really. Why would you wish it? You are a man free to do as you choose without reprisal! And not only a man, but one with power and position. Why would you deny that? Why would you ever wish to be anyone else?"

In those terms, Henry couldn't fathom it himself. "It doesn't matter. Except that I am in a position to assist you. I am here to visit with my relatives, the Duke and Duchess of Thornhill and their daughter, Philippa. She is sickly and the sea air helps her tremendously. Her governess has retired and I know she is very lonely. I think having a companion for Philippa, someone who is close to her own age, would be wonderful for her. If you will trust me to do so, I will speak to my aunt and uncle and arrange things for you. You will be our guest and a companion of sorts to Philippa until you can reach your Miss Darrow and make other arrangements."

"Why?"

"Why what?" he asked.

"Why are you helping me? We are practically strangers. In truth, given your deception at our introduction, we *are* strangers. So why?"

Because I can't bear to see you walk away from me again. He didn't say that, of course. How could he when she was so justifiably mistrustful of him? "Because it is the right thing to do."

"That is your second lie, my lord," she replied. "People in your position in society—well, they are rarely bothered with people from my position. Right or wrong."

Her expression revealed her dismay It also revealed no small amount of disappointment. If there was any question that he had permanently damaged things between them, then her expression laid that doubt to rest.

Henry shrugged, belying just how much her response meant to him. "I told you my name but withheld my title because pretending, even for a day, to be someone else, was freeing. I never thought I'd— well, it doesn't matter." How could he possibly explain it to her? The weight of expectations on him, of people who were forever dependent upon him for decisions and guidance, became oppressive over time. But the woman before him had no one. It certainly provided perspective on his own situation. "Please, Miss Upchurch, let me help you."

"Do I have any other choice?"

No, she didn't. They both knew it. And it would forever alter things between them, he recognized. His lark, his need to have an adventure had put the perfect woman in his path, and he'd destroyed it with dishonesty.

Chapter Three

"SHE'S SO TERRIBLY young, Henry. I cannot imagine any young woman being on her own in such a strange city. She must have been quite terrified!"

His aunt, Cecile, was pacing the floor in his uncle's library. Henry was standing before his uncle's desk with his hat in hand, both figuratively and literally. Meanwhile, Miss Upchurch was waiting on tenterhooks in the drawing room.

"She is young, Aunt Cecile, but that's rather the point isn't it? Philippa misses out on so much because she so rarely gets to go to parties and balls as other girls her age do. Having Miss Upchurch here will give her a friend, a companion to go to the shops with on days when she is well enough and to laugh and giggle as all young girls should. Philippa hardly ever laughs anymore. And in all honesty, offering our hospitality to Miss Upchurch for the next few weeks will mean the world to her at very little cost to us."

"I know that! This year has been terribly hard on poor Philippa... her megrims have become so much more frequent and she's developed a terrible melancholia as a result," Cecile said. "I suppose it couldn't hurt to have another young woman in the house she could bond with, that would be company for her."

"It would be good for her," his uncle intoned. "It's decided. The girl will stay. That way, Cecile, you can rest and not be party to all the quackery required to see the girl well! In your condition, you must be cautious, after all."

"Condition?" Henry asked.

Cecile blushed. "We weren't going to say anything yet... but I'm with child again."

Please let it be a son. Let it be a son and let it be healthy! He wanted that so much for both his aunt and uncle but also for himself and the freedom it would afford him. "Congratulations and best wishes to you both!"

"You won't mind not being the heir if it's a son?" Cecile asked.

"No, I will not mind," he stated emphatically. "I will be quite relieved to have the responsibility of the dukedom hovering over someone else's head for a change." It was quite true. He'd dreaded assuming even more responsibility for the family, because that's what the title meant. It meant being the head of the family and being fiscally responsible for all the various maiden aunts and cousins who invariably required upkeep.

His uncle shook his head. "Never will understand why a man wouldn't want to be a duke."

"Because then he gets to be too busy to be just a man," Henry said. "I'm going to go and let Miss Upchurch know that her future has been favorably decided."

"How did you meet this girl, again?" Cecile asked.

"On the stage," Henry replied. "She was traveling to Southampton for a position. Lady Parkhurst had retained her as a companion."

Cecile shuddered with distaste. "That woman! I know we aren't supposed to speak ill of the dead but she was just vile... vicious, mean and miserly... and every word out of her mouth was a complaint. The poor girl, despite all this uncertainty, will likely be better off!"

"I'm well aware," Henry said. He'd gotten pinned down by the woman at social gatherings once or twice over the years and had listened to her list of complaints on those occasions. What might have seemed terrible luck at first for Miss Upchurch, could ultimately be the best thing for her. "Now, I'll go speak with Miss Upchurch."

"I will speak with Miss Upchurch," Cecile insisted. "Frankly, this whole business is quite unorthodox enough. We certainly don't need you making it seem any more inappropriate. This girl is our guest now and all proprieties will be observed, Henry... no matter how pretty you find her."

Henry didn't bother to deny it. They would all know it for a lie, anyway. They had seen the girl, after all, bedraggled as she might be at the moment.

As Cecile exited the room, Henry turned to his uncle. "Julian was supposed to be at the Duke of Wellington Inn. I was attempting to waylay him there and send the boy home to face the consequences."

"Consequences?" his uncle asked. "What has he done now?"

"He's been sent down from University for gambling. And he's also quite in debt... to less than savory people," Henry answered. "It will only get worse from here."

"You'll sort it all out. No doubt he will show up eventually begging for sanctuary," the duke stated dismissively.

Henry shook his head. "It's a bigger problem than that, Uncle. This is not the first time Julian has done something like this. He's run through his allowance and he's racking up debts at an alarming rate."

"It's Horace's problem, really," his uncle said, waving his hand dismissively.

"And Horace is penniless," Henry reminded him. "He's run his estates into the ground and we've been supporting them for the last three years."

His uncle blinked. "Have we?"

Henry sighed. How did his uncle remain oblivious to such things? "Yes. Don't you read any of the reports from your solicitors and stewards?"

"There are too many of them," his uncle groused.

Apparently, he'd been working much harder as a prospective duke than the reigning duke did in his actual role. "On that note, I'm going up to my room to settle in. I shall see you at dinner."

"Your aunt will be here in the next few days with her betrothed. I'll leave it to you to ferret out anything problematic about the man. You can do that, can't you, Henry?"

He really didn't want to. He really wanted his uncle, the head of the family, to be the head of the family. But he would. Because he'd been asked. And that was simply the way of things.

⋙⫻⋘

SOPHIE HADN'T STAYED in the drawing room. It hadn't been her plan to snoop or to make free in someone else's household. Dirty as she currently was, she felt terribly guilty about sitting on any of the furniture, so she'd wandered about, pacing the perimeter of the room. It was then that she'd seen the pale, wan face of a young woman through the glass of the French doors leading to the garden. As she'd stepped closer to the doors to investigate, the girl had seen her. Her face, though still pale and tight, had warmed with a friendly smile and she'd beckoned Sophie outside.

Now standing on that terrace overlooking the garden, that same young girl settled in on a chaise with a light blanket draped over her, Sophie found herself feeling rather awkward. "Hello," she offered somewhat timidly.

"Hello. I'm Philippa. Who are you?"

Sophie wasn't certain how to answer that. "I'm Miss Upchurch. Your cousin brought me here."

"Henry? Henry is here?" The girl's face lit up. "Oh, I'm so glad he made it. Are you... oh, my goodness! Are you his betrothed?"

"No! Oh, dear heavens... goodness, no!" Sophie shook her head emphatically. "We've only just met, but I was having a bit of difficulty and he's been very kind."

"What sort of difficulty?" the girl asked.

"I was engaged to act as companion to Lady Parkhurst several weeks past and, unfortunately, word was not sent on to me that I should not come in light of her recent passing. So, now I find myself in a strange city with no employment. And your cousin, whom I met while traveling here today, thought that perhaps your parents might take pity on me and allow me to stay here with you all until I can sort things out."

The girl's smile lit up even more, her eyes glowing with vitality. "Oh, well of course you will stay! And you and I will have so much fun. You can accompany me when I go for my weekly sessions of sea bathing. Mama can't right now. She's... well, she needs to take care of herself for a change. No doubt she and father will be quite relieved to have you here to keep me company and to join me for my treatments."

Sophie stepped further out onto the terrace and seated herself on one of the chairs that flanked Philippa's chaise. "What sorts of treatments are you undergoing?"

"I have hydrotherapy twice weekly and sea bathing at least once weekly. The sea bathing is much preferred to the hydrotherapy. It's not enjoyable at all, frankly. But my physician insists that it will help with my megrims and with the melancholia that results from them."

"I'm so sorry," Sophie murmured. "What do you do when you are not suffering these terrible symptoms?"

"Oh, I don't know. I've been having these spells for so long, I can't recall what I did before. And honestly, I daresay that I've outgrown any such entertainments by now!"

"What sorts of things, aside from your treatments, do you do now?" Sophie asked.

Philippa sighed and waved her hand to encompass the garden. "This is what my physician has advised. Rest, sunshine, and hydrotherapy. I do occasionally, when I feel well enough, go to the shops. But the doctor has ordered no strenuous activity such as excessive walking or dancing, which means I cannot attend any parties unless they are hosted by mother and father. They must also be deadly dull as all excitement is to be avoided. But the megrims are so terrible that I will do anything to prevent them."

Sophie was overwhelmed with sympathy for the girl. "You poor thing! How long has it been this way?"

"I've always suffered terrible headaches, but they worsened as I became older until they were entirely debilitating," Philippa said. "But let's not talk about such awful things. Tell me how you met Henry! I'm so very curious. He has never brought anyone here before. He must think you very remarkable, indeed."

Sophie didn't wish to discuss that because she didn't want to tell this sweet girl that her cousin, despite his much appreciated assistance, was a liar. "I think it's more a testament to your cousin's charitable nature than any indication of his opinion of me."

Philippa grinned. "I think it must be more than charity, surely! Despite your slightly disheveled appearance at the moment, you must know you are very pretty. I daresay Henry knows that you are."

Sophie had no idea how to respond to that. Thankfully, the terrace doors opened and a woman in her mid-thirties appeared there. Dressed as elegantly as she was, Sophie knew she could be none other than the Duchess of Thornhill. Rising to her feet, she dipped a curtsy. "Your grace."

The duchess waved her hand. "No need for all of that, my dear. We are a much more informal household than most. With poor Philippa so ill, standing on ceremony is an exhausting waste of time in most instances."

"Certainly, your grace. As you wish," Sophie said. She had no notion of what degree of "less formal" was acceptable.

The duchess noted the high color in Philippa's cheeks. "You're certainly looking a bit livelier, dearest. I think Miss Upchurch's company must agree with you. Are you up for having a companion for a few weeks?"

"Oh, yes, Mother!" Philippa exclaimed. "It would be so lovely to have someone about who is my own age."

"Very well. Henry speaks very highly of Miss Upchurch, so even without references, I think we are well set to bring you into our household. Naturally, we will take care of everything for you while you are and the first order of business will certainly be your clothes! We have to see about improving your wardrobe, my dear!"

Sophie felt a flush creep over her cheeks. "Oh, that isn't necessary! I'm quite content with what I have."

The duchess laughed. "You will be taking your meals with us in the dining room. While we don't have guests all that frequently, I imagine we do entertain more than Lady Parkhurst had planned to do. I'm afraid you will certainly need a few gowns. And on the off chance that Philippa feels up to attending any parties or soirees as the summer progresses, you will certainly need appropriate gowns for that."

"The physician said—" Philippa began.

"The physician is a man," the duchess said firmly. "And all men are far more capable of being wrong than they will ever admit." Apparently realizing that her words might have been harsh, the duchess then smiled. "Come, Miss Upchurch. We will get you shown to a room next door to Philippa's and you may unpack your things and get yourself situated before dinner. The gong will ring sharply at eight. It is later than many of our neighbors dine but not so late as when we are in London. My husband is quite adamant about following the physician's orders that Philippa should get as much rest as possible."

"I'll see you at dinner, Miss Upchur—Sophie," Philippa corrected. "We are going to be the very best of friends. I'm so glad you're here."

Chapter Four

SOPHIE SURVEYED HER reflection. She'd dressed for dinner in the gown that had been delivered to her room by the duchess' maid. It was far finer than anything she'd ever owned. The pale green silk with its puffed sleeves and embroidered bodice and hem was a thing of beauty. It was also very flattering, the hue a perfect foil for her red-gold hair and pale complexion.

Then Philippa's maid had come to dress her hair. It was a much more flattering style than she was accustomed to, pinned in a loose chignon with curls framing her face. Typically, she followed Effie's advice about making oneself appear as plain as possible until one had the lay of the land in a new place of employment. Of course, she did not have any concerns on that score. She could not imagine that anyone in the household would be anything less than kind and considerate. She was also not an employee but a guest of sorts. Certainly the room she had been provided was proof of that. The chamber was spacious and quite luxurious, not at all the sort of place one would put the help. It was a very strange position to find herself in. But everyone seemed so welcoming and so warm.

You also thought Viscount Marchwood was only Mr. Meredith... because he lied. Willfully.

That little whisper of suspicious reasoning in her mind left Sophie very unsettled. She was terribly angry with him for lying to her, for deceiving her so wickedly for his own amusement. It didn't matter that, on the cusp of discovering his perfidy, she'd been contemplating the same sort of lie herself. Their situations were so different, after all! Still, it seemed somewhat ungrateful to her to be so unforgiving when he'd literally rescued her from heaven knew what. With very little in the way of funds and with no position, making her way back to London and to the relative safety and security of the Darrow School had seemed an impossible task. But forgiving his deception was not the same as trusting him.

It was all so terribly complicated. Perhaps because, when he'd only been Mr. Meredith, there had been a hint of possibility there. Perhaps he might call on her or seek her out, perhaps their flirtation might be something more. But he was a viscount and would likely one day become a duke. And men in that position required wives who were capable of assuming the role of viscountess or duchess and that would never be her. Her reaction to his lies was as much a reflection of her own disappointment and embarrassment as it was to his actions.

Pushing thoughts of the viscount, his terribly handsome face and the way her heart beat just a bit faster in his presence, firmly from her mind, Sophie considered her next steps. Effie, obviously, was the first thing to take care of. The letter she'd written to Effie explaining her new situation was face down on the desk. She'd read through it again after dinner to be certain she hadn't given too much away about the difficulties she'd faced, and if it was both vague enough and reassuring enough, she'd put it in the post the following morning. It was imperative to her that Effie not have cause to question her decision in allowing Sophie to take off and pursue her independence when she'd clearly had reservations about her abilities to do so.

The first dinner gong sounded then, signaling for everyone to gather in the drawing room. Sophie gave one last look at her reflection, sighed, and then exited her rather luxurious chamber. She paused in the corridor for just a moment and then Philippa's chamber door opened and two footmen came through carrying her in smaller scale version of a sedan chair.

"Isn't it ridiculous?" Philippa asked with an embarrassed smile. "I'm perfectly capable of walking but Dr. Blake says I mustn't. He fears I may be overtaken by dizziness while on the stairs."

Sophie was beginning to think that the physician was more of a hindrance than a help. Certainly taking away all of the girl's independence and not allowing her to exercise the parts of her body that were healthy would only create more illnesses in the long run. But then again, she was not so familiar with Philippa's condition that she could offer any sort of advice or criticism.

"Do you suffer from dizziness?" Sophie asked.

"I didn't before," Philippa admitted. "The pain in my head was always terrible, and would leave me quite ill and weak, but I never suffered from issues with my balance. But of late, that appears to be changing."

"Then I do not think it ridiculous," Sophie offered encouragingly. After all, she was a guest there on their charity. It was certainly not her place to question the doctor. "It is necessary for your safety. And, there are other benefits."

Philippa gave her a baleful stare. "What possible benefit?"

Sophie grinned. "Making an entrance."

Philippa blinked in shock then, after a moment, giggled. "I suppose there is that."

Sophie continued, "Indeed! It's rather exotic. Like Cleopatra!"

Philippa laughed softly. "Then there you have it. I am the Queen of the Nile and this is my barge."

They were still laughing at that jest when they reached the lower floor. Once there, Philippa was transferred from the sedan chair to a wheeled chair that would require only one footman to propel her. There was one on each floor for her to be able to get about as best as possible with the sedan chairs being used between floors. It was a great deal of shifting around and maneuvering in a small space. Still, it seemed that every possible step was being taken to grant Philippa as much mobility within the house as was possible.

Sophie walked behind her as the footman pushed her into the dining room. There was a noticeable gap in the chairs surrounding the table to accommodate her wheeled device. It struck Sophie then just how unique the family truly was. Such lengths had been taken to allow Philippa to be as much a part of things as possible despite her ill health. It was unlike anything she'd ever seen or heard of. Sadly, many families would just allow their loved one to languish away in a bedchamber, forgotten and abandoned. How remarkable they were to make such efforts to keep Philippa involved in the daily activities of the family as a whole.

The footman stepped back and a maid appeared to assist Philippa in situating herself properly in the chair to be able to sit at the table and enjoy her dinner with her family. Once she was arranged to her liking, Philippa gave the maid a slight nod. The maid stepped back, the dining room doors were opened and then the remainder of the family began to filter in.

The duchess entered first and right behind her came the Duke of Thornhill and Viscount Marchwood, both deep in conversation about something. It was immediately obvious to Sophie that he'd done more than simply conceal his title when they'd met on the stage. Dressed as he was in an elegant coat of blue superfine and a brocade waistcoat, it was clear that he'd intentionally dressed more shabbily than was his norm in order to "blend in". It sparked her ire. It *embarrassed* her. Pride wasn't something she had in abundance, but what little she did have recoiled at the notion that she'd never have encountered this man without him having gone to such lengths to lower himself. It stung.

When the entire family was seated about the table, the butler gave an almost imperceptible signal and the footmen began to serve. One dish after another was brought out then cleared away. And during each course of the meal, conversation flowed. The duke and duchess were delightful, Viscount Marchwood was charming, Philippa was not so lively, but still participated. It was apparent as the meal progressed that the young woman's energy was waning.

As for Sophie, she answered questions when asked, but she never volunteered information, nor did she insinuate herself into the conversations of others unasked. She was aware of her position, perhaps more so than she ever had been in her life. In truth, it wasn't about how they treated her. They did not act as if she were a servant or someone there only on charity, but rather as an honored guest in their home. Lady Parkhurst had not been that sort. It would have been very apparent from the outset that she would not be considered an extended member of the family at all but simply an employee. In some ways, that was preferable. It gave her a clearer vision of exactly where she stood in the household. It was not what she'd envisioned when leaving London, that was certain.

When at last the meal had come to an end, the duchess rose. "Rather than simply sequestering ourselves in separate rooms, I thought we might all retire to the drawing room tonight. We have much to celebrate, after all, with the arrival of Henry and the addition of the delightful Miss Upchurch to our household."

"A most excellent notion, my dear," the duke agreed. "Henry, we shall take a brief detour to the library so that I can go over that business proposition with you. That will allow time for Philippa to get settled—"

"Actually, Papa," Philippa spoke up. "I'm quite fatigued. I think I shall have the footmen take me upstairs to retire for the evening."

"Today has been too much for you," Sophie said in dismay. "I didn't mean to wear you out with all my talking!"

Philippa offered a wan smile. "Oh, it isn't that. Truly, your presence has been the best part of my day, Sophie! I had my hydrotherapy appointment this morning before you arrived and those always leave me exhausted. Normally on those days, I don't even come down to dinner. Your presence here has revived me like nothing else could have!"

"I'll come with you," Sophie insisted. "I can read to you or simply keep you company for a bit."

"Nonsense. Go to the drawing room with my parents and with Henry. You mentioned that you played the pianoforte and I know they'd greatly enjoy the entertainment."

"Indeed," the duchess insisted. "I adore music but my own abilities in that area are very limited. We'd be delighted to have you play for us."

"It's settled. We'll all go the drawing room together now while Philippa retires for the evening," the duke said, walking around the table to kiss Philippa's cheek. "Goodnight, my dear. Tomorrow you will feel better."

And with that, Sophie was stuck. Rising from her seat, she followed the duke and duchess from the room, with Lord Marchwood bringing up the rear of their party. She was acutely aware of him and of her own slightly irrational anger toward him. *He had rescued her. Because he was in a position to rescue her. Because he was far, far beyond her reach socially and to forget that, regardless of how his eyes twinkle when he smiles, would be a disaster.*

"If you will permit me, Miss Upchurch, I will turn the pages while you play," he offered as he fell in step beside her.

"Oh, that's hardly necessary," she said dismissively. The last thing she wanted was to be in such close proximity to him. There would be no way to end the interaction without appearing rude.

"I insist," he said in a firm tone but with a slight smile curving his lips. "After all, you are very graciously gifting us with your talents."

"My lord—"

He frowned and halted his steps. "I dislike the way you say that."

Sophie's brows shot up in surprise and she felt her heart stutter. It was not lost on her that she owed a great deal to him, despite her rather conflicted feelings about him. "I beg your pardon. I do not mean to be disrespectful."

"You are not disrespectful. You are entirely too respectful," he said, his voice pitched in a low, soft tone that was nearly a whisper. "And that is the problem. When you called me Mr. Meredith, your voice was warm and sweet. I didn't lie to you to hurt you or to embarrass you in any way. My intent was never to abuse your trust, but simply to enjoy an afternoon of freedom. Can you not forgive me that?"

Sophie gave him the only answer she could. "It isn't a matter of forgiveness, my lord. It's a matter of trust. I'm very grateful for all the aid you have afforded me, but I cannot help but wonder what else you might be concealing for your own purposes. It changes everything. It took what might have been a small gap in our social status and turned it into a chasm that I can see no way across. Men of your station do not have flirtations with women of mine, at least not with any honorable intent behind them."

HENRY WATCHED HER walk ahead of him, effectively leaving him in the dust and rubble of a ruin of his own making. Lying to her, impulsive as it had been, had not seemed so terrible at first, not when he'd thought they'd never cross paths again. It had been harmless, he'd thought. A lark for him and a meaningless encounter with a stranger for her. But fate had intervened and now he found himself feeling somewhat responsible for her and strangely protective of her. And she wanted nothing more to do with him.

He wasn't so foolish as to think her assertions about the gap in their social standing were insignificant. They were not. It was a matter that, if he had any real intent of pursuing her, would have to be addressed. He knew that. It was of no importance to him, but it would be to other people. Any relationship between them would always prompt some remark about it—how far beneath him she had been, or how ambitious she was. It would label her an adventuress or opportunist. It could likely see him labeled a dupe. When in truth, she had liked him better as a no one rather than a man of any consequence.

Frustrated, embarrassed by his own behavior and by the fact that he was trailing around behind his cousin's companion like some forlorn, calf-eyed fool, Henry nonetheless followed her into the drawing room. Once there, he stationed himself beside the pianoforte. He was determined to do exactly as he'd said he would and turn the pages for her. The best thing he could do now, he thought, to repair their relationship was to follow through on anything he said, no matter what it was. She needed to know she could trust him.

"It really is not necessary, my lord," she said. "I do not actually require the music. I know several pieces that I can play from memory alone. I would not want your attentions to me to be remarked upon."

"Then it is just as well that there is no one here who would remark upon it. And it saves me, Miss Upchurch. Turning pages for you keeps me from being drawn into conversations with my aunt which will invariably turn to my need to find a bride," he admitted. "It is Aunt Cecile's fondest wish to see me married off and she never ignores an opportunity to remind me that I am not so young that I should be avoiding the parson's mousetrap."

Miss Upchurch ducked her head in reluctant acquiescence. "Very well," she agreed, though her reluctance was quite obvious. After a moment of shuffling through the sheet music present, she selected a piece and placed it against the ornately carved scrollwork of the music stand. "Thank you, my lord."

"Thank you, Miss Upchurch. By the way, I should tell you that I was not aware that Lady Parkhurst had passed. My deception was not so ill intended that I would have allowed you to stroll blindly into such a terrible situation. If I had known, I would never have permitted things to escalate so quickly. You do know that, don't you?" It was imperative to him that she understand that.

She placed her hands on the keys, beginning with soft, tinkling notes. "I never suspected that you knew, sir. Despite your misrepresentation of your identity, I do not see you as an intentionally cruel person who would make sport of another's misfortune. I am grateful for all that you have done, during the journey here and after, my lord. Please do not think me so mean."

Relieved by that, he nodded. "One might argue that true cruelty would have been to allow you to put yourself at the mercy of Lady Parkhurst. She was not a pleasant woman, Miss Upchurch. I can only think that you will be much happier here with Philippa than with such a termagant. Though I daresay that Philippa may not be the best company on some days. Poor girl."

Miss Upchurch glanced up at him then, her expression no longer guarded and wary but one that conveyed deep concern. "How many physicians have been consulted about Philippa's condition?"

"Several, though I would hazard no guess as to the actual number. Some have offered no insight at all, simply shaking their heads in puzzlement. Others have said the megrims she suffers are naught to be worried over and that it's just the feverish brain of a young woman too sensitive for her own good," he answered with a sneer. "Her current physician, while not making her any better, does at least seem to recognize the severity of her illness. He has not made light of it or suggested that she belongs in an asylum, though I cannot see that his treatments and his restrictions upon her have had any positive effect. Why do you ask?"

Miss Upchurch bit her lip, her expression one of indecision. That indecision quickly gave way and she began to speak quite emphatically. "Megrims are truly miserable and I have the utmost sympathy for Philippa that she suffers them so frequently. But if the physician's treatments are not making her better then would it not be wise to seek a new physician? I cannot see that the restrictions she lives under—being confined to her bed or a chair and forced to live as an invalid when she is not one!—are of any benefit to her at all. It seems to me, my lord, that the prescribed cure is as incapacitating as the mysterious illness!"

It was a thought that mirrored his own, yet he did not feel it was his place to intervene or question his aunt and uncle about his cousin's treatment. As her parents, surely the provenance was theirs. "I understand your doubts, Miss Upchurch, but surely decisions about her care should be left in the hands of those who love her best and who would move heaven and earth to see her well. Would you not agree?" Except that he knew how his uncle made decisions, which is to say he avoided them as long as possible and then just simply chose the most expedient option.

"Well, yes, and I have no wish to overstep my bounds. While I do not know Philippa so well yet, I think I can see that these restrictions are crushing her spirit. I fear she shall grow despondent under such isolation."

"Better her spirit than her life," he said. But even as he said, it rang hollow to his own ears. There was no indication that Philippa's megrims were life threatening. They were painful and induced great sickness in her, but they were hardly fatal. And yet she was living in the most cloyingly cosseted way, as if she were impossibly fragile and couldn't withstand even the slightest excitement. The detestable sameness of her days must be a misery.

"You only say that because you aren't the one living like a prisoner," Miss Upchurch insisted. "What if it isn't the megrims that are the cause of her melancholia but the way she is being forced to live?"

And that was the rub of it. Philippa was a prisoner in many ways and he could not deny that. But he wasn't ready to wage war with his uncle by suggesting that the man did not know what was best for his own daughter. He might make slapdash decisions, but once he made them, he adhered to them with a stubbornness that was astounding. But could he, in good conscience, ignore something that was making Philippa miserable? "I will consider the possibility that I may need to speak to my uncle about this subject, Miss Upchurch, after a suitable period of observation."

"And what is that? A suitable period of observation? One day, one week?" Her impatience was evident in her tone.

"I had planned to stay two weeks in Southampton before returning to my estate," he said. "Before I leave, if I feel and if you still feel that Philippa's treatments are not appropriate to her condition, then I will approach him, but only on one condition."

"And what is your condition, my lord?"

Henry sighed. "That we can start over. That you will forgive me for my idiocy on the coach and know that I harbored no ill or nefarious intent toward you—then or now."

"Why on earth does it matter?"

"Because I like you, Miss Upchurch. I may more than like you. And I'd like to think there might be a slim chance you might more than like me also," he admitted. It hadn't been a thing he intended to say, but it was there now, hanging in the air between them. "I'd like to think that I may have a chance to prove myself to you... to prove that I am worthy."

Her fingers fumbled over the keys for just a moment before once more falling into the practiced playing that she had been indulging all along. "What does that mean precisely? More than like? And worthy of what?"

"It means that I may wish to court you, if you'd ever permit it." It was impossible to determine who was more surprised by his statement. "Will you permit it, Miss Upchurch?"

She blushed furiously, shaking her head. "I'm little more than a servant in your uncle's home! I have nothing to recommend me!"

Henry grinned at her scandalized tone as he gestured toward his aunt and uncle. She'd only addressed the reasons they should not. She had not stated she didn't wish for it though. "It isn't unheard of, you know? And Aunt Cecile was a governess when she and my uncle met." Her mouth dropped open in shock at that bit of information, prompting Henry to add, "We're not nearly the sticklers for propriety that you are, Miss Upchurch. We have a long history of scandalous matches, it seems."

With that, Miss Upchurch schooled her expression into one of proper passivity and resumed playing, but there was heightened color in her cheeks and he could see a slight tremor in her hands. She wasn't immune to him. Whatever she felt about his earlier deception, there was an attraction there and it wasn't one-sided. After a long moment of silence, broken only by the tinkling of keys beneath her fingers, she gave an almost imperceptible nod. It might not have been enthusiastic consent but it was consent nonetheless. He would be able to pay court to her as she deserved.

Chapter Five

PHILIPPA DIDN'T BREAKFAST below stairs but had a tray in her room. Rather than face Viscount Marchwood and his ridiculous proclamations of attraction to her and his assertions that he intended to approach her as an actual suitor, Sophie had elected to break her fast in Philippa's chamber and keep her company during the morning meal. Dr. Blake was expected to call that morning before noon and Sophie found herself quite eager for his arrival. She was quite curious as to what he might have to say regarding Philippa's condition.

"It's so very nice not to eat alone. I hate to go downstairs for meals because it's such a fuss and furor," Philippa noted. "I tend to stay in my rooms as much as possible, though I daresay I will have to rethink that. It would hardly be fair to you, would it? Stuck in here with me as if you, too, were some sort of invalid!"

Sophie sipped her tea and shrugged. "I am your companion. My duties, pleasant as they are, consist entirely of keeping you company. It's hardly a chore as you are a delight to be with. I am content to remain in your chambers as much as you like." And that would certainly aid her in her endeavors to avoid a certain viscount with very strong opinions and a streak of unconventionality.

"We shall go out tomorrow," Philippa declared. "I cannot wait! Sea bathing is truly the most invigorating thing I have ever experienced. Not that I have experienced very much. Have you ever been?"

Sophie shook her head. "No, I have not. I haven't a costume for it."

"Oh, I have an extra one, or Mother might have one that would fit you better. She never cared for sea bathing, but I enjoy it greatly. I find it quite invigorating. I never feel so well as I do after having indulged in the practice!"

It wasn't her place to make the suggestion, but Sophie couldn't help herself. "Then perhaps you should do it more than once a week."

Philippa sighed heavily, her expression tightening. "Dr. Blake would not permit it. He worries even now that I may be overtaxing myself. I should hate to defy his orders when he has worked so very hard to discover the nature of my illness. I do hate it so when I disappoint him."

There was something in Philippa's tone that alerted her to the shocking fact that Philippa might have romantic feelings for her doctor. Both curious and alarmed, Sophie asked, "Is he terribly old and gruff... your Dr. Blake?"

Philippa's answering blush was telling enough, even before she spoke. "Oh, no! Heavens no. He is quite young, perhaps a bit older than Henry though not by many years, I would wager. And he has a very pleasing way about him. I dislike the restrictions he has placed upon me, but I certainly understand the reasons for them. I can hardly hold him to blame for them. His recommendations are only for my well-being, after all."

"And does he have a wife?" Sophie asked.

"No," Philippa answered. "He is unmarried. He says that he is too devoted to his patients to have time for a wife."

"What an odd thing to say," Sophie noted. "How did that conversation come up?"

"We were discussing the possibility of my entering society and the marriage mart," Philippa admitted. "He thinks it will be unlikely, at least for the next few years."

Sophie rose and walked toward the window, peering out into the street beyond. There was a bustle of traffic though it was far less than what she was accustomed to in London. The pace of Southampton was much better suited to her nature than the bustle of the larger city. In London, she had often felt overwhelmed by the noise and the vast numbers of people. But she was at least somewhat free to roam and explore the city. For Philippa, her world was remarkably small and shrinking by the day. And this physician, this Dr. Blake, was the cause. If Philippa did have romantic feelings for him, it certainly wouldn't be a surprise. She had no opportunity to meet any other eligible men and, now, it seemed the doctor was telling her it would be years before that changed. Turning back to her, Sophie said, "I can't imagine what it's like... to be forever waiting for your life to begin."

Philippa dopped her head so that her chin rested against her chest for a moment. "That is precisely what I do... every moment of every day. I'm waiting."

It was Sophie's turn to let out a heavy sigh. "I'm terribly sorry, Philippa. I wish there was something I could do to make it all better for you."

Philippa reached out and clasped Sophie's hand. "Please do not feel sorry for me. I have so much when others have so little. My family has moved heaven and earth to try and make me well, and while my condition has only worsened, I have never been more certain in my life of how well I am loved. And now, I have you... a friend and companion to help me fill my days. It's wonderful, Sophie. Really!"

"I am not glad that Lady Parkhurst is no longer with us. But I am very glad that the situation has led me here to you," Sophie said with a sad smile. "I want nothing more than to make your days a bit brighter. We shall be the very dearest of friends!"

"Then let us ring for the maid and get you a bathing costume so that we can make our way to Hamble Common for some very bracing sea bathing tomorrow!"

Sophie had not yet seen such animation, such vivacity in Philippa. "I am quite pleased to see you so excited for this and to see you feeling so much better."

Philippa smirked. "Do you know what would please me even more?"

"What is that?" Sophie asked, as she placed her teacup back on the small table beside the bed. There was something in her tone that gave warning she would not much care for the turn the conversation was about to take.

Philippa leaned forward, her eyes alight with rabid curiosity. "To know the truth of how you and Henry came to meet... and what the nature of your acquaintance really is. He's quite different with you, you know?"

She didn't know. How could she? But it didn't matter how he was with others, despite the fact that she desperately wanted to know what Philippa meant by that. It only mattered that they were not suited for one another by virtue of their stations and expectations. "He was very helpful to me when I faced a terribly difficult situation yesterday. He singlehandedly saved my life and my reputation, I daresay. That is all there is, Philippa."

"I hardly think he would agree with you," the girl replied. "He watched you all through dinner... he could not take his eyes off of you. What I would not give to have a man look at me that way!"

"What way?" Sophie asked. Dismissively, she added, "You are likely making much more of it than there truly is."

"He looked at you with complete adoration. He looked at you," Philippa stated firmly, "as if you were the most beautiful, most charming, most intelligent, most articulate woman in the world. He looked at you, Sophie, as if you were everything!"

"One day, a man will look at you with complete adoration," Sophie insisted, "But that is not at all how your cousin looks at me. I daresay, you shall meet a bevy of gentlemen at some point who will be vying desperately for your hand!"

"Yes, because I am the daughter of the Duke of Thornhill. Not because they find me beautiful or exciting or compelling. Sickly girls who are only slightly better than bedridden hardly inspire such devotion." Philippa shrugged as if it mattered little to her, yet her disappointment was palpable.

"You will get better," Sophie insisted. "But I must ask you, are you confident in the skill and knowledge of your physician?"

Philippa smiled. "I could not be more confident. You will see when Dr. Blake arrives. He's so kind and so very handsome. He speaks to me with such compassion and such warmth that I know he could only ever have my best interests at heart!"

Sophie smiled, but she did not share Philippa's certainty. She would reserve judgment until she met the doctor herself, but she held little hope that her regard would be as easily won.

IN LONDON, IF one wanted information one went to his club. In the country, one went to church. In Southampton, there was only one option available to Henry, and it was neither of those. So he went to the Pump Room at the Long Rooms Assembly where he might overhear any gossip about Dr. Blake. Gossip that was not intended for one's own ears was the best sort of information, after all. If one wanted to know what was happening or to understand who the players in Southampton were, the Long Rooms were the place for finding out. For Henry, there was nothing he detested so much as gossip, but even he could not deny that it did occasionally have value. With that thought in mind, he braced himself and prepared for the onslaught of whispers and speculation that would occur when he made an appearance.

Entering the Pump Room, there was an immediate hush and then a low buzz that grew into a soft roar. His presence had been noted, likely because it was a very rare occurrence. No sooner had he stepped down into the room than an aging matron with a high-pitched and very shrill voice descended upon him.

"I say, Marchwood, I have not seen you in town for some time! Looking for a bride with a plump purse now that your uncle may be getting an heir out of his wife after all?"

Forcing a friendly smile, Henry reminded himself why he was there. "Not at all, Lady Hemsley. I am here simply to take the waters and enjoy the summer with my family."

The old woman clucked her tongue. "How is your dear cousin, Marchwood? Poor girl. Such a sweet thing. How is she these days?"

It was a surprise that Lady Hemsley had broached the subject of Philippa's failing health. Most people of his acquaintance tried to avoid discussion of the topic at all costs. "Not well, Lady Hemsley," Henry confessed. "She suffers greatly, but my uncle has obtained a physician for her here in Southampton... Dr. Blake."

"Dr. Richard Blake?" she queried.

"The same," Henry replied.

Lady Hemsley's lips thinned in an expression of obvious disapproval. "Your uncle has clearly not been in town for very long then. His choice of physician is quite unfortunate."

Feigning surprise, Henry said, "I am very curious to hear more. I confess to having some concerns about the man myself."

Lady Hemsley nodded, more to herself than to him. "Come to my home this afternoon for tea. I shall tell you what I know, but I am hesitant to speak of it here. He is not without support in society and those who do support him do so quite staunchly and vehemently. There are many here who would gladly carry tales back to him of any words spoken against him. He can be a formidable foe, Viscount."

Henry couldn't imagine why she would feel such concern to speak to him in any location. After all, Lady Hemsley was one of the most notorious gossips about and, as such, held a position of supreme power in society. Her late husband had been a powerful and well-respected man. She herself had the ear of Lady Jersey and they were known, despite their physical distance, to be dear friends. And she and Lady Parkhurst had been as thick as thieves. "Indeed, we shall discuss it thoroughly when I come for tea, then. And please, Lady Hemsley, allow me to express my sympathies for the passing of Lady Parkhurst. I know you had been bosom companions for some time."

A tight and rather pained expression contorted her face for a moment. "We shall discuss that this afternoon as well, Marchwood. It is all part and parcel, you see?"

He was beginning to see. Had the physician caring for Philippa been responsible for Lady Parkhurst's demise? Admittedly, the woman had been rather advanced in age, but she had always seemed to be in the very pink of health. In truth, that raised another question for him. Lady Parkhurst had hardly been infirmed, nor had she been particularly isolated. In truth, her need for a companion was very limited given just how active the woman had been in society. "Tell me, Lady Hemsley, were you aware that Lady Parkhurst had obtained a companion?"

"Oh, la, yes. I had encouraged her to do so! I cannot imagine what has become of that poor girl now," Lady Hemsley said with a slight chuckle, as if a person's fate weren't hanging in the balance. "I had thought having another set of eyes and a sympathetic ear might help Lady Parkhurst not to feel quite so dependent upon the goodwill of the doctor. But how do you know about this companion, sir?"

"She is currently residing with my aunt and uncle. Miss Upchurch is now acting as a companion to Philippa. In fact, it was Miss Upchurch who prompted me to question Philippa's care and to investigate Dr. Blake's competence." Henry wondered at the confluence of events which had brought them all together. Was it fate or merely a series of coincidences?

"I will see you this afternoon... and Marchwood, it's best if you keep any inquiries regarding this physician as discreet as possible. Advise your Miss Upchurch to do the same. He has quite the temper. And bring her with you to tea. I'd like to meet this very perceptive girl!"

To that, Henry smiled but it was hardly an expression of amusement. "He is not alone on that score, my lady. I myself can be quite fierce when it comes to protecting those I hold dear." Did he mean his cousin, Philippa, or was he thinking more of the lovely Miss Upchurch? It didn't matter. He would protect them both. Though he was not a man given to anger and violence, the idea that someone might be doing Philippa harm, intentionally or otherwise, sparked a recklessness and an anger inside him that he had never known. Compelled to protect them both, Henry bid a good day to Lady Hemsley and headed for home. He needed a word with Miss Upchurch.

Chapter Six

S HE'D TAKEN AN immediate and intense dislike to the man.

Seated in a chair near Philippa's bedside, Sophie listened to the physician as he placated and condescended to her new friend. He spoke to her as if she were simple in some way or perhaps like a spoiled child hovering on the edge of a tantrum.

"Now, Lady Philippa," he said, "Have you been getting your rest?" He glanced over at Sophie. "I understand that it must be very difficult for you to be so confined, but you must be cautious about overtaxing yourself!"

He spoke to her as if she were a small child or simple minded, Sophie thought.

"I assure you, Dr. Blake, I am following your instructions to the letter," Philippa said. Then the girl batted her eyelashes at him.

"I've told you that you may call me Richard," he said. "We are friends, are we not?"

Philippa looked very uncomfortable as she glanced away from him. "I know you are only looking out for me and I am very appreciative, and yes, of course, we are friends."

"I will do whatever is necessary to see you well, Lady Philippa. It is my fondest wish that you will be dancing waltzes and promenading with the other young ladies of society. But it will take time," he insisted.

"Yes, Dr. Blake," Philippa agreed.

"Richard! Now, are you still intent upon this sea bathing? I cannot tell you how terrible an idea I find it to be," he said. "In your weakened state, I think exposure to cold water in a more controlled environment, such as the hydrotherapy rooms, would serve you better."

Philippa's gaze shuttered and she seemed to recoil from that. "But the sea is not cold… or not so cold as the hydrotherapy baths are. I'm certain it can only be beneficial for me as it makes me feel better."

The doctor's expression became completely impassive, his gaze narrowing and tension filling him as he stared at the girl. In that moment, Sophie found herself fearful that he might harm Philippa outright. He appeared furious at having his authority questioned. Then the moment passed, his expression shifted again, softening and his eyes were once more downcast and his tone placating when he spoke. "I must disagree with your assessment. I adore cake but that does not make it healthful! Nonetheless, having a bit of it now and again is what makes the days brighter, is it not? You shall enjoy your sea bathing once per week. No more. I will have your word on it!"

"I solemnly promise," Philippa agreed with a soft and almost radiant smile.

Dr. Blake nodded. It was almost as if he'd forgotten anyone else was present. He reached out, his hand tenderly cupping Philippa's cheek before pushing a stray tendril of hair from her face. It was a decidedly intimate gesture, one that implied a relationship far beyond that of doctor and patient.

Observing it, Sophie was instantly uncomfortable. So much so that she cleared her throat more loudly and with far more force than was necessary. Still, it worked. The moment was broken. Dr. Blake withdrew his hand from Philippa's cheek and Philippa herself recoiled from it, as if realizing that, on the whole, it had been terribly improper.

Dr. Blake turned to Sophie then, a smile on his lips that did not match the coldness in his gaze. "And you, Miss Upchurch, I charge you with being certain Lady Philippa does not overtax herself... that includes your company. She must have hours of solitude and rest daily if she is to recover."

"I will only ever do what is in Philippa's best interests," Sophie hedged. "I shall endeavor to see to her comfort and health above all else."

He nodded, clearly choosing not to see the subtext of her reply. Then Dr. Blake reached into his bag and withdrew a dark green bottle. "Two drops in your tea in the morning, in the afternoon and three drops before bed," he said. "You must take it every day, never missing a dose, or it will not work."

"What is that?" Sophie asked.

"It's a tonic," he answered sharply, as if she were dimwitted.

"I'm aware of that, Dr. Blake. My question pertained more to the contents of the tonic. What is in it?" Sophie clarified.

The doctor's eyebrows rose, an obvious indication of his displeasure. "Medicinal herbs, Miss Upchurch. Shall I read you the list of ingredients or will you be satisfied to know that I am a trained physician who can adequately prepare and dispense appropriate treatments to my patients?"

Realizing she'd been too fervent in her question, Sophie smiled. "Oh, I did not mean to imply otherwise, Dr. Blake. It was merely curiosity. If the ingredients are so healthful and are appropriate for Lady Philippa's diet, I thought we might be able to ask the cook to incorporate more of those herbs into her dishes!"

"It is not at all the same," he snapped. "If you had any training beyond that of how to do needlework, you might know that yourself! These herbs have no benefit until they are combined in an elixir as I have made for Lady Philippa here. I trust, Miss Upchurch, that you will leave the doctoring of patients to their doctors and not attempt to take over Lady Philippa's treatment yourself?"

Trying to appear chastened, Sophie nodded. "Certainly, Dr. Blake. We are all certain that you will tell us how best to proceed with Philippa's care."

"Indeed, I do know what's best for her! Now I must be going. Lady Philippa, I shall see you at the end of the week. Naturally, you may send for me if you have need. I will always come for you, my de— Lady Philippa," the doctor said as he bowed his head in Philippa's direction. To Sophie, he gave a curt nod and then walked out. The door slammed just a bit behind him prompting Philippa to wince.

"I'm sorry. I didn't mean to offend him," Sophie said. "I really was only curious."

Philippa looked at her skeptically. "I understand that you have doubts, but he cares about my well-being. He was likely only frustrated because another week has passed and I am no better than I was before."

Or no worse. Sophie needed to find out precisely what was in that bottle. Was the doctor trying to cure Philippa or was he trying to maintain her state of dependence? If so, why? "Does he bring you a new bottle of elixir every week?"

"Always," Philippa said. "He insists that they are the key to my recovery, though to be perfectly honest, I see no improvement from it."

"And where do you keep them?"

"In the kitchen," the girl replied. "Cook takes care of it and makes certain that a cup of tea with the appropriate dose is sent to me as instructed. It's a vile tasting concoction and tea at least makes it tolerable."

"Well, I shall take the new bottle to the kitchen and leave you to rest for a bit. It has been a busy morning and I know you will be tired," Sophie offered. And she'd get the old bottle and take it to an apothecary to get his opinion on the contents.

Philippa handed the bottle to her. "You are too kind, Sophie. I am so very glad to have you here."

Sophie smiled back at her. "And I am very glad to be here, Philippa. Very glad, indeed."

Heading down the stairs, Sophie made straight for the kitchen. She found the cook elbow deep in pastry dough which was perfect for her plan. "I'm sorry to bother you. I've brought down Lady Philippa's elixir from Dr. Blake. If you'll simply point me in the direction of where it is stored, I'll be happy to put it away for you."

"Betsy, show Miss Upchurch where to put Lady Philippa's tonic," the cook said gruffly.

A scullery maid bobbed a curtsy, though it was hardly necessary to do so for her, and tittered nervously. "This way, Miss."

Down the winding corridor of larders and preparation rooms and laundry areas, Sophie was shown into a small pantry where various medicines, herbs, and other supplies were kept. There on the shelf before her, on prime display, was a bottle identical to the one currently in her hand. Sophie reached for the bottle on the shelf. "Oh, this one is empty." It wasn't. There was a small amount of liquid still in the bottom of the bottle but the maid couldn't possibly tell from the distance she stood. It would be just enough, Sophie hoped, to find out precisely what the contents were.

"I can take care of it, Miss. Cook will want to wash the bottle and reuse it."

"Actually, I've a bottle of rose water upstairs in my things that's chipped. This would be the perfect size to replace it. I'll just rinse it with some water beforehand. But thank you, Betsy."

"You might ought to let me see to it and give it a proper wash, Miss," the maid said nervously.

Sophie smiled blankly, trying to come up with an excuse but the cook saved her once more. The woman bellowed for Betsy who started like a frightened rabbit.

"It's all right. I'll take care of it, Betsy. Run along before you get into trouble."

The maid nodded and darted away. Placing the full bottle on the shelf, Sophie pocketed the nearly empty one and made her way out into the main corridor and up the stairs to the entry hall. She needed to find some reason to leave the house, some errand perhaps that she might complete for the duchess which would allow her to locate and obtain the services of an apothecary. She needed to find someone who could tell her precisely what was in that bottle.

Waylaying some passing footman in the corridor, Sophie inquired, "Is her grace in the drawing room or the morning room?"

"Her grace is out, Miss Upchurch," the footman replied. "His grace is in his study with the viscount if you require assistance."

"Oh, no! No. It's nothing that I would need to bother them about," Sophie said, quickly backing away. But her escape was curtailed by the opening of the study door.

"Ah, Miss Upchurch," the viscount said, "I thought I heard you out here. Might I ask for your company on an outing? I am to call on Lady Hemsley who was a great friend of Lady Parkhurst. She is quite keen to meet you as it had been at her behest that Lady Parkhurst deigned to obtain a companion."

Sophie stared at him in complete consternation. It was the opportunity she'd needed—a chance to get the tonic created for Philippa to an apothecary. But it was hours spent in his company. Realizing that she was stuck, she said, "What if Philippa needs me? I should hate for her to wake and have no one to assist her!"

The duke emerged then. "We've a houseful of servants, Miss Upchurch. Go and enjoy the day while you can. We have excellent weather for a change!"

"Of course," Sophie agreed. "Let me just get my shawl."

"Send a maid for it," the duke said, and gestured to the waylaid footman who was off then to see it done. "You're not a servant in this house, Miss Upchurch. I understand that your position with Lady

Parkhurst was that of a paid companion, but here you are a guest in our home who is thankfully providing much needed company and no small amount of joy to my daughter—both of which she desperately needs."

Sophie blushed. "Forgive me, your grace. I am not used to having servants to see to my every need and whim. It is quite an adjustment, but I am very grateful for your generosity and your hospitality, sir. Philippa is a delight and I hope that I may offer her some comfort while I am here."

The duke nodded, disappeared once more into his study and then shut the door behind him. Sophie found herself alone in the corridor with Viscount Marchwood. "Would it be possible to visit an apothecary while we are out?"

"Certainly. Are you ill?" he inquired.

"No," Sophie answered. From her pocket, she withdrew the bottle and showed it to him. "Dr. Blake provided a new bottle of Philippa's elixir today. I secured the small amount that remained in her previous bottle and I wish to have it examined. I want to know what he is giving her!"

⋙⋘

HENRY GAPED AT her. He was equal parts impressed and horrified. It was a tactic he should have considered himself, honestly. That she'd managed to do so in less than a full day in their household left him feeling somewhat uncertain.

"Tis a pity Wellington did not have your services, Miss Upchurch. The war would no doubt have ended much sooner," he stated.

Under his gaze, she blushed prettily, but he could see her bristling. "What would you have me do, my lord? It is apparent that Philippa has very complicated feelings for this man! He is her physician, he has authority over her, he is young and handsome—of course, she feels compelled to do as he bids whatever her instincts about him might say! And I must say that, while his behavior was not inappropriate with her, it skated very near to it."

It was Henry's turn to bristle. "What do you mean by inappropriate?"

Miss Upchurch glanced at the closed door of his uncle's study and at the footmen who were near the end of the corridor. "It's something we should discuss on our walk to Lady Hemsley's."

"No, Miss Upchurch. I think that is something we must address now. Do you think he has compromised her in some way?"

"No!" she protested immediately. "That is to say, I do not think he has. But what I observed today... well, his behavior seems more like a suitor than any physician of my acquaintance. It was, if I had to apply some sort of descriptive label to it, somewhat intimate. Even romantic. But not overtly so. I rather think he wants her to see him as potential suitor."

Philippa was an heiress. She was painfully young. Not even sixteen yet. And her illness kept her from most social activities where she might meet suitable young men. In short, she was especially vulnerable to such attentions and, therefore, the ideal candidate for such schemes from a well-disguised fortune hunter. "And what do your instincts say about him, Miss Upchurch?"

"That he is a charlatan. That perhaps he has some ulterior motive. Philippa is the daughter of a duke, after all. What if he is making her sick—or failing to make her well—only to miraculously cure her later on? What if he is banking on her gratitude, and perhaps her family's gratitude, to earn him a more permanent place in her life?"

It wasn't so different from his own suspicions aroused by his prior conversation with Lady Hemsley. "I owe you an apology, Miss Upchurch. While I did not dismiss your suspicions out of hand initially, I did not take them as seriously as I ought to have. I've reason now to suspect that your interpretation of the situation is more accurate than you might realize. And our outing today… well, it has quite a bit to do with that."

Henry went quiet as soon as the maid that had been dispatched by his uncle returned with Miss Upchurch's shawl. She donned it quickly and then they were off. He did not bother having a maid or groom to accompany them as they would not be in a closed carriage but on foot. It wasn't improper, though it wasn't quite the done thing either. Still, the fewer people who overheard their conversation the better. Henry held his arm out to her.

Miss Upchurch smiled a tad too brightly as she placed her finger-tips on his arm. "Well, let's be off then. I'm quite anxious to see Southampton." Exiting the house, they'd gone some distance down the street before she said, "What have you learned?"

"Lady Hemsley informed me that Dr. Blake came to be Philippa's physician by way of recommendation from Lady Parkhurst," Henry answered, keeping his voice pitched low. "And while Lady Parkhurst was somewhat advanced in her years, she was always in very keen health until Dr. Richard Blake became her physician. And apparently, she is not the only one. Several people have experienced worsening symptoms while under his care. But he has a great deal of support in society. I cannot understand why people will continue to seek out the aid of a physician who does not provide cures or relief from symp-toms!"

"Because he is young and handsome and tells people what they wish to hear," Miss Upchurch stated. "And I'm beginning to think his elixirs might be part of that, as well. He prescribed an inordinate amount of it to her. Two drops in the morning, two in the afternoon and three at night!"

Henry was more than a bit confounded by her continued refer-ences to how handsome the doctor was. "What on earth does his handsomeness have to do with anything? And I confess to knowing next to nothing about what quantities of mysterious elixirs one should be taking."

"Because he is appealing to the vanity of his female patients," Miss Upchurch stated. "He flirts with them, he pays particular attention to them. In the case of Philippa, and perhaps other young women, he plants the seed that his interest might be more than just that of a physician for his patient! When someone is isolated by illness, when their world shrinks every day, that sort of brightness and hope can be a very powerful motivator."

Henry couldn't deny any of that. But he wasn't quite ready to accept it entirely. "And what is his end then in making them sicker?"

Miss Upchurch considered her answer for a moment, chewing on her lower lip in a way that drew his eyes and sent his thoughts into very dangerous territory. At last, she said, "By making them sicker, he limits their access to the outside world even more and increases their dependence on him. It allows him to cast himself in the role of both friend and savior. It's quite diabolical really."

Henry wondered if that could really be the case. Was it truly so simple? For some reason, he could not bring himself to believe that was the whole of it. Reluctant as he might have been to be sucked into this *investigation*, for lack of a better term, he now found himself wholly invested in it. "There must be something more."

"I agree. I, too, suspect there may be something more to it than that. I cannot help but wonder why he sees Philippa twice per week. No other physician does such unless it is truly warranted. While she is not well, her condition does appear to be stable at least. Unless that harkens back to my earlier suspicions regarding the nature of his attentions toward her and that his interest in her is more than professional. Do you think—would he have designs on her virtue?"

"Possibly," Henry conceded. "I think it more likely that he has designs on her fortune, however."

"You do not see her, do you?" Miss Upchurch asked.

"What do you mean by that?"

Miss Upchurch sighed. "You think Philippa is still a child. But in truth, she is only about two years younger than I am. Do you think me a child?"

Heaven help him, he did not. He saw Miss Sophia Upchurch as the very definition of womanhood, and that was a disaster for them both. "You know that I do not."

"Then do not presume that, simply because you cannot see her that way, that other men do not look at Philippa and see her beauty and her youth and the fact that she is, whatever your beliefs on the matter, on the cusp of womanhood," Sophie stated. "And girls at that age are especially vulnerable to the attentions of men who understand that about them... who understand that they very much want to make that leap from being a girl to a woman."

"And did some man take advantage of your vulnerability that way?" He had to ask. It would not change his opinion of her, but it would explain her caution and her reaction to his deception.

"No," she answered sharply. "But I have seen it frequently enough with other girls. You have but to look around you, my lord. It is nothing to see young women married to men who are twenty, thirty and sometimes even forty years their senior. It is also nothing to see that women who have been turned out into the street are often not much older than I am. Meanwhile, the men with whom they committed their sins bear no consequence at all. If ever there was proof that women are exploited by men, the very existence of the Darrow School should provide it."

They walked on in silence for a moment, Henry digesting what she had said and Miss Upchurch, if her sidelong worried glances were any indication, wondering if she had gone too far. But she hadn't. She'd pointed out some universal truths—truths so accepted as simply being the way of the world that the terrible wrongness of them had ceased to be noted.

"How much further to Lady Hemsley's?" she finally asked.

"Not much further, but we will detour a small bit. We shall find your apothecary first," he said. "Lady Hemsley is not expecting us until later in the afternoon. We are to join her for tea." If what Miss Upchurch suspected of the doctor and his intentions were true, then the man was far more diabolical than Henry had first imagined him to be.

Chapter Seven

T HE INTERIOR OF the apothecary shop was quite dim and dreary. Located below street level in what had once been the kitchen of a terrace house, the door was so short that the viscount had to duck his head entirely and bend at the waist in order to enter. Inside, it was a bit roomier, but not by much. The ceiling was still so close that he was forced to dip his head. It had the effect of making her feel surrounded by him. It was not an unpleasant sensation and that was the most terrifying part of it. His nearness, the way he towered over her, the breadth of his shoulders—it made her feel safe and protected. It also made her very aware of all the mysterious ways in which they were different. It piqued her curiosity and left her feeling flushed and warm in a way she didn't quite understand.

For her own peace of mind, Sophie forced herself to pay more attention to her surroundings than her companion. Surveying the shop, she made note of all the various tools of the trade that were evident. There were bundles of herbs and flowers hanging from the rafters of the ceiling, drying for use in future concoctions. Glass bottles of various sizes and tools of unidentifiable origins and usefulness littered every surface. But along one wall was a glass-fronted cabinet laden with cures. Bottles upon bottles of tonics, elixirs, purgatives, poultices and tinctures lined those shelves, each one carefully labeled.

"Hello!" The cheerful greeting came from the back of the shop, one of the rabbit warren of rooms from the shop's former use as a kitchen.

"Hello. We have need of your services, sir," Viscount Marchwood called out.

"Right! If you didn't, then you wouldn't be here!" the man called out again, then laughed. In fact, he chortled all the way down the long, skinny corridor until he stepped into the light from the shop's small front window. "How can I help you?"

Sophie removed the bottle from her pocket. "Would you be able to identify any of the ingredients in this?"

The little man accepted the proffered bottle, tipping his head back and peering at the label through his spectacles. "I might be able to tell you some of the ingredients, but I could not identify all of them. My concern, young lady, is why you wish to know?"

"It's been given to a friend of mine," Sophie answered. "But I am worried about the contents."

The man pulled the stopper from the bottle and gave it a whiff. He made a terrible face. "And well you should be. You, sir, flip the sign to closed and lock that door."

If Viscount Marchwood took exception to being ordered about by a tradesman, he didn't indicate it at all. Instead, he did as instructed and then returned to Sophie's side.

"Come this way," the apothecary said. "My workroom is back here."

Following him along the narrow corridor, it dawned on Sophie that they'd chosen the man at random. He might have a relationship with Dr. Blake. He could be a villain, as well, for all that they knew.

"Do you know Dr. Blake, sir?" Sophie asked.

"Who?"

"Dr. Blake," Sophie stated. "He's the physician who prepared that elixir for my friend."

"Ah," the apothecary said. "Not much of a physician, is he?"

"I'm not sure I take your meaning, sir," Sophie answered.

"What I mean, Miss, is this physician, best as I can tell, is poisoning your friend. That or turning her into one of those hollow-eyed souls that chase the dragon," the apothecary answered, a note of bitterness in his voice.

Sophie was still frowning as he stepped through a doorway into a larger room, this one more brightly lit from the candles all about it. "I'm afraid I don't understand what that means."

"Opium, Sophie," Viscount Marchwood stated. "Chasing the dragon is a term applied to those who are addicted to opium."

Sophie glanced back at the bottle in horror, almost as if it might reach out and bite them. "Oh, but... well, she does have terrible megrims. Perhaps he truly intends it to ease her pain?"

"Not likely. There's a bit of henbane in here, as well," the apothecary said. "Thought I smelled it. All this concoction will do is make the girl's head ache worse than it already does, make her feel weak and tired and still have her reaching for this bottle because she'll crave what else is in it. Lots of physicians and apothecaries have no issue in prescribing laudanum, or it's stronger parent—opium—to their patients. I find it often does more harm than good. Unless the person is at death's door and unlikely to recover, I'll not give such a substance."

"You were quite right, Sophie. It seems that Dr. Blake does mean to make his patients dependent upon him," the viscount said. "But he means to use far more than his handsome face to do so. Come, we must go."

"Might I keep this?" the apothecary asked. "There are other ingredients that I might identify with time to do some tests."

"Yes, sir," the viscount said. "Keep it."

"Wait," Sophie said. "Is it safe for our friend to stop taking opium immediately? Will it not make her terribly ill?"

"It will, Miss," the apothecary said. "But with the other ingredients in this bottle, I don't know that she could tell the difference."

"Then transfer those contents to another bottle and refill that one with a harmless substance. We shall replace the bottle in the cook's cupboard with it and we shall begin weaning Philippa off his concoction with no one the wiser... not even her," the viscount stated.

The apothecary gave him a wink and a nod. "Quite right. Let the devil hang himself."

⟫⟫⟫⟪⟪⟪

AN HOUR LATER, they were being shown into the drawing room at Lady Hemsley's. Henry was still reeling. What he'd discovered that day, both about Dr. Blake and his wicked intentions, as well as Sophie Upchurch and her uncanny criminal mind, had left him feeling entirely out of his depth.

"Good afternoon, Lady Hemsley," he said.

"Good afternoon, Marchwood," Lady Hemsley replied. She was giving Miss Upchurch a thorough once over, her gaze traveling over the girl in a way that could only be called insolent. "You do not look very much like a companion, Miss...?"

"Upchurch. Miss Sophia Upchurch. I wasn't aware that companions looked any way at all, Lady Hemsley," Miss Upchurch replied.

Lady Hemsley let out a harumph, though it was clear she was amused. "Old Bess would have enjoyed you! Oh, not openly. She'd have complained and groused as she was wont to do but, secretly, she'd have liked that you had a bit of spirit about you."

"Old Bess?" Henry asked.

"Lady Elizabeth Parkhurst. Or, if you'd known her for as long as I did, Old Bess," Lady Hemsley said. "She wasn't always old. Neither was I for that matter. Once upon a time, young man, we were bold and scandalous women." That statement was accompanied with a wink and a grin.

That was a terrifying thought and one he felt compelled to avoid further acquaintance with. "We have information about Dr. Blake, Lady Hemsley."

The woman eyed him speculatively for a moment. Then she waved all her servants away. "What do you know about that charlatan?"

"He's prescribing laudanum without telling his patients they are taking it. In fact, his elixirs are little better than poisons that also happen to be addictive in nature," Henry stated.

"I knew it," Lady Hemsley said triumphantly. "Bess changed, you see. Her personality, her energy—everything that made her who she was became muted or dulled after she began to see him. But she refused to hear a negative word about him. And I do not need to tell you, Viscount Marchwood, that for Bess to refuse to gossip about anyone was truly a rare occurrence!"

"We will defer to your knowledge of Lady Parkhurst's nature and character as my own acquaintance with her was so very limited," Miss Upchurch offered diplomatically.

Lady Hemsley laughed softly. "Oh, yes. You'd have led her on a merry chase. But we're not here for that, are we? Let me tell you what I've heard about the good doctor. He's deeply in debt and looking for a way out of it."

"A wife," Henry surmised.

"Indeed. One with access to significant wealth and powerful connections... I find it quite telling that he was most insistent upon Bess making a recommendation to the Duke of Thornhill that he should be sought after to treat the duke's ailing daughter."

"If that is true, then perhaps he chose to permanently silence Lady Parkhurst so there would be no one to bear witness to the fact that the recommendation occurred at his behest," Miss Upchurch suggested.

Lady Hemsley's eyes gleamed. "You are a smart girl! Quite right. He's forever moving up a step in terms of how influential or prestigious his patients are. Oddly enough, most of his patients are also women. He is a man who is very certain of his appeal to the opposite sex. Do you not think, Miss Upchurch?"

"I think him handsome and I think him well aware of it, Lady Hemsley. I believe that he does trade upon his good looks in order to sway his patients to compliance."

Lady Hemsley nodded. "You are an excellent judge of character, it seems, for you have read him quite clearly. He treats many matrons of local society for their various ailments. Because he is handsome and charming, they all presume him incapable of wickedness. I know better! And because he is giving them all laudanum, they have all sworn by his remedies. Well, naturally, they feel better when taking whatever tincture he's provided! Or rather, they do if they serve no other purpose for him. So you must be careful to whom you say anything about him. It will get back to him, you see? They all want to curry favor with him and will inform him of your plots against him for their own gain! Do not act until you have proof of what he's about."

"What sort of proof?" Miss Upchurch asked.

"I will start with the moneylenders," Henry stated. "If he has markers, I can buy them up. That will give us leverage."

"What sorts of debt has he incurred?" Miss Upchurch asked. "Is he gambling?"

"I do not know, my dear girl, but I do know he is living well beyond the means of a simple physician. Bespoke clothing from the finest tailors around. Boots that would rival Hobie. And he has a carriage that is quite fine. Not to mention that house of his. End of the terrace and four windows across the front. It would cost more in a month than he earns in several years to lease such a residence," Lady Hemsley explained. "There's no connection to any sort of family money that I've been able to discern. Which leaves only credit."

"He lives quite high then," Henry mused.

"Indeed. He's often seen at the racecourse, though I do not believe he is betting. I think he simply likes to see and be seen," Lady Hemsley said. "Start with the moneylenders, Marchwood, as you said. That is a most excellent notion. Now, I may not look it, but I am quite old and quite tired. You may disagree with me on both counts, but not strenuously."

Henry couldn't stop a grin. "Indeed, Madam, you appear to be the picture of vitality."

"Well enough, young man. The two of you run along and begin your investigation. I am quite intrigued to see all of this play out. And for once, I intend to keep my mouth shut and not go blathering what I know to the masses," Lady Hemsley stated. "Good day to you both."

Dismissed, Henry escorted Miss Upchurch from Lady Hemsley's home. Once outside, he asked her, "How did you know that about Dr. Blake? How did you so easily identify his character?"

Miss Upchurch shrugged. "Effie—Miss Darrow—has always en-couraged us to follow our instincts about whether or not a person meant us harm... if they were trustworthy or not. And I found him questionable from the first."

Henry nodded. "And yet when we met, I was lying to you about my name... still you trusted me. Perhaps because instinctively you knew then, as now, that I would never mean to harm you." With that bit of logic, he'd pinned her. Standing there on the street, watching as she tried to formulate some response to it, he simply waited.

After a long moment of silence, she said, "You may not have in-tended harm. But, you have to see that it changes things. You said you wished to determine whether or not you wanted to court me... but I am not the sort of woman a man in your position should court. I know how attachments for people in your position work. Marrying for love alone is the only luxury the poor possess."

"Not every peer must marry for wealth or position. I don't need further wealth and my position in society is something I could not care less about! I am currently jumping for joy that my aunt might present my uncle with an heir and I will not have the dukedom hanging over my head. I don't want any of it, Miss Upchurch. I want to live a simple life on my country estate, hopefully with a wife who likes me for who I am… who might even love me a little as I hope to love her. Is that so very wrong?"

She didn't answer the question. Instead, she glanced up at the sky which had filled suddenly with clouds that mirrored her own troubled gaze. "We should return home. It will begin raining soon."

Henry didn't lose heart. He took her lack of an answer as a good sign instead. She would come around. He was certain of it.

Chapter Eight

PHILIPPA WAS AWAKE when they returned. The sky was still cloudy and overcast but the rain had held off, so she was taking the air on the terrace just off the drawing room again. While Sophie had expected that she and the viscount would part ways upon their return, when she made her way out to the terrace, he accompanied her.

"Henry!" Philippa cried happily. "Thank you for taking such wonderful care of Miss Upchurch while I was resting. I cannot abide the thought that she would grow bored or languish while here with us."

The viscount grinned. "I shall endeavor to keep Miss Upchurch well entertained when you cannot, Cousin." Leaning forward, he kissed Philippa's cheek. "I'm so glad to see you up and about."

"Up, hardly about," Philippa replied. "Where have you been?"

"We called on Lady Hemsley," Sophie answered. "She was apparently very dear friends with Lady Parkhurst and was instrumental in Lady Parkhurst's decision to take on a companion. She's the reason I'm here, I suppose."

Philippa's expression never altered. "Lady Parkhurst was a patient of Dr. Blake's. He's terribly disappointed because she had stated she would see him remembered in her will and, alas, she did not."

Sophie seated herself on another bench on the terrace and took in that bit of information. "What an unusual topic to come up in conversation."

"Oh, well... it was last week. Right after she'd passed but before you'd arrived," Philippa explained. "I suppose I was impertinent when I asked him if he was part of the social scene here, if he was, perhaps, looking for a bride."

"And how did he answer such an impertinent question?" Henry asked her, as he strolled along the perimeter of the small terrace.

"Only that without the inheritance he'd expected from Lady Parkhurst, it would be some time before he'd be in a position to marry."

"Unless he finds a wealthy bride," Sophie stated.

Philippa frowned. "Well, yes, I suppose so. But he never said such a thing. I cannot imagine that he would have such an expectation."

"My lord, would you please excuse us for a moment?" Sophie asked. "There is a delicate matter that I need to discuss with Lady Philippa."

"Certainly. I'll go in and arrange for a tea tray. I'm sure after our call and our walk you are quite parched, Miss Upchurch."

When he'd gone back inside, Sophie looked at Philippa and asked very bluntly, "Has Dr. Blake been inappropriate with you?"

"I don't understand what you mean," Philippa denied.

"He should not be discussing his marital prospects with you, first of all. Secondly, Philippa, I saw how he touched you this morning. Cupping your cheek. Brushing your hair back. Those gestures are very..."

"I know," she said. "But he's never done anything more than that."

"But he shouldn't be doing that at all. When did he begin making such overtures to you?"

Philippa clasped her hands in her lap, clenching them so tightly that her knuckles went white. "It hasn't been very long. I know he shouldn't and that perhaps I should say something to him or to Papa, but—I just want to be well, Sophie. I just want to laugh and dance and do the things other girls do. Dr. Blake insists he can make me better.

He can give me the life I want to have. I'm afraid to say anything!"

The anguish the girl felt, the desperation that she clearly lived with every day as she felt life simply passing her by, that weighed heavily on Sophie's heart. "What if there was another way to have what you want, Philippa? What if Dr. Blake's restrictions are not designed to help you?"

"What else would they be designed to do?" Philippa asked. "I don't wish to discuss this anymore. My head is beginning to ache and I simply can't bear it. I know you mean well, Sophie. I do. But I'm just so very tired!"

How much of that was Philippa's condition, Sophie wondered, and how much was the noxious elixir that Dr. Blake had prescribed for her? She would need to speak with the apothecary again to determine how long the effects of not having her daily laudanum would last for Philippa.

"I shall leave you to enjoy the air then," Sophie said and rose.

"No," Philippa said. "I really am tired. Would you have a footman come to take me upstairs? I need to rest."

"Very well," Sophie agreed. She moved back into the house, rang for the footman, and when he arrived almost instantaneously, she relayed Philippa's request. Within seconds, it seemed, servants were scurrying to do her bidding and return the girl to her chamber. *Her prison.*

Sophie hoped that once the drug was entirely out of Philippa's system, things would alter significantly for Philippa. If they did not, then the notion that Dr. Blake was doing her harm might become very difficult to prove. It would be even more difficult to secure Philippa's cooperation.

Alone in the drawing room, Sophie stepped outside to the now deserted terrace. Moments later, a maid stepped through the door carrying a tea tray which she placed on one of the tables, dipped a curtsy and then bustled out. Seconds later, Henry came striding through.

"Where is Philippa?"

"I pressed her too hard," Sophie admitted. "I asked her impertinent questions about Dr. Blake. She pled exhaustion and was taken upstairs to rest."

⫸⫷

HENRY SIGHED HEAVILY as he settled onto the chair recently vacated by Philippa. "Does she care for him?"

"No," Sophie replied thoughtfully. "I believe that Philippa's loyalty to Dr. Blake is not an indication of her feelings for him as a man but her desire to believe the promises he has made to her about making her well."

Frustrated, Henry clenched his fists at his sides. It was better than the alternative of tossing things about. "How can he make such a promise when he has yet to fully ascertain what her condition is?"

"He will likely call it some sort of hysteria and blame it on the fact that she is a woman," Sophie replied bitterly. "It's enough to get one locked in an asylum, after all."

"I'd never considered it, but yes, I suppose it is," Henry admitted. "You're quite the reformer, aren't you, Miss Upchurch?"

"Hardly that," she replied. "It's impossible to be a reformer when you have no power or position from which to demand change. I'm aware, of course, of what it means to be a woman in this world, of what it means to lack any sort of control or power over one's own life. That's why I find Effie—Miss Darrow—to be so remarkable."

Curious but also a bit concerned, Henry asked for clarification. "Because of her school?"

"No. Because she has elected to retain her independence. A woman, once married, is little more than property. But women like Miss Darrow and me, those who are parentless under the letter of the law and who do not have husbands, we have a kind of freedom that other women will never know. It is the primary reason I have always been content with the idea of being a governess or companion. It will never afford me great wealth or even moderate financial security, but it will allow me to remain independent."

"And your independence is very important to you," he surmised. It was telling. He could see that Miss Upchurch had given a great deal of thought to her future. The question remained of whether or not he could sway her to think there were alternatives.

"Precisely."

"And if you could find a husband who would not treat you as property, but who recognized your worth and treated you according-ly?"

She cocked her head to one side, a quizzical expression on her face. "Does such a mythical being exist? If so, I might be tempted. But it doesn't change the law, does it? And the laws are the problem, really."

"You are remarkable, Miss Upchurch. And your vision of the world is enlightening to say the least."

"And you, my lord? What is it that you found the need to run away from?" she asked.

"This," he said, sweeping his hand all around them. "Last year, my uncle decided he wanted the gardens redone. So I hired a designer, I hired a time, and the gardens were redone. Then he decided he didn't care for it. So I hired a different designer and another team to attempt to return the garden to its prior state. And while doing that, I was managing his estates, managing my own estate, addressing issues with distant relatives who were then and now spending beyond their means. Regardless of that, we cannot let them starve or be evicted."

"You take care of all of them?"

"To some degree, yes," he replied.

"And who takes care of you?"

He laughed at that. "It was my ability to take care of myself from an early age that prompted my uncle to place more and more responsibility on my shoulders."

"And your parents?" Sophie asked. "You've never said what became of them."

"My mother died when I was a very small boy. I do not recall her at all really. My father died when I was twelve. He... umm... well, he was not himself without her. He frequented the opium dens of London with regularity. Outside of one of them, he was robbed, stabbed, and left for dead. Someone discovered him, brought him home and he died several days later after infection set in."

He'd said it all rather matter of factly. But when he looked up, he knew that she'd heard something in his voice that hinted at his past pain. "It's all right," he said. "It was all a very long time ago."

"Not so very long. Is that why you take care of everyone? Because you think you failed to take care of your father?"

The question pierced him to his soul. He'd never considered it. But it was likely true. "Perhaps. Which begs the question, Miss Upchurch, do you prefer independence because you believe no one can be depended upon?"

She was saved from answering by a great commotion from inside the house. Even from their position on the terrace, the noise was undeniable. Servants could be seen scurrying to and fro beyond the open drawing room door.

"Shall we go and see what that is all about?" he asked.

"Yes," she agreed. "And let's leave old wounds alone. Shall we?"

He nodded his agreement and offered her his arm. She accepted and, together, they made their way inside.

Chapter Nine

W HEN SOPHIE EXITED the drawing room on the viscount's arm and stepped into the main corridor, there were boxes, trunks and valises everywhere. It appeared as if the entire household were on the verge of vacating the premises. "Heavens, what has happened?"

"My aunt, Horatia, has arrived," Viscount Marchwood explained. "It's always a bit of a… well, a mess. Aunt Horatia likes to make an entrance."

Sophie stared at the chaos before them. "That is putting it quite mildly. Does she always travel so—that is to say, she seems very well prepared." It was a relief to be talking about someone or something else. Their inadvertent confidences and speculation about one another's innermost motivations had created a feeling of intimacy between them that left Sophie very uncomfortable and that only confirmed for her that their relationship was a dangerous one.

The viscount laughed. "I think it is worse than usual. Aunt Horatia has been a confirmed spinster for many, many years. And she has recently met a gentleman and they are betrothed. He is from the north, you see, and involved in trade. I believe he owns several quite successful textile mills. Aunt Horatia is likely concerned about what will be said when they enter society together here and so she means to dress to the nines to display her social superiority lest anyone think to challenge her choice."

"Would they challenge her choice then?" Sophie asked. It didn't take a great deal of intelligence to see that he was trying to illustrate how remarkably unconventional everyone in his family was.

"Never to her face," he admitted. "I daresay many people will say unkind things when her back is turned. But she will not know about them, will she? Thus freeing her from any obligation to care."

"You say that as if it is so very simple!"

"It can be," he stated. "One simply has to decide what is more important: one's own happiness or the opinions of others. I personally know what I value more. But come, let me introduce you to my aunt."

Sophie permitted him to escort her into the morning room where the duchess preferred to receive guests, dodging servants who were carting boxes and cases to and fro. The duchess had returned and was seated next to a woman on a settee who was much older than Sophie would have first imagined. The duke was standing behind the duchess. And standing next to whom she could only assume was Horatia was a man that Sophie instantly recognized. In fact, taking one glance at him, she recalled the countless times she had seen him and felt her gut clench. He was known to her because he'd come once per quarter to the Darrow School, met with Effie, paid her a significant sum of money for the care of one of her pupils and then left without ever actually seeing the girl, whomever she was, that he was there to support.

A glance at his face showed that he recognized her, as well. He stared at her with something akin to dread. She knew his secret shame and they were not at all on equal footing. As someone who would be marrying into the family, he was on far more secure footing than she could ever hope to be.

"Ah, here you are," the duchess said with a warm and welcoming smile. "Henry has been showing Miss Upchurch around Southampton today. We are ever so happy to have her with us. She's been a true blessing for poor Philippa. Miss Upchurch, this is my sister-in-law,

Lady Horatia Meredith and her betrothed, Mr. William Carlton. Horatia, Mr. Carlton, please meet Miss Sophia Upchurch. And Mr. Carlton, of course, you know Henry."

"How lovely for Philippa to have such good company," Lady Horatia said, though there was a slight sneer to her lips and a coolness to her tone that belied her kind words. "But how odd that you should be on Henry's arm today instead of with her."

There had been no attempt at all to disguise her disapproval and Sophie found herself bristling under it. "Lady Philippa was just with us on the terrace but, alas, after her visit with Dr. Blake this morning, she was quite exhausted and has gone upstairs to rest. I'm certain, after your long journey, that you are in complete sympathy, Lady Horatia."

"Of course, she was. Poor dear! And yes, we are naturally very tired from our journey, but I am more hale and hearty than poor Philippa," Lady Horatia said. Still, the woman's gaze roamed over Sophie and then over Henry, as if they had been engaged in something scandalous.

"Where were you off to, Henry?" the duchess asked. "You are normally not so sociable! Why, we must threaten you on pain of death to make you engage with society! Yet, you show no qualms about squiring Miss Upchurch around!"

"I had run into Lady Hemsley this morning," he said. "Apparently she had been instrumental in getting Lady Parkhurst to seek a companion. She felt quite responsible for Miss Upchurch's current situation and wished to meet her to be assured all is well."

The duchess snorted in derision. "Unlikely. She was no doubt hoping for some bit of scandal or gossip to pass around. That woman! Good heavens."

"Lady Hemsley?" Lady Horatia parroted. "My goodness, I would have thought she'd given up the proverbial ghost some years back. Though I daresay it is a pity about Lady Parkhurst. She could be difficult, but she was a good woman. Still, I suppose it is to the benefit of Miss Upchurch, is it not?"

"How so, Lady Horatia?" Sophie asked. She had the distinct feeling she would not like the woman's answer.

"Well, my dear, rather like a cat, you've landed in a much more pleasant position than the one which you started in. After all, it's well known that Lady Parkhurst, despite being very deserving of my good opinion of her, could also be quite difficult and very exacting, particularly of those in her employ."

The duchess made a slight moue, a clear indication of her disagreement. "That woman was wicked. How you can think so highly of her, Horatia, I'll never know. I shall never forget how horrid she was to me when I first married. She said all manner of awful things about me. I was called a fortune hunter and an adventuress!"

"Well, she's hardly here now to be punished for it and continued discussion of her character flaws hardly does any of us credit," the viscount pointed out. "I am curious about something, though."

"And what is that?" the duchess asked just as a maid entered with a tray bearing refreshments.

"If you disliked Lady Parkhurst so much, how is that she came to recommend Dr. Blake's services for Philippa?" He posed the question as if it were simply idle curiosity, but it was quite pointed, even if no one else clued in to that.

The duchess shrugged. "I didn't like the woman, but she was a font of useful information. Nothing occurred in Southampton without her knowledge. I believe that we spoke in passing about Philippa's need for a new physician when we'd gone to take the waters, that she simply offered up the suggestion. It is rather strange now that I think about it, though!"

"How so?" the viscount pressed.

The duchess poured tea with a steady hand as she answered, "Lady Parkhurst, to my knowledge, did not aspire to be helpful to anyone. Ever. Certainly not to anyone in this family. As for our own long-standing tolerance of one another, we made it a point to be civil to one another at social events but we never sought out opportunities for conversation. And that day, Lady Parkhurst made a concerted effort to engage us in conversation. Perhaps it was an olive branch. Maybe she had some sort of inkling that her time on this earth was at an end and wished to mend her fences, so to speak."

"I think that is an excellent observation, your grace," Mr. Carlton stated. "Very insightful. I feel most people seek to mend fences, as it were, when they sense their time is at an end."

What an ingratiating little toad he was! Sophie watched him simper and smile with a feeling of disgust. Every time she'd ever seen him at the Darrow School, he'd been snide and superior. As if, in spite of being there as a direct result of his own indiscretions, the entire sordid mess was somehow beneath his dignity.

"Mr. Carlton, please forgive me, but I cannot help but think perhaps we have met before," Sophie stated. "Are you much in London?"

The man's face paled and his expression became pinched. But he didn't answer. As he stammered helplessly, Viscount Marchwood's aunt stepped in.

"William goes to London quite frequently," Lady Horatia said. "He has many business interests there. Though, I cannot imagine where the two of you might have crossed paths. You are a companion, after all, and he has no reason to pay calls on anyone sickly or elderly enough to require such a person."

"I have only recently left school to begin to such a career, my lady," Sophie said. "Perhaps you are a benefactor for the school? It is not a charity school, per se, but Miss Darrow does often take on students who are not in a position to afford tuition. Despite that, it is very well respected."

"If not a charity school, then what? If students' families cannot pay—if they have them at all—and others must provide for them, how can it be anything else?" Lady Horatia harrumphed. "For women? It ought to be a charity matchmaker! Teach young women to get husbands and not careers!"

The duchess frowned. Her expression was one of confusion, as if she didn't understand her sister-in-law's vitriol. "I hardly think that is necessary. Many young women, if they have no family to ensure that the match made for them is in their best interest, should certainly have some sort of skill to support themselves in the world. Horatia, I am shocked at you. I had always thought you something of a reformer when it came to strictures placed on women in our society. You have been a staunch supporter of such causes for as long as I can recall!"

Lady Horatia's expression tightened into a smile that was anything but amused. "Perhaps all it took was meeting a gentleman of quality, a man of his word, to help me see the error of my ways. I have learned now that a woman, when faced with the right man, does not need independence."

The duchess let out a sigh. "I see." Then she looked up at the viscount for a moment before her gaze drifted to Sophie and a slight smile curved her lips. "Sometimes fate is all the matchmaker a girl requires. Don't you think, Miss Upchurch?"

With the tables turned and all gazes expectantly on her, some warm and others quite glacial, Sophie felt a flush creeping over her cheeks. "I think we are hardly in a position to understand something so capricious as fate, your grace. If you'll pardon me, I'd like to go up and check on Philippa."

"Certainly, my dear."

"It was lovely to meet you… for the first time, Miss Upchurch," Mr. Carlton stated, his tone infused with a warning.

"Indeed," Lady Horatia said, looking at Mr. Carlton with surprise. "Quite lovely, for however long our acquaintance should last."

HENRY HAD NO notion of what was going on. But he was certain that Mr. William Carlton was not the upstanding gentleman his aunt claimed and he was quite certain that Miss Upchurch had seen him before. The man's expression when they had entered the room had been one that could only be described as terror. He'd looked at Miss Upchurch as if, well, as if she knew his secrets. Both curious and concerned, Henry knew he'd have to get it out of her later.

"Forgive me, my dear," Mr. Carlton said. "But I must go out. There is a business associate in town that I must meet with and time is of the essence."

"Of course, my love," Horatia said, her voice so sickeningly sweet it was a wonder that such a tone could come from a woman who had routinely been described as acerbic.

When Carlton had left, Henry noted her pinched expression. Not all was well in that relationship, whatever she might choose to say. "Tell me, Aunt Horatia, how did you and Mr. Carlton meet?" Henry asked casually as he took one of the remaining seats.

"He was most gallant," Horatia said. "My carriage was disabled as I was traveling back from Birmingham to Manchester. If it hadn't been for Mr. Carlton, I might well have frozen to death on the roadside."

Henry had never understood has aunt's desire to remain at a crumbling estate in the north, but then there was a great deal about Horatia that he didn't understand. She'd worn her spinsterhood like a badge of honor for as long as he could remember. There had been countless speeches from her on why she never wanted to be some-thing so menial as a wife. And, yet, here she was, on the cusp of tying herself forever to a man who appeared to be less than forthright.

"That small bit of misfortune was clearly a stroke of luck for you then, as it seems you are quite taken with him and he with you," the duchess remarked.

"Indeed, Cecile," Horatia agreed, ducking her head as a blush stole over her cheeks. "I adore Mr. Carlton and he has certainly given every indication that the feeling is mutual. He is most gracious and most gallant and I count myself very fortunate to have found him when I did."

It rang with sincerity. She meant it, Henry thought. Whatever secrets Carlton was hiding, it was apparent that Horatia was completely enamored with the man. Did he feel the same for his aunt, or was it some sort of charade? Horatia, despite being somewhat stern in demeanor, was a handsome woman. But she was also a woman of remarkable wealth.

"How very romantic!" the duchess cried, clapping her hands together with glee. "Pay attention, Henry! That's the sort of thing that will turn a girl's head, you know."

"And have you found a *suitable* girl that you wish to court, Henry?" Horatia asked.

"I have expressed a fondness for Mr. Upchurch and have informed her of my intent to court her when she is amenable to such," he stated.

"When she is amenable?" Horatia snapped. "What in heaven's name does that mean? Amenable? Does she have so many suitors then? Does she not realize what a great honor you pay her when she is clearly poor and has no family? And yes, I know all about this school of hers in London. Everyone knows about it. Castoffs and bastards!"

"Horatia!" the duchess snapped. "That is quite enough! Miss Upchurch is a guest in our home. As for where she came from, I am far more interested in who she is and how she comports herself. She is all that is elegant and kind. If Henry wishes to court her, I say I am all for it. And if she has her reasons for wanting to be cautious in such a thing, well, more young women should certainly take her example."

Horatia was far from chastened. "It is terribly irresponsible of you, Cecile, to condone such an attachment! The girl's very existence is tainted by scandal."

"Enough!" Henry hadn't intended to shout, but the word echoed about the room and every inhabitant had grown so silent that even the sound of a pin dropping would have been like cannon fire. "When it comes to my attachments and entanglements, they are my decision. They will not be reached by committee. And as for your opinions of Miss Upchurch, Aunt Horatia, they are for your consumption only. While you are here, I expect that you will treat her not only with civility, but with warmth and kindness—even if the latter are completely without sincerity."

Horatia drew back as if deeply offended. "You have never spoken to me in such a manner."

"I have never, until today, had cause. I am ashamed of you, frankly. You have brought your betrothed here... a man who is not of the peerage and who is even in trade. He has been welcomed with open arms and your choice in the matter has not been called into question. Why you would indulge in such hypocrisy as to then challenge anyone else's choices, I cannot fathom," Henry stated. "Now, I expect that at dinner your treatment of Miss Upchurch will be dramatically different. Good afternoon."

Chapter Ten

PHILIPPA WAS STILL sleeping. Drugged, Sophie thought. She would have gotten a dose of Dr. Blake's *special* tonic the night before and again that morning. Was it any wonder the girl had been so unwilling to discuss the matter downstairs? She likely couldn't make much sense of anything.

Standing in the doorway of her chamber, Sophie felt a wave of protectiveness for the girl. It was immediately followed by a flood of anger toward Dr. Blake. There was no question that he'd taken a legitimate medical condition, worsened it and exploited it to make her entirely dependent upon him. And that would stop. The bottle that had been refilled with harmless ingredients by the apothecary was in her pocket. She'd need to get it down to the kitchen and replace the other one, but that would have to happen in the dark of night when the rest of the house was abed.

Stepping back out into the corridor, she closed the door softly. When she turned around, she let out a soft squeak of alarm. She'd thought she was alone, but Henry—*Viscount Marchwood*—was there.

"I need to apologize to you, Miss Upchurch… for my aunt and Mr. Carlton. They were terribly rude downstairs and I will not have you treated that way," he stated emphatically.

Sophie's breath caught. This time, it had nothing to do with being startled. It was simply him. Once more being her champion, just as he had on the coach, just as he had when she'd wandered into that inn—bedraggled and nearly penniless. It seemed that Henry Meredith, Viscount Marchwood, had made a habit out of defending her and rescuing her. And he'd done so without asking anything in return but forgiveness for a harmless omission that hadn't really been about her at all as much as it was his need to escape from the responsibilities of his position. Something she had grown to understand about him more so in the last few hours. With the weight of Philippa's well-being resting on her shoulders, Sophie could understand wanting to escape responsibility. It could be a terrible burden, feeling responsible for others.

"You have nothing to apologize for, my lord," she said. "Not on behalf of your aunt and Mr. Carlton, and not for anything in your own behavior either. I think that I am beginning to understand why you wanted to escape being Viscount Marchwood for a day. They all depend upon you and expect so much from you, don't they?"

His face flushed, clearly embarrassed that she'd seen so much. "I've taken on a lot of the responsibilities for running the estates as my uncle has been grooming me as his heir for quite some time now."

"That's not what I meant. It's not about the estates or the business part of things, though I suspect that also takes a toll. You are almost like a parent to many of the people in this family, despite the fact that you are considerably younger than all of them. And here I've asked you to take on this issue with Philippa. I've burdened you even further, on her behalf, and on my own, as you seem to be perpetually coming to my rescue. But it's important and cannot be entrusted to anyone else," she said.

"The truth is, Miss Upchurch, I like being there for my family. I like being the one they come to with their problems and I like that, more often than not, I have the answers. I simply sometimes wish they'd bother to look for those answers on their own first before they come to me. As for coming to your rescue, well, there is little that I would not do for you."

He needed someone to take care of him so that he could continue taking care of everyone one else, Sophie realized. No wonder the duchess was forever pushing him to get married! The very thought of him marrying someone else was painful to her, but her own position had not changed. She was far beneath him socially and from a practical standpoint, she lacked the necessary skills to manage estates and grand houses. Much as she might wish otherwise, she was not the wife for him. "Perhaps you should allow the duchess to play matchmaker for you?"

"No," he said. "I'll do my own matchmaking, thank you. It may well be a moot point now at any rate."

"You can't pursue this... flirtation with me," Sophie insisted. "You must see it's impossible. Even your aunt, Lady Horatia—"

"Needs to remember that she is now betrothed to a man who is in trade. Frankly, in the eyes of the *ton*, that's worse than being a foundling or being illegitimate," he pointed out. "Besides, I've no wish to be in society. I'm happy enough to rusticate at my estate in the country. Besides, it isn't as if I've proposed... yet."

"You did state you wished to court me! If not for marriage, then for what, my lord?" Sophie demanded. Then it occurred to her precisely how he had phrased his statement about a proposal. "And what do you mean you haven't proposed 'yet'?"

"I'm not saying that I wouldn't propose, Miss Upchurch. Only that I haven't done so at this time, but it could very well happen in the future. It likely will happen, at that. And you are a confounding creature. On the one hand, you act as if a proposal is entirely unwant-ed, and on the other, you act as if you are offended that one has not yet been offered. Which is it?"

Sophie bristled at that. She understood the contrariness of what she'd just expressed but that didn't mean she wanted it pointed out to her. "Wanting to receive the proposal and recognizing that accepting it would be foolish are not mutually exclusive, sir!"

From inside Philippa's room, there was a loud bang. Concerned, Sophie turned away from him and stuck her head inside the door. A book came sailing past her, remarkably close to hitting her directly on the nose.

Philippa, terribly grumpy and sleepy eyed, snapped, "If the two of you must argue, would you do it elsewhere, please?"

Chastened, Sophie nodded and ducked back out of the room, closing the door softly. Turning back to him, she gestured for quiet.

"Walk in the garden with me... tonight after dinner," he said.

"We can barely have a conversation without arguing, though to be fair," Sophie whispered, "that is primarily my fault. I know I've been difficult."

"I lied to you," he said, as if that justified her bad temper.

"Yes, but I know why you did so... and I'm not angry about that. Not anymore. But, I am worried. I am worried that one misstep could see your aunt and uncle withdraw their charity to me—charity that I am uncomfortable accepting as it is but nonetheless entirely dependent upon for the moment. I worry that this is just another lark for you, such as traveling under a false name was. I worry that your interest is more indicative of your boredom than any real attraction!"

"You doubt my attraction for you?" he asked.

"Well, we hardly know one another!"

HENRY STARED AT her for a moment. Did she really have no idea how appealing she was? Yes, he realized. She really was, entirely and without guile, oblivious to her appeal. With that, he knew there was only one option if he wished to convey to her just how appealing he found her.

"Then allow me to demonstrate," he said. Without further preamble or warning, he simply dipped his head, leaned in close and placed his lips over hers.

It had been intended as a relatively chaste kiss, as simply a way to show her that he did, indeed, find her very attractive. But then she'd let out a small gasp of surprise, her lips parting beneath his in an age-old invitation that he simply could not deny. The kiss depended, becoming something carnal and incendiary. The heat that swept through him, the clawing and aching need to possess her—it left him stunned.

Her lips were beyond sweet. Her response, though untutored, was not tentative or timid in the least. As much as he kissed her, she kissed him back. It was unexpected but so very, very welcome.

Raising one hand to her chin, he tipped it up slightly, tilting her head back and changing the angle of the kiss. It opened her mouth more fully to him, allowing him to explore more freely the wonders of that kiss.

And then as abruptly as it began, it ended. A loud harumphing sound echoed in the corridor behind them. Sophie stepped back and Henry looked up and over his shoulder to meet Mr. Carlton's gaze. The man was dressed to go out, having traded his traveling clothes for those more appropriate to pay a call.

"Companion, indeed. You are certainly a companion to someone, Miss Upchurch, but it does not appear to be the daughter of the house," he offered with a sneer.

Henry's temper flared and he whirled, ready to challenge the man for what he'd said. He wouldn't permit anyone to be so blatantly disrespectful to her. But Sophie caught his arm, her grip firm.

"Do not," she urged. "We were being inappropriate and we were caught. That is all. If you take any sort of action, it will only make things worse. Mr. Carlton understands that saying anything at all about this would not go well for him."

Mr. Carlton laughed. "Really? What would induce me to keep

your secret?"

"The duchess is with child and is quite tired most of the time," Sophie stated. "If you disclose what you saw, they will have no choice but to ask me to leave, thus putting the strain of helping Philippa daily back on to the duchess' shoulders. That is something no one wants. You will be making both Philippa and the duchess unhappy when, quite frankly, they would both cheer if the viscount and I were to make a match. I think carrying tales of any impropriety on my part, whether they were spurred to action by it or not, would only make them resentful of you as I am serving a purpose in this household. And as your own position here is somewhat... precarious, I'd hardly think you would wish to draw attention to yourself in that way."

Carlton's face flushed. "Are you threatening me?"

"I'm merely pointing out, Mr. Carlton, that we are both out of our element and moving beyond the sphere of our natural class," Sophie stated evenly. "For both our sakes, we should be as circumspect as possible." With that, she cut her gaze reproachfully toward Henry. "In all things—regardless of whether or not we may be observed. Good day, gentlemen."

Chastened, quite aware that he had crossed a line that perhaps he should not have, Henry was still not entirely remorseful, however. That kiss, unwise as it might have been, had offered all the proof he needed that Sophia Upchurch was not indifferent to him. Far from it. She was just as inexplicably drawn to him as he was to her. Nor was she impervious to his touch. They, it seemed, were one another's weakness.

After she'd walked away, he leveled a warning glance in Mr. Carlton's direction. He'd not let the man make her life any harder than it had already been. "Whatever you've seen here today, you should know that my intentions toward Miss Upchurch are entirely honorable. I intend for her to become a very permanent part of this family. You would do well to remember that before you speak ill of her to anyone."

"It's a pretty speech, but we both know a viscount such as you will only ever have one use for a girl like her," Carlton replied with a superior sneer.

Sophie wasn't there to halt him. There was no cooler head to prevail when his normally placid temperament failed him entirely. Henry reached out, snatched the other man's shirt and neckcloth, hauling him up on his toes until they were eye to eye. "You know not of what you speak. You insult both Miss Upchurch and me. More to the point, you malign the honor of my entire family by even hinting that such a thing would be permitted in this household or that I have been brought up to be such a cad by the very people who have welcomed you here."

Carlton stammered, "You—you can't be serious! No man in your position would marry someone so low!"

"You've no notion what I would and would not do, Mr. Carlton," Henry stated, letting the man go so abruptly that he staggered backward.

"She will never fit in—and you may think that an insult, but we both know it to be true! That girl cannot be a viscountess of note. She hasn't the breeding for it."

"And you are little better than a shopkeeper," Henry snapped. He didn't believe in such notions. Being noble for him, having a title and wealth—he hadn't earned it. It was an accident of birth and made him no better and no worse than anyone else. "Yet you have set your sights quite high indeed! Haven't you? What entitles you to a better life that does not also permit her entry into what you view as a rarefied circle?"

"I'm not a bastard!"

Henry's gaze narrowed as he considered, not for the first time, how satisfying it would be to knock the other man directly on his arse. "That, Mr. Carlton, is a topic of much debate."

"Were it not for the sensibilities of your dear aunt, and the rest of your family, I would call you out for such a remark!"

"Do so," Henry answered. "Please, I beg of you, do so. It will be the last challenge you ever issue."

Carlton's face purpled with rage and the man turned abruptly on his heel to walk away.

Thinking over the man's earlier statement about Sophie's parentage, he called out. "One more thing, Carlton!"

Carlton halted, but did not turn. "What do you require?"

"How do you know what she is?" Henry demanded, stalking toward the other man and closing the distance between them. When he stood beside him, staring at Carlton's somewhat hawkish profile, he went on, "You denied any knowledge of the Darrow School, after all."

"I denied having been there," Carlton answered dispassionately, still not looking at him. "But everyone knows of it... and knows precisely where those students come from. The wrong side of the blanket the lot of them."

"You may have managed to keep the true nature of your character a secret from my aunt. But it would take only a single word from me to my uncle to put a halt to it. And I will, if I deem it necessary. I'd caution you to remember that the next time you say anything insulting regarding Miss Upchurch, or anyone I care about for that matter. Good day, sir."

⇛⇚

WILLIAM CARLTON'S HEART was pounding. His gut had drawn tight and he could feel a hot, burning sensation in the pit of his stomach as he considered all the implications of what was happening and the many ways it could go wrong. *It was all slipping away.*

He'd spent his entire life working his way up through the ranks of society. He'd clawed. He'd groveled when needed. He'd lived like a miser for years, scraping together every penny until he'd have enough to give the appearance of a gentleman. From the outset, his goal had been to marry a wealthy woman of good breeding with impeccable social position. There was no denying that Horatia Meredith fit that description to a veritable "T". She was everything that he had ever desired in a wife. He didn't believe in love. It was nonsense for women. Even if it were not, it wasn't for a man like him. Pragmatic and driven, he understood the necessity of playing the part and of having her believe in it and to love him.

The idea that his secret shame and his less than noble past might come back to haunt him, just when he was on the cusp of having everything he'd ever wanted and more—it was a risk he could not take. The girl needed to go. She'd been an inconvenience to him for long enough.

To imagine that he'd come all the way to Southampton, to finally meet the family of the woman who'd agreed to become his wife and give him access to the kind of society and respectability he had always craved only to find his own illegitimate offspring inhabiting that house as a guest, would have been impossible.

Was it intentional? Was she there to ruin him?

William entered his chamber and paced back and forth. There were hard choices to make. He'd always been so careful to give no indication of why he had come to the Darrow School to make those payments. But he'd been smart enough to make them in person. The last thing he needed was documentation floating around in anyone's hands but his and Miss Euphemia Darrow's. Even then, he'd always given her a false name. He'd called himself Mr. Smith, a dubious moniker at best. But it had allowed him to not provide a name while allowing her to know, without question, he was providing an alias only. It had been, in short, an acceptable lie. He'd never told her which of the girls was his responsibility. Instead, he'd gone once per quarter, and "sponsored" one student per annum. There had only been a handful of girls there on actual charity, one of them being Sophia.

He'd never acknowledged her, never admitted that there was any connection. But he'd thought that Miss Darrow had guessed. There was enough of a similarity in their appearance that it would only be a matter of time, with the two of them occupying the same house, that someone else would remark upon it.

"I will not let this opportunity pass me by," he said to the empty room. "I have not worked so hard and sacrificed so much to be undone here and now by an embarrassing youthful indiscretion!"

And with that, his decision was made. It was either her or him and he was not about to give up his newfound position so easily. The only question that remained was how. But as he turned, pacing the room, he saw the small case on his dressing table that contained his stick pins. There were only a few in there and they were not so valuable really. Not enough, he thought. But if it was something larger, something more significant and with a far greater cost, then it would do.

There were few unforgivable sins in a grand house such as that of the Duke and Duchess of Thornhill. But theft... theft was never something the quality would overlook.

"Sabotage it must be," he declared.

If there was even a qualm, a tiny frisson of guilt, he ignored it. He'd done more for her than most men did for their bastards, after all. His hands were tied. There was much at stake, and he meant to come out on top.

Chapter Eleven

"**G**OOD EVENING, EDWARD," Horatia said as she entered her brother's study. He was seated at his desk, already dressed for dinner, and enjoying a brandy.

"Do tell," he said, gesturing toward the drink. "What brings you here, Horatia?"

Horatia stepped deeper into the room. "I don't wish to upset Cecile, but I felt compelled to ask how Philippa is doing. How she is really doing, Edward?"

He sighed wearily. "I do not know. This new physician swears she will improve but I do not see any evidence of it. He cautions us to be patient but I am nearing the end of mine."

"And this companion of hers? Miss Upchurch? What do you know of her?"

"Very little," the duke confessed with a soft laugh. "She is one of Henry's strays. When he was a boy it was wounded birds and pups. Now it is young women stranded by the death of their employers."

"Is her story not somewhat suspect?" Horatia questioned. "I have never known Lady Parkhurst to employ the services of a companion. She was such a particular person that I would have thought she would not hire someone so very... well, I do not wish to speak ill of the girl."

"So very what? What is she, Horatia?" he asked.

"Why are you impatient? Brother, I have never known you to be so cross."

"You're here to complain about Miss Upchurch. I've already had conversations with Henry because he has doubts about Dr. Blake and your Mr. Carlton. I simply don't wish to be bothered with it all!" he snapped. "Can't a man have some peace in his own household for pity's sake?"

"Well, I'm terribly sorry, Edward. But you are the head of the family. Being bothered is part and parcel with that position," Horatia pointed out. "Now, about Miss Upchurch. She is illegitimate. Raised in that school for girls where we honestly have no notion what sort of radical ideas have been put in her head. Are you certain she's a good influence on Philippa?"

"Frankly, I'd be happy if Philippa were to display some gumption to do something inappropriate! Not too inappropriate mind you, but the girl is like a ghost these days! If I didn't know better—" He broke off abruptly, running his fingers through his hair.

"What is it, Edward?"

"If I didn't know better, I'd think it was laudanum. She sleeps for days on end. Always tired, always quiet and subdued. What sort of life is it that she's living?"

Horatia sighed. "She will recover… eventually. She will, Edward. And in the meantime, you must not let this girl sway her to a path that would see her ruined. I caution you, Edward, to think of her future."

"I will investigate Miss Upchurch further, Horatia, and determine if aught must be done," he replied defeatedly.

"That is all I ask, Brother. We must all make sacrifices for the sake of family. Henry seems to be overly fond of the girl."

"You will leave Henry to me," Edward insisted. "I can handle him."

WILLIAM WAS WAITING patiently for Horatia to return from her brother's study. He'd hatched a plan to recover some ground. That plan hinged on pitting the viscount and his uncle against one another. She was key to its efficacy. She'd gone to see the duke to offer a well-timed warning about the possible dangers that Miss Upchurch could present. It was the first step in a much larger goal. When at last she entered the drawing room and offered him a nod and a smile, he breathed a sigh of relief. Immediately, he crossed the expanse of the room to her and bowed over her hand.

"My darling, Horatia, I feel like it's been ages."

"I, too, dear William," she agreed.

"Would you care to take a turn in the garden before dinner?"

"That would be lovely!"

Leading her to a set of French doors that opened onto the terrace, they stepped out into the evening air. It was still quite warm, muggy even, and not at all comfortable.

"I did it. I spoke with him. He says he will look into her," Horatia said as soon as they were outside. "Whatever is the matter?"

"That girl is an opportunist. An adventuress!" William said. "She means to trap your nephew into marriage. I do not think looking into it will be quite enough."

"Well, as he wishes to marry her, I hardly think her plan constitutes a trap," Horatia replied, a snap to her tone. "Why have you taken her in such instant dislike? I trust and defer to your judgment on the matter, of course, but is there some reason?"

William considered lying, but the truth, so long as it was carefully edited, would be more effective. "When I was a young man, just making my fortune, Horatia, I was not wise to the ways of the world and I was led astray by a shameful woman... a woman much like Miss Upchurch. It took years to recover financially from the havoc she wreaked in my life and longer still to recover from the emotional and mental toll her lies and betrayals wrought. I would spare your nephew that fate if I could—and the rest of you. It could be damaging to your entire family, after all."

Horatia reached for his hand. "Oh, William… you are so kind and so generous. I know that you would spare Henry such a fate, but he is a stubborn, stubborn boy! We may hold no sway over him at this point. It appears this young woman has well and truly gotten her claws into him."

"Well, I have my suspicions about this school of hers," he said. "I think that requires further probing. But there is something else we can do in the interim." He needed to find out exactly how much Miss Euphemia Darrow knew or suspected about Sophie Upchurch's origins.

"We must be cautious," Horatia said. "She has clearly gulled both my brother and his wife. We cannot afford to anger them, especially if you still wish for my brother to invest in your new venture… and to maintain his blessing for our marriage."

"We must do more than simply ask questions and let her answers paint her for the adventuress she is," William replied. Of course, that wasn't all he intended to do. But it would be a start. "I'm certain it would happen, but it would take far too long. We must make our own opportunities."

"How so?"

"The necklace, Horatia," he said.

"It was a gift," she protested. "One far too dear that I should have refused."

He stroked her cheek. "It was a testament to the depth of my feelings for you. Now it will be the key to saving your nephew from a fortune hunter. Tomorrow, you will hide it in her chamber."

"Me? Why should I?"

He sighed. "Horatia, I cannot go into her chamber. If I were discovered, it would look terrible for us both. But you can enter her chamber under the guise of asking to borrow a hairpin or some such nonsense. It would be easy enough to explain it all away. Will you do it?"

Horatia dropped her head for a moment. Then she nodded. "Yes, I'll do it."

At that moment, the dinner gong sounded and they returned to the drawing room, following the small group gathered into the larger dining room which had been laid formally. They found their respective seats, and with a nod to one another, they were ready to begin the next campaign.

DINNER WAS A guarded affair to say the least. From the moment Henry had come downstairs to join everyone else in the drawing room, it had been uncomfortable. But now, one course in, the tension in the dining room was thicker than the soup. His uncle, the duke, was seated at the head of the table and his aunt, the duchess, at the other end. Henry, himself, was seated to his uncle's right and directly across from him was his Aunt Horatia. Miss Upchurch was seated to his right and Mr. Carlton was seated directly across from her, a most unfortunate placement.

Henry noted that Sophie kept her gaze on her plate and very rarely looked up. She spoke only when a question was put to her directly. She was clearly embarrassed at having been discovered in such a compromising position in the corridor. He could certainly understand that. He only prayed that she did not have regrets about allowing him to kiss her or about kissing him in return. It was truly one of the most glorious moments of his life.

"It is a shame," Horatia intoned, "that poor Philippa did not feel up to joining us. I would so love for Mr. Carlton to have an opportunity to meet her. The poor dear is so isolated."

"I'm certain Philippa will be feeling up to coming down for dinner at some time during your visit. Perhaps for tea tomorrow or the next day," the duchess offered. "What can you tell us of her current state of health, Miss Upchurch?"

Sophie's head popped up, a guilty flush stealing over her face. Because she'd been woolgathering, possibly thinking of the kiss they'd shared, or was it because she was secretly circumventing the duke's and duchess' will regarding their daughter's care at the hands of a less than competent physician?

After a moment's hesitation, and a brief glance in his direction, she answered the question. "I expect she is only overly tired due to the excitement of the day. Visits from Dr. Blake can be quite taxing, especially as she had her hydrotherapy appointment the day prior. We are expected to go tomorrow for a sea bathing treatment and Philippa states they always leave her feeling much improved."

"Indeed, they do," the duchess said with a slight inclination of her head. "I am ever so relieved, Miss Upchurch, that she will have you to accompany her on such outings. I must admit, I would have gone daily to the shore to aid my sweet girl. But I dislike the water terribly. Looking at it is quite fine, but being in it? I find it terrifying!"

"I've taught you to swim," the duke stated balefully. "You do so remarkably well and yet you despise the water. It makes no sense. Women are such perverse creatures!"

The duchess cast a sharp look in his direction. "In the ponds and still waters on our country estates, I will do so happily. But the sea, even in calm estuaries, is a different matter. The vastness of the sea is terribly frightening to me. I feel very small and very powerless in such a body of water. No. I understand that it aids Philippa, but if I do not need to place myself within its depths, I will happily keep both my feet on dry land," the duchess reiterated. "And now, with Miss Upchurch here, I may do so."

"Do you swim, Miss Upchurch?" the duke asked, somewhat distractedly. "Though I can't imagine it makes any difference now."

Henry noted his uncle's preoccupation. Whatever was on his mind had kept him from fully attending to the conversations taking place around the dinner table.

"I do, your grace. Though I haven't had much opportunity and my experience is somewhat limited, I do possess the skill," Sophie replied.

"Excellent," he said. "I can't imagine it was an easy skill to acquire in London."

"Indeed. Pray tell, where, Miss Upchurch, did a London-bred girl such as you attain such a unique skill?" Horatia asked. "Not in the Thames, certainly. I cannot imagine swimming in such disgusting muck."

Henry didn't intercede because he was quite curious himself. Still, he was aware of the undercurrent of suspicion and possibly even accusation in Horatia's tone. He also hadn't missed that his uncle was behaving strangely.

"Miss Darrow, the headmistress at our school, took us to a country estate outside of London where all the students were given swimming lessons," Sophie replied. "She felt, given that many of us would take positions well away from London, that riding and swimming, as well as the ability to utilize pistols and swords effectively, were requirements for our future safety."

Horatia's eyes widened. "That is quite an unorthodox approach to the education of young women! Pistols and swords. Did she also advocate riding astride and wearing trousers?"

"Not at all," Miss Upchurch answered. "Effie—Miss Darrow—was quite adamant that her pupils should act as ladies at all times, but that we should also be able to defend ourselves against men who were not gentlemen."

"An excellent notion," the duchess interjected.

Horatia continued, "Though, I suppose most of her pupils do not have family members that would object to such a thing."

"That is quite enough, Aunt Horatia," Henry said.

All wide-eyed innocence, Horatia blinked at him. "Did I say something untoward?"

"Near enough to it," Henry answered. "I personally am very grateful that Miss Darrow has taken it upon herself to educate women on something more useful than needlepoint. A finely stitched pillow or chair covering is all well and good, but the skills she's taught these young women will allow them to be self-sufficient, to be able to make their own choices and defend themselves when the occasion calls for it. I think it is rather remarkable."

"I could not agree more," the duchess chimed in. "Why, I rather regret not having the opportunity to attend such a school myself!"

"You would never have been admitted, my dear," Horatia stated smugly. "You had two parents."

"Did I?" the duchess asked. "I do not recall that we ever discussed my family of origin, Horatia."

And with that, the entire table became quiet. No one dared say a word. It was only the arrival of the next course and the footmen serving that eased the tension in the room.

"It is true, Lady Horatia, that many of the students at the Darrow School are illegitimate. In fact, most of them are. But there are exceptions. For myself, I do not know my parents at all. If they were married, if they were not, if they are dead or alive—I am ignorant of it. I cannot even tell you their names," Sophie stated flatly. "I was left on the doorstep of the Darrow School as a foundling and Miss Euphemia Darrow, despite the fact that I was far too young to be her pupil, took me in and kept me there with some anonymous person paying for my education over the years. I am quite fortunate to have found myself in a household such as this one, where people of such elevated stations as the Duke and Duchess of Thornhill, seem not to care in the least about my humble beginnings."

"Quite right," the duke stated, finally seeming to be aware of what was going on around him. "It isn't how one begins, after all. It's what one accomplishes along the way, and you, Miss Upchurch, are quite an accomplished young woman."

The remainder of the meal went on in a similar fashion. Thinly veiled barbs, pointed questions, and all of it hidden behind polite smiles and feigned innocence. For his part, Henry could see the triumph in William Carlton's expression. The man had clearly put Horatia up to her interrogation because he himself was in too precarious a position to do so. Henry knew that he'd have to find a moment to discuss the issue with Sophie, to determine what it was that made Carlton take her in such instant dislike.

Henry was well aware of the strange undercurrent about them. Suspicion and snobbery seemed to be at the root of it all. He wanted say something, but was uncertain where to begin or whom to direct his disapproval at. He was also fairly certain that Miss Upchurch would not appreciate any interference on his part. She was rather independent. And he didn't want to risk her ire. He wanted that walk in the garden with her after dinner. Of course, that meant taking the risk of being alone with her again. With the memory of their kiss still very fresh in his mind, that was a dangerous prospect, indeed.

Glancing in her direction once more, he watched intently as she sipped her wine. He envied the glass. Watching her lift it to her perfect lips and sip from it was both pleasure and torment. Then she looked up. For just a moment, over the rim of her glass, their gazes locked. It was quite obvious that she was recalling that same moment, as well. Her cheeks flushed. He could see a slight hitch in her breathing, then she quickly averted her gaze.

"Tell me, Viscount Marchwood," Mr. Carlton said, "how your own estate is faring in your absence. Is it not some distance from here?"

"It is just north of London, Mr. Carlton," Henry replied, gritting his teeth at the man's friendly tone despite their earlier altercation. There was not a doubt in his mind that it was well remembered, after all. "And I have an excellent steward who will see to all things while I am away. And your business ventures in… Birmingham, isn't it?"

"Manchester," Mr. Carlton replied. "They do well enough. Again, as you say, I have a trusted man who will oversee things while I am away. He knows the business inside and out. So your visit to Southampton will be an extended one?"

Henry glanced once more at Sophie. "I had thought to stay a few weeks. But I may stay longer still. One never knows."

"Indeed," Cecile offered up her agreement. "And what a delight it is to have a house brimming with guests. It is the most wonderful thing."

"That would depend on the guests, would it not?" Horatia asked. The pointed quip was greeted with an absolute void of sound. No one spoke. It seemed as if no one dared even breathe. The remainder of the dinner passed in silence, not even a hint of false civility was uttered.

Chapter Twelve

ALL BUT TIPTOEING, Sophie made her way to the servants' stairs. She should have given the bottle to Henry earlier, but she'd dared not seek him out after what had occurred earlier in the day. And given what had transpired between them, being alone with him had seemed equally unwise. Opening the door cautiously, she peered into the darkness and saw no one. Not even daring to light a candle, she made her way by feel. Keeping one hand on the wall, she placed one foot on the next tread, testing her footing with each step. It might have been a tedious task, each movement so carefully measured, had her heart not been pounding out of her chest from the fear of being caught.

Dinner had been a terrible ordeal. Every glacial glance and pointed barb from Lady Horatia and Mr. Carlton had hit its mark and left her feeling raw from the exchange. She owed no one apologies for her origins. It was the one thing in her life, after all, that she had absolutely no control over. But for the first time in a very long time, she hadn't felt that confidence Effie had helped to instill in her. Instead, she'd wanted to crawl beneath the table and hide, to apologize for who she was and where she'd come from, if only she'd known where that was.

"Now is not the time," she whispered softly to herself. "You cannot do what you need to do if you are focusing on them."

Buoyed by that thought, she continued on. Creeping carefully, soundlessly along the corridors. When at last she finally reached the kitchen, there was no sigh of relief. There was no time. Without knowing beyond the shadow of any doubt that every single servant in the household was abed, she simply couldn't afford to linger. Easing down the long corridor of small workrooms, she found the small pantry and eased the lever down. The door opened inward and she stepped inside, closing it softly behind her. Once there, she reached for the small candle and tinderbox on the shelf beside the door. With hands that trembled, she struck match to the tinder and the dim glow illuminated the small space and she quickly touched the lit match to the wick of the candle.

Placing it carefully on the table, she went to the shelf where all of the medications, curatives and remedies were stored. Finding the bottle with Philippa's elixir, she switched it with the one she'd brought and then backed away. But as she reached the door, a noise in the corridor beyond rooted her to the spot. Snuffing the candle quickly, she stood there in the dark and waited to be discovered.

But then she heard it. Humming. It was followed by singing, though not very good singing. Thankfully, that off key voice was quite familiar. Her response was complicated. There was relief certainly, but nerves as well. She'd avoided him after dinner, despite their earlier agreement to walk in the garden. In light of everything else, it had seemed the safest course of action.

Huffing out a breath, she opened the door and stepped once more into the corridor. Henry stood there, leaning against the wall, arms folded across his chest which was clad only in a linen shirt. He wore breeches and boots, but his cravat, waistcoat and jacket had long since been discarded. His hair was disheveled, too, as if he'd been abed.

"You'd make a terrible housebreaker," he said. "Were you dancing a jig on those squeaky floorboards or perhaps simply jumping up and down?"

Her eyebrows shot upward and her mouth gaped for a moment. "I was trying to be quiet."

He grinned. "You failed. Miserably."

"I tiptoed and crept along quite clandestinely," she insisted.

"It's an old house, Miss Upchurch—Sophie."

"I've never given you leave to use my given name," she protested.

"We are co-conspirators are we not? It's a liberty I feel comfortable in taking."

"You have been quite free in taking many liberties, my lord. And how is that you are such an expert on clandestine matters?"

"I may have taken a liberty or two, but I have not taken all that I wish. That should count for something."

Sophie's pulse began to pound again but for an entirely different reason than before. What liberties did he desire that he had not taken? Why did she wish that he might have taken them anyway? Deciding that it was safer by far to steer the conversation to a different topic, she addressed the other issue at hand.

"I didn't realize the floors were quite so telling," Sophie insisted. "Was it terribly loud? Did it wake anyone else?"

"My uncle poked his head out of the door to check on things," he said. "Luckily, I was in the corridor and told him I was heading down to the kitchen for a bite to eat. I apologized for waking him. He grunted and then returned to his rooms. That's the trick to clandestine outings such as this, Sophie. One must simply act as though they have the right to go wherever it is and whenever it is that they are headed."

Sophie sagged against the door to the pantry. "You've had so many clandestine outings, then?" Where in heaven's name did that flirtatious tone come from? *Not to mention that tiny spark of jealousy that she was absolutely not entitled to feel.* Why was she smiling at him in the kitchen while they were alone in the dark of night and she wore nothing but a nightrail and a wrapper?

"More than a few… most of them involved sneaking the last of the tea cakes, however," he admitted sheepishly.

"And those that didn't?"

He cocked an eyebrow at her, "I don't wish to scandalize your poor innocent ears. Regardless, they all pale in comparison to this very moment."

She didn't want to be flattered. She didn't want to admit that her heart thudded in her chest at his flirtation or that she wished desperately she knew how to flirt back. "You'd say that even if it weren't true. I heard you offer the same sort of nonsense to Lady Hemsley this afternoon!"

He nodded. "But only when she asked me to do so. I take it this is your first attempt at sneaking through a house in the dark of night?"

"It is," Sophie admitted. "I'm not very good at subterfuge, I'm afraid."

He grinned. "I do not think that is something to be apologized for. Is it done then? The bottles have been exchanged?"

Sophie nodded. "They have. The bottles are switched. Now, the question remains, how do we prove that the good doctor is anything but? And how long will we have to continue this charade? Week after week?"

"I'm working on that, and I certainly hope not," he told her. "But we have another issue that requires the sharing of information."

"And what is that?" Sophie demanded, though she certainly had an idea.

"How do you know William Carlton?"

"I do not know him… not by name," Sophie admitted. "But I have seen him. He came at least quarterly to the Darrow School and made a *donation*. It was an arrangement that several gentlemen had. It was a way for them to provide for their illegitimate offspring without ever openly acknowledging them or forming any sort of relationship with them."

"Surely, if that was how he wanted things, he could have had it taken care of via his bank."

"That means other people are privy to it or that there is evidence of his generosity. Many men take care of the fees at the Darrow School in person to avoid anyone else knowing their business... or their secrets." Sophie walked down the corridor toward the main part of the kitchen. He fell in step beside her and the silence between them was companionable. "Why do some men care so little for their children?"

"There are people in this world, sadly most of them do appear to be men, who think very little of anyone else. I very much think Mr. Carlton may be one of them. Could you find out more from Miss Darrow about him?"

"Possibly," Sophie replied. "I will write to her. But she may be limited in what she can say. The school functions so well, in part, because it offers anonymity to those gentlemen who wish it. I doubt she would break that confidentiality even for me."

As they made their way into the kitchen proper, Sophie stumbled, her slipper catching on an uneven stone. He caught her, his arms wrapping about her, holding her tightly to him as she let out a squeak of alarm.

"I have you," he said. "You're fine. Everything is fine."

And it was. And that was the biggest problem of all.

IT HAD BEEN instinct more than anything that had him reaching for her. It was luck, pure and simple that had allowed him to catch her before she fell. The consequences of it—injury and potential discovery—could have been catastrophic. But as he held her close, as he felt the soft press of her body against his, he was acutely aware of just how few barriers remained between them.

"You aren't hurt?" he asked.

"No," she replied. Her voice sounded breathless and slightly tremulous.

Was it the fright she had from nearly falling? Or was it him? Henry knew which answer he preferred.

He made no move to let her go. If anything, his arms drew more tightly about her, pulling her closer. "I told myself I wouldn't do this again. I know that I shouldn't. But I haven't been able to think of anything but kissing you again."

She didn't push him away. Nor did she attempt to right herself and put distance between them. But she did softly utter the words, "We shouldn't. It would be very unwise."

"It would," he agreed. His hand was pressed against the small of her back, his other hand splayed over the delicate arcs of her shoulder blades just beneath the fall of her hair. It was like silk against his skin.

And then the choice was taken out of his hands entirely. She rose onto her tiptoes and pressed her lips softly against his. A sigh escaped him at that whisper-soft contact. His arms tightened about her, holding her close, feeling her flesh yield to his own. It was beyond sweet and beyond temptation. And there was not a power on earth that could have prompted him to let her go in that moment.

There in the darkness, the kiss simply took on a life of its own. His lips played over hers for the longest time—gentle and without demand. But like all things, it shifted, altering, evolving. For a man who'd spent most of his relatively young life being responsible and practical, in the presence of Sophie Upchurch, he became anything but. With her, reason and sense fled and he was left with only his need to be close to her, to hold her and to protect her, but also to possess her in a primal way. She filled his senses and consumed him. And it was that, recognizing his own lack of control and the very precarious position they were in, which prompted him to break that kiss abruptly and step back from her. Immediately, he felt the loss.

There was a small amount of moonlight filtering in through the high windows of the kitchen. It was just enough that he could see the stricken expression on her face.

"I don't know what came over me," Sophie said softly. She sounded positively stricken and completely embarrassed. "I'm so terribly sorry."

"I am not. I am not sorry that I kissed you in the corridor and I am not sorry for the kiss we just shared," he said. "And if I trusted myself more, if I had any faith at all in my ability to resist the temptation to take liberties far greater than a kiss, I'd be kissing you still."

Her lips parted on a soft "o". "I don't understand."

"No," he said. "You don't and in a darkened kitchen, where we are entirely alone, is not the place for explanations. You are going to the sea with Philippa tomorrow?"

"Yes," she said, nodding slightly. "We are leaving midmorning."

"I will meet the two of you there in the afternoon. While Philippa rests and enjoys the sun, we will walk—and talk—in a place where we will not forget ourselves," Henry stated. "Where I will not forget myself."

"I need to return to my room," Sophie stated, "before anyone discovers us."

"Yes. Go on," Henry replied. "I'll be a few paces behind you just to be certain you are safe."

"What could I possibly have to fear in this house now that our perfidy is complete?"

"Give me the bottle," he said. "I'll dispose of it so you will not have to."

She passed it to him, their fingers brushing slightly. It was like the static charge in the air before a storm.

"I told you that I meant to court you," Henry said softly. "But that isn't the truth."

"You don't?" she asked, her voice reflecting her dismay.

"No. Not now. Now, Miss Sophia Upchurch, I mean to marry you. As soon as possible. And I will not take no for an answer," he said.

"We've only known one another for three days. It seems terribly impetuous, don't you think?" she asked.

"Yes," he agreed with a smile. "It does. It was impetuousness that led me to you in the first place, after all. What could be more perfect? We could elope. Tomorrow or the next day."

"No… yes, we could. And I'm not opposed to the act of it—of eloping—but the timing," she explained. "We cannot leave until we know Philippa is safe, what plots Dr. Blake has afoot and until we know what Mr. William Carlton is about."

"Right… three days. Give me three days, and I will have answers to all of it," he vowed.

"That's very ambitious."

"I'm very motivated," he replied.

Chapter Thirteen

EFFIE READ THE letter. Then she read it again. After reading it for the third time, she placed the missive on her desk and reached for the scandal sheets that were her only real vice, especially as she'd severed all ties with Highcliff. That man certainly constituted a vice, at least for her. Just thinking his name made her blood boil! But he was not the issue and she could not afford to let herself be distracted by thinking of him. No. Sophie was the issue. More to the point, Sophie being far from London, in the home of people who had not been properly vetted—that was the issue.

Of course, Effie had heard nothing but good things about the Duke and Duchess of Thornhill over the years. Her concern stemmed more from something she'd read in the gossip rags that morning as she'd indulged in a cup of decadent chocolate and enjoyed her morning meal. Lady Horatia Meredith, the spinster sister of the Duke of Thornhill, had very recently announced her betrothal. *To William Carlton.* It was quite possible, of course, that Sophie's temporary position with that family would never result in her crossing paths with Carlton. It could also be that it was a different Mr. Carlton altogether. It was, after all, not so uncommon a name. But the odds—Effie didn't like them. And when it came to her girls she would always err on the side of caution. If she'd learned one thing since they started leaving the nest, it was that the graduates of the Darrow School were a magnet for trouble. Could Sophie have really found herself in an unanticipated position in the home of the brother of her potential father's betrothed? It seemed completely implausible. But there was always a chance. Stranger things had happened. One only had to look at Calliope Hamilton nee St. James for proof of that, not to mention the recently resurrected mother of Lilly Burkhart.

"Well, this is simply terrible," she murmured. Mr. Carlton had never disclosed his relationship to Sophie, he'd certainly never indicated that she was his daughter. But he'd arrived once per quarter to pay tuition for her. Per his request, she'd never revealed to Sophie that Mr. Carlton was her benefactor. But she'd always had her suspicions. There was a similarity in their appearance that was rather marked. Would anyone in the duke's household take note of it?

"What's that, Miss? Is the breakfast not to your liking?" Mrs. Wheaton asked as she bustled into the office, inspecting the dishes.

"What?" Effie asked in confusion. Then realizing she'd spoken aloud, she added, "Oh, no! The breakfast was quite delicious, Mrs. Wheaton. It's something else that is amiss... but it's a matter I'll take care of. Not for you to worry about." Her appetite had been a bit off since her terrible argument with Highcliff. But she wasn't heartbroken. She was angry and she was embarrassed.

"Ah, well, then. I know it's early for callers, but Miss Wilhelmina and Miss Lillian—ahem—Lady Deveril and the Viscountess Seaburn are here. Can't quite get it right, can I? Addressing them by titles! Imagine our sweet girls grown up and married so well!"

"Thank you, Mrs. Wheaton. I'll see them in the drawing room... no need to trot them into my office and remind them of their past infractions." It was quite fortuitous that they'd come for a visit as she now needed to ask them for quite the favor.

Leaving her small study, Effie made her way to the drawing room where her former pupils waited. Both were now married to men of substantial rank. More importantly, they were both deliriously and happily in love with their respective husbands. There was a small pang of envy, of regret that she herself would never experience such a thing, but it did not dampen Effie's happiness for them. There was nothing she wanted more than perfect happiness for all of her girls.

"Willa, Lilly!" she said, entering. "It's so good to see you, but whatever are you doing here so early?"

"We've come to take you shopping," Lilly said.

"You mean you haven't bought out Bond Street, yet?" Effie teased. Lilly's love of all things that sparkled was quite notorious.

"The merchants have recently restocked," she replied cheekily. "Besides, I'm annoyed with Valentine and there is no better way to exact my vengeance than by spending ridiculous sums of his money."

Effie's smile slipped. "Alas, I cannot. A situation has arisen that requires my attention. It's about Sophie and her placement with Lady Parkhurst."

Willa's expression shifted to one of concern. After all, both of them had attended school with her and had helped care for her when she had arrived as such a young child. "Is Sophie all right?"

"She's quite well, I think. I hope, though her current situation is… well, complicated."

Willa pursed her lips. "Explain what that means precisely. Complicated."

Effie sighed. "Lady Parkhurst has passed away and Sophie is now in a more temporary position with another family. But I fear there isn't just one complication. There are numerous complications… and please do not ask what those are because I am not at liberty to say. What I can attest to is that I am afraid Sophie's poor heart will be broken if I do not fetch her home. Suffice it to say, the sooner I retrieve Sophie and bring her back to the school the better for everyone involved," Effie explained.

"Does this heartbreak have to do with her past or her future?" Lilly asked. It was a question that displayed just how adept she was at reading people and situations.

"Both, I fear," Effie answered. With another deep sigh, she moved directly into the request. "And to that end, I am very happy you are both here. I know it's terribly short notice and that your respective husbands may be less than pleased to share you, but would it be possible for you to manage the school for a few days? You needn't stay here. Mrs. Wheaton and the maids will be in overnight to supervise the girls, but my classes and the administrative aspects will need tending to while I fetch Sophie."

"Well, of course, we will," Willa said. "But you don't mean to go after her alone! It's dangerous."

"I do mean to go after her by myself. Who would go with me?"

"Highcliff," Lilly answered. "I mean, he would have to ride beside the coach and, of course, you couldn't tell anyone he accompanied you. But if anyone could keep you safe on the journey—"

"It's hardly a journey," Effie insisted. "One day's travel on the mail coach to Southampton. Naturally, once I have retrieved Sophie, we will use a hired conveyance to bring us both back to London." She wouldn't ask Highcliff for anything. In fact, she never wanted to see him, speak to him, or hear his name uttered ever again. It wasn't fury, though she certainly had more than her fair share of anger directed at him. It was the hot, burning humiliation she felt when she recalled the expression on his face when he'd summarily and without even a hint of regret refused her request completely. Facing him would be too devastating for words. After all, what did one say to a man one had begged to make love to them only to be rejected without qualm?

"Still, the road can be dangerous," Willa added softly, always the voice of reason. "There must be some precaution—"

"And I will be prepared. I do not need the aid of a man. I have done well enough in my life without one," Effie insisted.

"But what of your reputation?" Lilly asked. "Surely a woman traveling alone—"

Effie held up her hand to stay any further protest, even as she rolled her eyes. "I'm hardly a young woman, am I? By every account, I am considered to be a long in the tooth spinster. It will be fine. I will be fine."

"Are you certain?" Willa persisted.

"Yes! Please, will you tend the students?"

"Of course, we will," Willa agreed. "We would never refuse you. But I suppose that curbs our own shopping agenda for the day. I'll need to return home and make some arrangements for Marina and little Douglas."

Effie smiled. "You are the most perfect mother... to your son and to your sweet little niece. Thank you, Willa. And thank you, Lilly. I know Bond Street will miss you."

The women said their goodbyes and Effie made her way upstairs to pack.

⟫⟫⟩⟨⟨⟨

LEAVING THE DARROW School, Lilly looked at her half-sister in surprise. "We're really going to let her just take off on her own? Frankly, I'm appalled. What if something happens to her?"

"Oh, heavens no!" Willa answered. "We will be sending a note round to Highcliff this instant to meet us at our favorite tea shop. He will be informed of what she plans and I've no doubt at all that he will be here before Effie can even leave the school."

Lilly considered that for a moment. "Is that what we want though? To stop her?"

"Well, yes!" Willa exclaimed. "We can send someone else to fetch Sophie."

Perhaps she'd spent too much time with Valentine's scheming grandmother, but Lilly was formulating a plan. "Or we could let Effie do as she sees fit. Let her depart on that mail coach and potentially put

124

herself in some sort of jeopardy. If we were to inform Highcliff over tea, possibly, then he might have to go off on a dashing mission to rescue her."

"Rescue her from what?" Willa asked, shaking her head. "We don't know that she'll be in danger, only that she might be. Perhaps we shouldn't meddle in it at all. Effie is a woman grown and quite capable, I might add."

"I'm not worried about her capability, Willa. I'm worried about her heart. She's unhappy," Lilly stated. "We both know it. *He* is unhappy, too. We've seen it. You know what they were like over the holidays." They'd been distant and polite, civil but clearly avoiding any interaction with one another as much as possible. And yet their awareness of one another had been palpable. Why two intelligent people were so adamant about denying themselves the thing that would likely make them the happiest, Lilly could not fathom.

Willa sighed again. "I do know. But they are both adults and what they mean to do about their feelings for one another, obvious as they may be to those who care about them, is, ultimately, up to them."

"But it doesn't have to be," Lilly cajoled. "If a situation was created where they were forced to be alone together, where they were thrown together in a way that they had to confront their feelings, then maybe... maybe they might finally find some happiness."

"Or they could part ways forever. There is no guarantee that they will confront their feelings for one another."

"If Highcliff is angry enough, and we both know that he will be when he discovers she's put herself in jeopardy, his temper will get the better of him. That temper is precisely what will lead them to discussing their feelings. We need to rattle their control, Willa."

Willa was silent for a moment. Then she huffed out a breath. "I wish to go on record as stating I think this is a terrible idea and that it could go horribly awry. But as it's the only idea we have at the moment and something clearly must be done, I will agree."

"Fine," Lilly agreed. "They need to be together or they need to be completely apart. But right now, they both hover like ghosts on the edge of one another's lives. And they are both equally haunted by the things they want and the things they believe they cannot have! What I do know, is that the current situation cannot continue as is. We must provide some sort of catalyst that will spur them to either be together or be apart forever!"

Willa stared at Lilly for a moment before tossing up her hands. "Fine. I foresee utter disaster, but... fine. What do we need to do?"

Lilly grinned. "Do you know anyone who might be willing to indulge in a bit of faux-kidnapping?"

"No," Willa replied balefully, looking at her half-sister as if she'd gone stark raving mad. "I can honestly say that I do not."

"Stavers it is. But if you tell my husband I sought this man out, I shall never speak to you again."

"If this man murders us, it will not matter," Willa replied.

"He's a butler, not a murderer," Lilly protested. "I think."

"You hope!"

Lilly laughed at that. "We both do. Come on, he isn't far from here!"

Willa held up her hand, staying her half-sister for the moment. "I think I may have a slightly better and less ridiculous idea than kidnapping, faux or otherwise."

"Fine. Then you can be the mastermind," Lilly acquiesced. "You're much better at that sort of thing than I am, anyway. What is your plan?"

"We will simply tell Lord Highcliff that Effie went off, entirely on her own, to rescue Sophie."

Lilly blinked at her in confusion. "You think that is enough? Just telling him? But where is the danger in that?"

"Highcliff is a man of the world, Lilly. He will imagine every sort of danger. There is no need to manufacture any. Trust me."

Lilly sighed. "Fine. I like my plan better though. It is much more dramatic!"

Willa grinned. "Yes, dear. I know all about your flair for the dramatic. I also know it always results in trouble. Trust me?"

"Always."

Chapter Fourteen

SOPHIE FEIGNED EXCITEMENT as they climbed into the carriage and headed toward Lymington and the waiting bathing machines. It wasn't that she didn't wish to go sea bathing. In truth, it was an experience she'd often been quite curious about. It was more that she found herself distracted by the fact that she'd somehow embarked on a secret engagement with Henry Meredith, Viscount Marchwood. Would they detest her? Would Philippa forgive her for keeping secrets? Would they think her a fortune hunter? Would they convince him to renege as she was so impossibly far beneath him?

"The water isn't very deep," Philippa said, mistaking the source of Sophie's very obvious nerves. "And while it is saltwater, it's very calm. We can even have a guide if you like."

Sophie smiled somewhat nervously. "Oh... well, yes, that would be all right."

Philippa held up her hand as if swearing an oath. "I promise that you will love it. It's so invigorating. Even when you aren't ill!"

"I am certain I shall love it," Sophie offered with false assurance. "I must apologize. I am not some scared rabbit of a woman who is terrified of everything and everyone. I'm really quite excited to try sea bathing. Just perhaps a bit uncertain of what to expect."

"I don't think that at all! You are so very brave to have set out on your own," Philippa exclaimed. "I could never have done so. Not even if I were well. I think this school you attended sounds perfectly remarkable. I wish…" the girl stopped talking altogether. Her expression became rather bleak and she looked to be on the verge of tears.

Concerned, Sophie braved the rocking of the carriage to close the distance and clasped Philippa's hand in hers. "What is it? Are you in pain?"

"Not physically," Philippa stated. "Yesterday was just so terrible. My head ached. My entire body hurt. I felt sick and weak and hopeless, frankly. But today is a good day. And on days like today, I feel almost normal, like I could do anything. The truth is, I wish I could be like you, Sophie. I long for independence, as much as any young woman can have independence in this world. I'm told what to do by everyone! Dr. Blake, my mother, my father! Even my own servants."

"Then I shall endeavor to never tell you what you may or may not do. And I vow, that if you choose to throw off the edicts of others, I shall keep your confidence—barring any situations that might be considered life or death," Sophie swore solemnly. *But hadn't she already? Hadn't she switched Philippa's tonic without ever telling her the truth of it?*

Shaking her head slightly, Sophie reasoned that it was different. Dr. Blake, though they had no proof yet beyond his concealment of the nature of his elixir, was a scoundrel. She and Henry were trying to save Philippa from him. "Has Dr. Blake ever been inappropriate with you, Philippa?"

The girl looked askance. "He is my physician. I daresay that what he does would only be considered liberties if another man were to do so—one who is not doing so to gauge my health and well-being."

"Such as?"

Philippa blushed. "Well, naturally, he must from time to time perform examinations."

"Without your clothing?"

"Not entirely," Philippa replied. "I am permitted to wear my chemise throughout and a wrapper until the examination begins."

Sophie frowned at that. She'd certainly never been as ill as Philippa was purported to be—potentially as ill as Dr. Blake was making her—but she'd never been examined in such a manner by a physician. "What do these exams entail?"

Philippa blushed. "Well, he looks at various parts of my person and palpates them for any irregularities."

"But I thought your primary complaint was megrims," Sophie insisted.

"Well, it is. But Dr. Blake insists that the megrims I suffer could be a manifestation of an ailment elsewhere in my body that has yet to be identified," Philippa explained.

"Does your mother know?"

"Oh, goodness no," Philippa said. "She'd have apoplexy! Dr. Blake has admitted to me that his methods can be viewed as somewhat unorthodox by those who do not understand the science of medicine. Thus, he instructed me to keep the nature of his exams to myself. But I can trust you, can't I, Sophie?"

Sophie looked away. "Philippa, I—yes, you can trust me. But you must not submit to these examinations again. Not until I've had a chance to research this science he is referencing. I know that you trust Dr. Blake—"

"I want to. I want to trust him because he promised me he could make me better!" the girl cried. "He swore that if I trusted him and did as he asked, I would have my life back. But I do not. It's been almost a year!"

"Tell me, Philippa, what do your instincts tell you?" Sophie demanded.

"My instincts—" Philippa broke off abruptly and looked away. "They are as dulled as everything else most of the time. I go through entire weeks where I feel like I am moving in a fog. Followed by spells of terrible weakness and pain. Then I'll have a few days where I feel well and then it all starts again in some vicious cycle. My instinct tells me that the treatments are having no effect at all, or if they are having an effect, it isn't a positive one… I'm afraid that what he's said and what he's done are all part of some elaborate scheme. Is it? What do your instincts say?"

Sophie decided then that she must tell the truth. All of it. "I have something to tell you… I took your nearly empty bottle of his elixir to an apothecary and had it analyzed. It's full of herbs that will make you feel sick or ill but do not do long-lasting harm. But it also contains a not insignificant amount of laudanum. And from what I understand, people who use laudanum regularly often suffer ill effects from the lack of it."

"Laudanum?" Philippa gasped, her face paling. "Papa has refused to let any physician treat me with laudanum. He insists that with my megrims, it is better to deal with the pain another way as the risks of using such a substance—he lied, Sophie. He lied directly to my father's face!"

"Well, you may take the current elixir as you like. I had the apothecary replace the contents of that bottle with something harmless. It is actually intended to aid with megrims but does not contain any opium derivatives. But you must not allow any of the elixirs provided directly from Dr. Blake to be consumed. I understand that stopping usage of opium can be terribly painful. I can only imagine that would prove worse if one had to do it over and over again."

"Why wouldn't you tell me? And why would you undertake such a thing without consulting me or any member of my family?" Philippa's tone showed her hurt.

Sophie sighed. "I didn't want to lie to you. But I felt that perhaps you had some romantic feeling toward Dr. Blake that might make you less willing to hear any critique of his methods. And from the moment I met him, I had no trust for him at all. You asked what my instincts tell me of Dr. Blake… that is it. He cannot be trusted. The man is a charlatan and I fear these examinations he performs are much more for his benefit than yours."

The significance of that seemed to sink in and Philippa's face paled. She appeared quite stricken. "I feel so foolish. Why didn't I question him? Why didn't I demand some sort of explanation? I am not stupid or incapable of understanding the complexities of whatever science he was referencing!"

"Because you were desperate," Sophie stated. "Because he preyed upon your desperation to have some relief from the pain of these terrible megrims. You are not to blame for any of this. There is only one guilty party here and that is Dr. Blake! As to your family... well, Henry is helping me. He's looking into the doctor's past. And whether or not he might have had a hand in the passing of Lady Parkhurst."

"Henry?" Philippa asked. "Not Viscount Marchwood, but Henry? What else aren't you telling me?"

Sophie let out a deep shuddering breath. "I might have become secretly betrothed to your cousin last night in the kitchen while I was switching out the elixir Dr. Blake had given you for the placebo from the apothecary!"

Philippa blinked at that. "You have been remarkably busy. Plotting, subterfuge, engagements!"

"You hate me, don't you?" Sophie asked. "I really only have your best interests at heart! I swear it."

"I don't hate you at all," Philippa said. "The truth is, I find myself quite envious. You've done all that in two days and I've all done is lie abed!"

"To be fair, I am *your* companion. If you'd been up and about, I'd never have accomplished so much," Sophie said.

Philippa's eyes widened and then she laughed. She began to giggle. The sound was infectious, filling their small carriage. "Oh, heavens! I suppose if one is determined to find the bright side of my current predicament, that might be it!"

"Even if it weren't for my secret betrothal, even if not for meeting Henry—Viscount Marchwood—I'm happy to be where I am. I'm so happy to have met you and, I hope against hope, that my presence here will effect some sort of change for you... whether that involves parting ways with Dr. Blake or not."

Philippa smiled. "I'm glad for your presence. But no more secrets. None. Please talk to me about things. And if what you suspect, and what I now suspect, about Dr. Blake is true, then I will say good riddance to him."

Sophie nodded. "Then let me tell you about Mr. William Carlton."

WHILE SOPHIE AND Philippa were off to Lymington to enjoy a morning of sea bathing, Henry was off on a quest of his own. In order to get to the truth about Dr. Blake, he needed to know where the man had originated from. He also needed to find another doctor to see to Philippa's care once Dr. Blake was no longer given run of the household.

So he went back to the place where it had all started: Lady Hemsley. But he needed to catch her before she went into the Long Rooms for the morning gossip and taking the waters. After all, if he wished to speak freely with her, a public place was hardly the best location.

To that end, he'd set out early enough to catch her at home and ride with her in her carriage. Rushing through the streets, he arrived just as the front doors opened and Lady Hemsley stepped out of them. She caught sight of him, arched one well-drawn brow and then beckoned with a quick jerk of her head.

"You are making a habit of this, Marchwood," she remarked in an imperious tone.

"I sincerely hope not, Lady Hemsley. I merely needed clarification on a few points from our earlier conversation."

"Help me into the carriage," she said on a sigh. "And then I suppose you may accompany me."

Henry smiled and did as he'd been bade. Climbing into the carriage behind her once she was settled, he waited until the wheels began to turn and the sound of the horses' hooves would mask the content of their conversation before he began to speak. "Where did Dr. Blake come from? Before he was practicing here in Southampton, where was he?"

"Salisbury, I think. I vaguely recall Bess mentioning something about it," she said. "Though that is what he has put to her, that does not make it true. The man has barely a passing acquaintance with the truth, after all."

"He did not go very far then. Salisbury is but a half-day's ride," Henry mused.

Lady Hemsley made a humming sound. "Who do you know in Salisbury?"

Henry considered the question. "No one that I can think of. Why?"

"Precisely. Salisbury and Southampton are so close together they might as well be a world apart. The people from there rarely venture here and there is very little in Salisbury to draw anyone from Southampton. And people traveling to Southampton, that close to their destination, are unlikely to make a stop there."

It was true. Given the location, if a person in Salisbury required something that could not be found within its confines, they would surely just go to London which was no further than Southampton was. "You make an excellent point. I shall go to Salisbury and make my inquiries."

"You do that, but first, you will answer my questions, Marchwood," Lady Hemsley commanded imperiously.

"If I can, I will," Henry hedged.

"What is the nature of your attachment with Miss Upchurch?" The woman's brow rose and there was more than a hint of disapproval in her tone.

Henry sighed. "That is really between me and Miss Upchurch, Lady Hemsley."

"But it is not," she said. "I do not know the girl, truthfully. But in some small way, I am responsible for her being here. I will not be responsible for luring her to her ruin! To that end, I feel I must ensure that she is not being treated with any impropriety. What, Marchwood, are your intentions?"

"My intentions are entirely honorable," Henry replied.

"How honorable? Honorable in that you mean to marry the girl or honorable in that you intend to leave the girl be? I'm not blind, you know. I have eyes! I saw how the two of you looked at one another yesterday," she said. "I may be old, sir, but I am not dead, nor is my youth so far beyond me that I cannot recall what the flush of infatuation looks like!"

The old bat was like a dog with a bone, Henry thought. "When there is news to share regarding the nature of my attachment with Miss Upchurch, I have no doubt, Lady Hemsley, that you will be the first person to be apprised of it."

She sat back and crossed her arms, a satisfied smirk playing about her mouth. "You said when, Marchwood. Not if. Is that a slip of the tongue or a way to answer my question without necessarily *answering* my question?"

Henry sighed. "I cannot tell you more than I already have. Suffice it to say, I have a deep regard for Miss Upchurch and would never deal badly with her."

"Again, that is not a denial that there is more to tell. But I shall let it pass for now. I will even keep your secrets for the time being. But make no mistake, this is the sort of gossip that, if one gets to break the story, it can make or break one's social standing."

"Lady Hemsley, there is naught that could be done to break your social standing," he remarked.

She grinned rather triumphantly. "Indeed. I have cut a wide swath, haven't I? I was considered the most beautiful debutante in London my first season. Did you know that?"

Henry studied her. There were hints of that beauty remaining. "I did not know it, but I am not surprised by it."

She inclined her head. "I found very quickly that nothing will diminish the power of beauty like familiarity. People look at a pretty face so long and it suddenly requires no more notice than the wallpaper or that vase on the hall table that you take for granted. But information— gossip, if you will—that is a thing that holds sway, Marchwood. No one ignores you when they think you know things no one else does. So while my position is secure, I'm not quite willing to rest on my laurels yet."

"You are a diabolical woman, Lady Hemsley. I am glad I do not have to count you among my enemies," Henry noted.

She beamed in response, as if he had just paid her the highest of compliments. "Indeed. You'll send me a note when you're ready for the world to know what precisely you intend to do with Miss Upchurch and then I, Marchwood, will do what I do best."

"And what is that Lady Hemsley?"

She chuckled. "Talk, of course. I shall talk."

Chapter Fifteen

THERE WAS NEVER truly a lull in activity in a house with so many servants and so many guests. But there were times of the day when the activity was centered more thoroughly below stairs. It was midmorning, thus the beds had all been made, laundry gathered and rooms tidied. All of the younger members of the household were out for the day. Cecile was tending to household duties and Edward had gone on an outing with William under the guise of getting to know her betrothed better. Besides the servants, she was alone in the house. It was a rare occurrence and an opportunity that could not be squandered.

As such, Horatia did not creep down the hall. She simply walked with her head held high, as if it were her right to go anywhere in the house of her choosing. And in truth, to her mind, it was. The home belonged to her brother, after all. Her purpose might be suspect, but no one, if seen, would dare to question her. In the pocket of her day dress, the necklace was a heavy weight against her hip.

There was a part of her that recoiled at what she was doing. If Miss Upchurch was *only* her niece's companion, she would never dream of committing such an act. But she wasn't. She was a young and beautiful woman who had caught Henry's eye. He would throw his future away on her and that could not be permitted. The whole of it, the girl showing up to be the companion of a dead woman, encountering

Henry on the road as she had, it all smacked of a conspiracy. It was too convenient, too indicative of the girl being a consummate adventuress. And Henry had to be protected from such. After all, he would very likely be the next Duke of Thornhill! Despite what Cecile had said at dinner the night before, she could not condone such a match.

Of course, Henry would call it hypocrisy. He would point out that, in the overall scheme of things, William Carlton was far beneath her own standing. But she wasn't the heir. She wasn't the scion of the family. She was naught but an aging spinster who had always been more handsome than beautiful and for whom even wealth and rank had not been adequate inducement for a husband that met her exacting standards.

It was a funny thing how those standards lowered year by year. Now, hovering dangerously close to forty, a time when most women were dandling grandchildren on their knees, Horatia found herself on the cusp of marriage. Her first proposal had come when she was so firmly on the shelf most people had forgotten about her entirely. Yes, it was marriage to a man that, in her youth, she would have snubbed. Not that William wasn't handsome. He was. But he was in trade and that was something that, even with her limited options, she'd considered carefully. Ultimately, she'd been so charmed by him and so taken by his obvious infatuation with her that she'd elected to simply overlook it. She was also terribly tired of being alone and of being an object of pity when anyone deigned to notice her at all.

But she adored Henry and she adored Philippa. She looked upon her niece and nephew as the children she'd never had. In truth, she wanted nothing more for them than to be happy. She wished to spare Henry the pain of marrying a woman he so clearly loved and who was more than likely naught but a fortune hunter. And there was nothing she would not do in order to spare Philippa the pain of a life such as hers had been. Whatever it took, she would see her niece well and not relegated to the life of a lonely spinster. Someone had to look to preserving their family—not only the line but the reputation, as well.

As she reached Philippa's room, she looked about her. There were no servants in the corridor. No one was about at all. Moving quickly, she bypassed it and slipped quickly into the chamber that had been assigned to Miss Upchurch.

It was a lovely room and one she herself stayed in on previous visits. The dressing table was positioned near the window, where the best light would reach it, but also near enough to the fireplace to aid with the always monumental task of drying one's hair. It was the most likely place for the necklace to be discovered, as well.

There were a few personal items placed carefully atop it. A small bottle filled with a delicate scent. A box of hairpins. There were no cosmetics, but then a woman of Miss Upchurch's youth and beauty would hardly require them. A lovely comb and brush set backed intricately with carved wood rested there as well. They were fine pieces but not overly extravagant as befitted a woman of Miss Upchurch's limited means. The center drawer just beneath the mirror was slightly ajar. From her own experience, Horatia knew that drawer had a tendency to stick. Pulling it out entirely, she placed the necklace in the void created and then eased the drawer back in place. It took some maneuvering but when it was done, the drawer appeared undisturbed and the damning evidence had been planted.

Another pang of conscience swept her. Edward could be unpredictable. What if he had the girl arrested? Or transported? Or heaven forbid, what if she were hanged? She had nothing more to go on than her own cynical and suspicious opinions... and William's. Horatia reached for the drawer once more, but the doorknob rattled and she quickly pulled her hand back and hurried toward the door as a maid entered.

"Oh! My lady! I'd not have come in if I'd known you were here!"

"It's quite all right," Horatia offered. "I was looking for Philippa and Miss Upchurch. I thought we might spend some time together today."

"They've gone for Miss Philippa's sea bathing today," the girl offered with a shudder. "Can't stand the thoughts of it myself. All that water, black as pitch, and frothing around you! Terrifying. I want to see what's in the water with me and I want it no deeper than a bathtub."

Horatia smiled. "I quite agree. Thank you for reminding me about their appointment. By the way… I'm missing a necklace. I'm sure I've simply mislaid it. But it's a rather dear piece and has very special significance. It was a rather extravagant gift from Mr. Carlton."

The maid smiled. "Oh, yes, my lady! Should I see it, I'll let you know straightaway!"

"Thank you."

Horatia left the room and made her way downstairs to the morning room. It would be best to be in company with Cecile when the discovery was made. It would allay any suspicion.

As she reached the foyer, William was entering with Edward. The two of them had gone riding. She met William's questioning gaze and offered a smile accompanied by a slight nod. It was done. Now they had but to wait.

IF ONE WANTED to know about a physician, the best place to start, Henry reasoned, was with his competition. There were few enough physicians in Salisbury, fewer still that catered exclusively to the upper class. It was to those men that Henry turned his attention. Tracking down the first one, who had offices on New Street, Henry rang the bell and a woman garbed all in black answered the door. Rail thin and with a hawkish nose, she did not inspire feelings of welcome.

"Are you ill?" she asked.

"I need a word with the doctor."

"It's five shillings to walk through this door, young man."

Dutifully, Henry reached into the pocket of his coat and produced a small purse from whence he paid her. She immediately pocketed the coin. "He's upstairs. You wait in the parlor and I'll fetch him."

Henry did as he was bade, stepping into a parlor bedecked with furniture that could use reupholstering and curtains that could have done with a good washing. After a few moments, a man who appeared to be near his uncle's age stepped into the room. He still wore the powdered wig of his youth and, judging from the strain on the buttons of his outmoded waistcoat, it was from another era of his life, as well.

"I am Dr. Howard Almstead. How may I help you, sir?"

"Lord Henry Meredith, Viscount Marchwood, Dr. Almstead," Henry said, sketching a brief introduction. There were times when a title was quite a useful thing, after all. "I am here to inquire about another physician who may have left the area not long ago. A Dr. Richard Blake."

Dr. Almstead shook his head, powder raining down upon his shoulders. "No, my lord. To my knowledge there has been no Dr. Blake in Salisbury."

Henry had feared as much. "He's a young man, handsome. Treats primarily women. And prescribes laudanum quite generously but may disguise it as something else entirely."

The elder doctor's expression hardened, his lips firming into a thin, disapproving line. "His name is not Dr. Blake. Here, he was known as Dr. Albert Evans. To put it mildly, Viscount Marchwood, the man was run out of town. He married one of his patients—not unheard of—but somewhat unusual given that she was quite young. Sixteen to be precise. She died within months of the marriage under somewhat mysterious circumstances and conveniently for him, too, as her family had just cut them off. But he had what he wanted from her, I suppose. He'd gotten her dowry and apparently spent it on fancy clothes, a barouche and all the trappings of wealth that a physician truly cannot afford."

"Do you know from whence Dr. Blake—excuse me—Dr. Evans had come? Where did he practice before?"

Dr. Almstead shook his head again. "I knew little enough about the man. We did not associate. I think perhaps London, based only on his clothing on the few occasions I saw him. He had what one might refer to as town polish. Beyond that, I could not say. What is your interest in the man?"

"He is currently treating a young woman in my family and concerns have arisen about the efficacy of his treatment and about his intentions toward her," Henry admitted. "You said his young bride died under mysterious circumstances. What were they precisely?"

Dr. Almstead sighed heavily, as if the entire matter were too distasteful to discuss. "Given the reason for your investigation into the man, I can make an exception to my rules regarding the repetition of gossip. Normally, I would consider it far beneath my dignity."

"Dr. Almstead, I assure you that I have no interest in gossip myself. I only seek to protect my young cousin from someone who may exploit her illness and isolation for his own gain."

"Quite right. The girl had suffered spells of megrims and dizziness. Oftentimes, she would also have fits. Seems to me, she was far more ill and far more frequently ill after her marriage to that man. Her family was advised to have her committed but she was their only child."

It was all sounding terribly, terribly familiar, Henry thought with a sinking feeling in his gut. "Go on."

"She was found at the bottom of a flight of stairs. Her neck was broken. But there were servants who reported hearing the doctor and his bride arguing the night of her fall. It was also very unusual for her to be out of her rooms in the middle of the night. Given her health issues, she rarely went below stairs at all as I understand it. Anything she required, she would have had a servant fetch for her... even in the wee hours."

"I see," Henry said. And he did see. He was beginning to see very, very clearly. "I appreciate your candor."

"My advice to you, my lord, would be to bar him entrance to the house and never let him near anyone you care for."

Henry nodded. "Thank you for your time, Dr. Almstead, and for the information. It is much appreciated. I mean to act upon your very sound advice at once."

"Good luck and good day to you, sir," the doctor said stiffly.

Leaving the man's offices, Henry retraced his steps to the Red Lyon Inn where he'd stabled his horse. There, he made arrangements to have the mount returned at a later time and obtained a fresh horse for the journey back to Southampton. He couldn't afford the necessary time to allow the horse to recover. He was overtaken with the feeling that something was terribly wrong and that it was imperative he return at once. He needed to speak to his uncle about Dr. Blake. Or Dr. Evans as it were. The sooner they limited that man's access to Philippa the better. He also needed to see to Sophie's safety. If Dr. Blake-possibly-Evans knew that it was she who had called his position into question, it would not go well for her at all.

Chapter Sixteen

WHEN THEY REACHED the house, Philippa was utterly exhausted. It was apparent in her slow steps and the fact that each one seemed to become more difficult for the girl. Sophie knew better than to offer the girl her assistance. It was bad enough that the footmen were waiting with a sedan chair for her just inside the doors. It was something Philippa had confessed to her during their outing. She would allow herself to be squired around indoors in such a manner, but her pride would not permit it in public where she might be observed.

"You've done too much! You are completely worn out," Sophie clucked her tongue in concern as they reached the top step and the butler opened the door for them. They had stayed at the bathing area for longer than intended, but it had been remarkable to see Philippa so full of joy and life.

"Perhaps," Philippa agreed with a wan smile. "But I'm quite pleased with the day. And I strongly suspect that tomorrow shall be even better. Especially given what I now know. I cannot thank you enough for that."

"Do not thank me," Sophie said. "I'm just so relieved that you believed me."

They had not quite reached the stairs and the footmen waiting for her when the duke emerged from his study at the end of the corridor.

His expression was dark and there was a tension emanating from him that was unmistakable.

Even in her exhausted state, Philippa sensed it. Her steps faltered and the last vestiges of color fled from her pale face. "Is everything all right, Papa? It isn't—how is Mother?"

"Your mother is fine, Philippa. This does not concern you, Child. You will go on to your room. But, Miss Upchurch, we require your presence in my study."

"We?" Sophie asked.

"Yes. My sister and her betrothed have some questions for you. I presume you know what this is in reference to," he stated coldly.

"I do not, but I shall be there directly," Sophie answered.

"Now, if you please, Miss Upchurch. This is not a matter that can wait," the duke stated firmly. His tone was cold and snappish, indicating that he was at the end of his patience.

Sophie's heart sank and bile rose in her throat. Whatever was happening, it could not be good. There was something foul afoot and she was without allies. Philippa was too weak to do anything and she had no notion of where Henry had gone to. There was no doubt in her mind that William Carlton was the architect of it all. He saw her as a threat. That much was clear. It was apparent he would mitigate that threat by any means necessary.

"I will come with you," Philippa offered, clutching Sophie's arm.

"I don't think your father will permit it," Sophie stated. "And you need to rest. You've overtaxed yourself today."

"But I fear they will send you away!" Philippa said.

Sophie stepped closer and hugged her friend tightly. She very much feared the same thing. Next to Philippa's ear, she whispered, "Ask one of the maids what occurred. The servants always know. And when Henry returns, tell him to find me at the inn where I found him my first day here."

Philippa nodded. "All right. You will be well? You have funds?"

She had some. She had the small amount she'd traveled with. So long as she didn't have to secure a room for the night, all would be well. "I will be fine. Let me face whatever this is and get it done."

Philippa hugged her then, tightly. "Be careful. I've never seen Papa so angry. So cold! Whatever it is, I know you didn't do it. You couldn't have. You're the most wonderful person I know and the dearest friend I could ever have made!"

"Do not trust Mr. Carlton," Sophie warned. "He has your aunt in thrall, but the man is a scoundrel. I know it. Remember what I told you!"

Sophie turned away from her friend and made her way to the study. Stepping inside, she found the duchess softly sobbing into her handkerchief while Lady Horatia sat cold-eyed and unbending beside her. Mr. Carlton was standing near the window, looking inordinately pleased with himself.

"There she is," Carlton said. He pointed one long finger directly at her. "The thief."

Someone had seen her sneaking to the kitchen the night before, Sophie realized. It was all just a misunderstanding. When she explained about the elixir and what she'd learned from the apothecary, all would be well.

"I'm not certain what I am meant to have taken, but I assure you I am no thief, your grace. I believe this must be some sort of misunderstanding."

The duke reached into his desk drawer and pulled out a necklace. It was a stunning piece of jewelry, all but dripping with diamonds and pearls as it draped over his hand. "Do you have an explanation, Miss Upchurch?"

"An explanation for what?"

"Why was Lady Horatia's necklace found in your room, Miss Upchurch?" the duchess demanded. "If it is a misunderstanding as you say, then surely there will be a logical explanation."

Fear was an ugly and dark thing. It swelled inside her, making her feel as if she could not breathe, like there was not enough space left inside her for the very air she required. Swallowing with some difficulty, Sophie managed to say, "Well, I can't imagine why it would have been there. I certainly did not place it there, your grace!"

"It was in her room because she stole it. She saw me wearing it at dinner last night, coveted it for herself and took it," Horatia stated. "I saw the way you stared at it, Miss Upchurch!"

"I assure you that is not so. Not to mention, I would have had no opportunity to take it from your chamber," Sophie replied.

"How could you betray us this way? We've been nothing but kind to you. We welcomed you into our home!" the duchess wailed.

"I have no explanation," Sophie stated. "Your grace, I have never seen that necklace before. Lady Horatia states she wore it last night, but if she did, I certainly paid it no heed. If it was in my room, it was not because I placed it th—"

"Enough!" the duke shouted.

It was so loud, the bark of his voice so vicious, that Sophie flinched and drew back. She didn't say another word. Instead, she went completely still and simply waited. Because while they had welcomed her into their home, it was quite clear that in the overall scheme of things, she would not be believed. *Because she was beneath them.* In their estimation, she would never be above reproach. Impoverished and illegitimate, why would they believe her when a successful business-man and his betrothed were willing to swear against her?

"Your thievery is bad enough, but I will not be lied to, Miss Up-church!" the duke snapped. "You will tell me the truth. Where were you last evening?"

"I was in my room," Sophie replied.

"And when a maid saw you in the corridor in the wee hours of the morning... where were you going then?" Mr. Carlton demanded.

"Which maid?" Sophie asked.

"Does it matter?" Carlton countered. "When Horatia discovered her missing necklace and one of the maids discovered it in your chamber, you lost the right to ask any questions. A servant stepped forward and admitted she had observed you skulking about. Do you deny it?"

"I do not deny that I had left my room, but the only place I went was to the kitchen," Sophie admitted. "Henry—"

"Viscount Marchwood!" Horatia corrected. "Address your betters as is their right, girl. The poor boy will be devastated to think he brought such perfidy into this house!"

"And what were you doing in the kitchen in the middle of the night?" the duke demanded. "Did we not feed you well enough at dinner? Must you raid the larders in the darkness, then?"

Sophie had no reply. She didn't wish to tell a lie but she could not tell the truth, because they were unwilling to hear it. Nothing she could say to them would make them question the narrative they'd been provided by Lady Horatia and Mr. William Carlton. And telling them about Dr. Blake in that moment could make them dig in their heels and insist that he continue treating Philippa regardless of her feelings on the matter.

One question burned inside her. Why? What possible thing could she have done to deserve such treatment? Yes, she knew William Carlton's secret, that he'd likely sired a child out of wedlock. But she'd not speak against him to Lady Horatia or the duke. Why would she? "Am I to be arrested then?"

The duke sighed. The duchess wept. Carlton smirked. Lady Horatia simply remained stoic and cold.

"No, Miss Upchurch. My daughter has a true fondness for you and I would not see her hurt further by watching you dragged from our house to the gaol. It is for her sake and the sake of my nephew that the matter will go no further," the duke stated flatly. "Your bags have been packed for you. You will leave this house with precisely what you entered with and nothing more. You may wait in the foyer under the watchful eye of our butler. I want you gone from my sight. And should you show your face here again, this mercy I have shown you will be rescinded. No matter the cost or upset to my family."

Dismissed, disgraced and more hurt than she cared to admit, Sophie did just that. She left the study without another word and retreated to the foyer where the servants whispered and stared. Ultimately, a footman delivered her bags, dropping them at her feet with a tad more force than necessary. Silently, the butler opened the door for her, a cue to exit.

Picking up her valises, Sophie straightened her shoulders, lifted her chin and exited the house. But as her feet touched the first step, a tear fell. It was followed by a stream of others; hot, silent and utterly pointless.

Chapter Seventeen

THE SMALL TAVERN was full of the more unsavory elements of Southampton. Most of the men there would do honest work when they had to, but preferred dishonest work over it. At a small table in the back corner, a small man in a dirty waistcoat was rubbing an apple against his scrawny chest.

William Blake, formerly known by a slew of other monikers, entered the building and made straight for that table. "Is it done?"

The little man looked up. "Which part?"

"The apothecary. It's done?" The man had come to his home the night before, asking all manner of unfortunate questions. It wasn't a great leap to imagine that Miss Upchurch had been the one to spark the man's interest. She would be dealt with soon enough, though.

"Done," the man said, and took a bite out of the apple. Given how terrible his teeth were, it was a wonder the man could eat an apple without losing the half-rotted nubs. "He won't be making no trouble for you. Won't be asking no questions either. But he's not your only worry. Miss Ruby sent some men round what to collect. Only there ain't enough. Even selling off everything that squawking old bird owned that her relatives ain't scarfed up, you'll not get enough to cover the debt."

"I've got something else in mind to cover the debt. The usual meeting place?" Miss Upchurch would serve as a partial payment. Miss

Ruby held sway over the criminal elements of the southern coast. The Hound of Whitehall ruled in London and she ruled in Brighton. A young, lovely and well-mannered woman such as Miss Upchurch would command a great deal of money in any one of Ruby's houses. That Miss Upchurch was likely virginal meant that there could well be a bidding war to determine who'd get her first. It would buy him the time he needed to cover the rest of his debt to her. Especially as Lady Parkhurst's pockets had been far emptier than the old biddy had let on. It had taken months to have himself written into her will and longer still to be named executor.

"The Crooked Leg in Salisbury," the man stated. "You'll be lucky not to hang going back there!"

"Well, I can't afford to be seen meeting with that sort here. Meeting with you is dangerous enough," the doctor insisted.

"What about the other one? The young one," the man asked.

"In a month, I will be able to convince her to marry me so that I can look after her all the time. I think I could convince her parents by tomorrow desperate as they are for a cure. Dupes," he sneered. "They'd do anything to see her well, including seeing her marry so very far beneath her. It won't be like Salisbury. They'll give me all I ask for and more."

The little man took another bite of his apple, and as he chewed, warned, "I best get what I ask for. I know enough of your secrets, *Doctor*. Don't think I won't spill my guts if it means saving my own hide."

"I have your money. But I won't give it to you in here. The alley is best. The fewer people in this establishment that know either one of us has a fat purse, the better off we are," the doctor insisted. He did indeed have what the man was asking for. But it wasn't money. He'd get a blade between his ribs and nothing more.

"Right. You go first. I'll follow," the little man said.

Chapter Eighteen

SOPHIE WAS NUMB. It was impossible to really process what had just happened. Branded a thief and literally tossed out into the streets, it was far worse than she had ever imagined it could be. Even discovering that Lady Parkhurst had died unexpectedly and her waiting position was no more had not left her so low. It was worse perhaps because she'd held the Duke and Duchess of Thornhill in great regard. The warmth and easy welcome she'd been shown had been revoked so quickly and without compunction. Even on their short acquaintance, she'd thought them kind and pleasant people. Philippa was already a dear, dear friend and now she might never see her again. And what of Henry? Would he believe the lies? Or would he see it for the Machiavellian twist that it was?

Oh, how she prayed that he would see through the machinations that surely originated with Mr. William Carlton. As for Lady Horatia, she had no notion of whether the woman was a knowing participant in the scheme to see her ruined or if she was simply a dupe, as well.

As she trudged toward the inn, valises in tow, she had more questions than answers. How could they have believed it of her so quickly? The answer was, of course, class. She was illegitimate and impoverished. While Mr. William Carlton was still in trade, he was wealthy. It was simply the way of the world.

"Miss Upchurch? Are you quite well?"

Sophie looked up to see Dr. Blake walking toward her. Panic hit her then. "I'm quite well, Dr. Blake, thank you."

"Nonsense! You are quite pale, Miss. Peaked even. Let me escort you back to the Thornhills' home," he offered.

"I am not going in that direction. I will not be returning there. I shall be returning to London on the public stage today," she stated and hoped very much to leave it at that. He was the last person to which she wanted to explain her current situation.

His expression shifted to one of quiet knowing. There was a hint of satisfaction behind his eyes, even as his tone filled with feigned sympathy. "I see. There has been some sort of falling out?"

"I have no wish to discuss the matter, Dr. Blake," Sophie stated.

He nodded. "I do understand. It is not easy, Miss Upchurch, to be in this terrible limbo between servitude and respectability. As a physician, I find myself there, as well. I am forced to take a fee for my service which makes me part of the trade, and therefore somehow less than. Yet, because of the nature of the service I offer and their dependence upon me, I am not entirely outside of their social sphere. It makes them very uncomfortable to be confronted with people they cannot simply place in a familiar box."

Sophie shook her head. "I'm certain it's all a misunderstanding, Dr. Blake. I shan't speak ill of them when they've been so terribly kind and gracious to me." *Until today.*

He smiled sympathetically. "Of course, Miss Upchurch. And it speaks volumes about the nature of your character that you would be so willing to forgive any slight. Allow me to see you to your destination, at least. There has been a flurry of ships just in at the docks and the streets of Southampton are no place for a young woman to be unescorted. Where are you going?"

Sophie didn't want his assistance. She didn't trust him at all. But even in her state of upset, it had been impossible to miss that there were far more sailors roaming the streets than was the norm. Many of them had leered at her already and called out things that, had she understood them, would surely have put her to blush. "To the inn, sir. The Duke of Wellington," she answered.

"You are departing Southampton for good then? You have a position waiting for you in London?" he surmised.

"Perhaps. I... do not know yet if my departure will be permanent," she stated honestly. Surely there was no danger in disclosing that?

"Let me get a carriage and see you there myself. Those bags must be terribly heavy and you do look unwell, Miss Upchurch," he stated again. "I insist upon it, in fact."

She couldn't protest. If she continued to say no, he would suspect that she suspected him. "Thank you, Dr. Blake. You are most kind."

Sophie waited there while he hailed a hack for them. When it arrived, she noted that it appeared far nicer than the hacks in London. This coach was newer, cleaner and far less worn.

"Let me take those," Dr. Blake offered, reaching for her bags. He had them plucked from her hands and tucked inside the hack before she could even respond. Then he offered her his hand to help her inside.

Reluctantly, Sophie accepted it. She didn't know what else to do without making a scene. If she refused him there on the street, he could take off with her bags which also contained the only bit of coin she possessed. Not to mention that it would likely have no effect. He was a respected physician, regardless of whether or not he deserved it and she was no one of consequence. He could simply claim her to be an overset patient and others would likely help him load her into the coach despite any protest. Cooperation and the hope that he did not know how much she knew already and what she suspected him of was her best chance.

Reluctantly, Sophie climbed into the coach and then the doctor climbed in after her. It was only when they were underway that she noted his medical bag. He hadn't been carrying it on the street, yet it was sitting on the seat beside him. A feeling of trepidation overtook her. "This isn't a hack, is it?"

"No, Miss Upchurch," he said. "How remarkably observant you are!"

Sophie didn't care how it looked. She reached for the door, ready to leap out. But he caught her wrist, twisting it so viciously that she cried out.

"You may scream if you wish. This is my coach. The driver is loyal to me and will not aid you," he warned.

"Why are you doing this?" Sophie demanded.

He smiled coolly, his grip loosening on her wrist slightly. "Now isn't the time for your questions. It's the time for mine."

"What questions are those?" she asked.

"Why are you and Viscount Marchwood interfering in my affairs?"

"He only wanted to be certain you were the best physician to be treating Philippa," she stated.

"Did her father ask him to undertake this investigation?" Dr. Blake demanded. "No. I do not think that he did, Miss Upchurch. No one had even the slightest suspicion that I might be less than a most excellent physician until you arrived in Southampton. Is that a coincidence, Miss Upchurch?"

The carriage turned down another street, carrying her away from the Duke of Wellington Inn. Sophie jerked her wrist, trying to pull away, but he held firm. "Where are you taking me?"

"You will not be harmed, Miss Upchurch, so long as you cooperate. But I cannot have you spoiling my plan."

"What plan?" Sophie asked.

"I mean to marry Lady Philippa Meredith," he stated boldly. "I will have her as my bride. Then all of my financial woes will be far behind me. Her mother and father will be so grateful for the tender care I give her and the care I take in nursing my dear, sickly wife, they will be quite generous, I'm sure."

Sophie considered her options. She could jump from the coach, assuming she could break free of his hold. It wasn't going overly fast yet as it was still town. But if she did, and managed to not injure herself terribly in the process, where would she go? She could wait until the coach stopped and attempt to make a run for it, but she had no notion of where they were going or if there would be people around to offer aid, or at least witness the situation. "I see. And Lady Parkhurst? Where did she fit into your nefarious plot?"

Dr. Blake smiled. The carriage had picked up enough speed that he must have felt safe in letting her go. He thrust her wrist from his hand with far more force than was necessary. "It is impossible to enter society, even in the guise of a physician, without having proper entree. I began with other ladies of slightly lower standing and worked my way up to Lady Parkhurst. You see, she had the reputation that was required. I needed her stamp of approval before I could ever get near one such as Lady Philippa Meredith."

"You've done this before," Sophie stated. "How many young women have been laid to waste in your wake?"

"They haven't all been young," he said. "My first wife was an aging widow with a generous annuity... which I borrowed against heavily. My second wife was another young woman who suffered from similar symptoms to poor Philippa. It was a bit of trial and error to figure out how to worsen her symptoms without just poisoning her outright. And then I chanced upon laudanum. Oddly enough, withholding it produces significant megrims. So I would alternate. One bottle of my elixir will have it and the next will not. That insures Philippa will not get so well that she no longer needs me."

"And the most recent bottle?" she asked.

"Without," he said. "But the one before had it aplenty... but then you know that don't you? Your apothecary was asking questions, as well. Sadly, he was not very discreet. He'll ask no more questions, however."

He wasn't simply a greedy and unscrupulous fortune hunter as she'd initially suspected. He was a monster and quite possibly a madman. "What did you do to him?"

"He had an unfortunate accident. Terrible thing, getting into one's cups and then falling drunkenly into one's work bench. Head wounds bleed terribly, you know. Alas, it happens all too often," he offered with a sad half-smile. "'Tis a shame really. He was very good at his work."

Sophie felt positively ill. He was dead. That kind man, who had done nothing more than help two strangers had now lost his life because of it. "And me? What is your plan for me?"

"Many young women meet misfortune on the road, Miss Up-church. It's an unfortunate fact of life that your sex makes you a target for all manner of wickedness. Alas, I owe a bit of money to a woman in Brighton who will be able to put your many assets to good use."

It didn't require a great deal of imagination to deduce precisely what assets he was referring to. She needed to distract him, to delay him. "Surely escorting me as far as Brighton will take you too far from your patients," Sophie insisted. "However will you explain your absence for so long?"

"Oh, I don't have to get you all the way to Brighton. I only need to get you as far as Salisbury. I've a man there who acts as an agent for the woman in question… he'll pay me, she will pay him, and you will have all the work, as it were, that you can manage."

Sophie's gaze shifted to the window. They were heading out of the city, likely already on the road to Salisbury. If she didn't attempt an escape now, she'd be too far from anyone's assistance for it to matter. Wracking her brain, she tried to imagine where she might go.

Lady Hemsley.

Would the woman help her? Or would she have been turned against her, as well? Had word already spread through polite society that she'd been branded a thief?

"Don't even think it," he warned.

"Think what?" she asked.

"Escape. You cannot. I will catch you. And while I have no real desire to hurt you, Miss Upchurch, I will if you force my hand. We're the same, you and I," he said, "Miss Upchurch. Sophie. May I call you Sophie?"

"How are we the same? And you may call me Miss Upchurch, though to be honest, I'd prefer not having to speak with you at all!"

"Bastard children who have been forced to make their own way in the world. Oh, yes. I know all about your Darrow School. I also knew that I couldn't afford to keep Lady Parkhurst around when she'd have a nosy companion to poke into things. I added arsenic to her elixir when I found out she'd hired you. A little bit every day until she simply couldn't hold out anymore. Poor old bird."

"And is that what you will do to Philippa? See her dead? Poisoned by your hand?"

He shrugged. "That will depend upon the generosity of her father. So long as the funds flow freely in my direction while we are wed, she may languish in an opium-induced stupor for as long as she lives. Now, should he decide to stop providing for us, then I will have to look into other options."

Sophie considered her options carefully. She had only one. Escape. But this was not a man who knew what being a student of Effie Darrow's entailed. She waited for just a moment, long enough for the carriage to hit a particularly deep rut. And then she clutched her stomach. "Oh... I don't feel well."

"Do not try these ploys with me!" he shouted at her.

"I always suffer such sickness when traveling by carriage, but especially if I ride facing backward. Perhaps if we moved seats?" she suggested.

He stared at her for a moment, weighing and measuring. The truth was Sophie did feel quite ill, but it wasn't the motion of the carriage. It was disgust at him and being in his presence, coupled with fear, that left her thus. Still, whatever he saw must have swayed him.

"Fine," he ultimately agreed and rose, levering himself onto the seat beside her.

Sophie rose then, moving toward the other seat. There she stumbled slightly, pitching forward onto the seat and knocking his medical bag to the floor of the carriage where all the instruments spilled out.

She felt him grab her hair, pulling her head back roughly. But even as she was jerked to her feet, she managed to place one of her walking boots over a scalpel on the floor of the carriage, kicking it until it rested against the wooden block beneath the seat. He shoved her forward onto the seat, her head connected painfully with the wooden seat back. But the stumble allowed her to drop to her knees, to slide the scalpel forward enough that she could grasp it before pulling herself up.

"Do not toy with me, Miss Upchurch. The fate in store for you may not be the one you desire, but I could just as easily see you dead," he warned coldly.

"There is one major point of disagreement, Dr. Blake," Sophie replied.

"And what is that?"

"You are not the one who will decide my fate," she said softly. And without warning, she lunged forward, scalpel in hand, and slashed at his face.

He let out a roar of rage and pain as he clasped one hand to the wound which bled profusely. With his other hand, he reached for her, blinded by the blood flowing into his eyes. Sophie evaded him, continuing to lash out with the scalpel as she pushed open the carriage door. She discarded the blade just as she leapt free of the carriage. There was no way to land safely with it and she couldn't afford to be slowed down by a puncture wound.

Her only hope for survival would be that he was bleeding too profusely to give chase. Regardless, she couldn't afford the isolation of ducking into the woods to conceal herself. Her only real protection would come from being in a crowd with witnesses. To that end, Sophie ran. She headed back toward Southampton, her legs pumping beneath her and her breath billowing as she ran as hard and fast as she could.

Chapter Nineteen

H E WAS RIDING hellbent for leather, chasing down a woman who would surely be the death of him. Nicholas Montford, Lord Highcliff, was a man on a mission. How, he wondered, even as the horse's hooves thundered beneath him, could she be so foolish? If ever there was a woman who ought to understand the dangers of traveling alone, it was her. Wasn't that how they'd met after all? He'd come upon her after her carriage had been halted by brigands intent on robbing her and divesting her of her virtue. Of course, she'd flouted their plans quite soundly, but that didn't mean she would be so lucky every time.

From the very moment he'd received the missive from Lady Seaburn and Lady Deveril requesting his presence, he'd known it would be nothing but trouble. Were they ever anything else? But as the whole ridiculous tale had spilled out of them, that their esteemed former teacher, Miss Euphemia Darrow, had taken off entirely on her own, aboard a mail coach, no less, to track down one of her students who—well, he drew a blank. At that point, he'd been so overwhelmed with visions of Effie lying dead on the roadside from a carriage accident, or worse, shot by brigands who'd held up the mail coach, he'd stopped listening to them. He didn't know precisely what sort of turmoil Miss Upchurch was in.

He'd ushered them out the door of the tea shop, gone home, had his mount saddled and taken off after her, even though he'd sworn the last time they'd met that she would never set eyes on him again. Now, he was eating those words and that was her fault, as well.

He could throttle her! How could she be so reckless and so foolish? It would serve her right if he didn't come to the rescue, he thought. Of course, they both knew that would never happen. He'd cut off his own arm before he'd ever let harm come to her, but this—this was just going too far.

It seemed all he did with his life anymore was rescue Effie, her wayward students, or procure special licenses for other people to marry. *Fine way for a master spy to end up.*

Up ahead, he saw a coaching inn tucked into a bend in the road. He also saw the mail coach easing into the inn yard from the road, no doubt to swap out horses again. The occupants would be ushered inside to utilize the facilities, of course. It was the perfect opportunity to confront her and to escort her straight back to London where she could remain safely inside her school while he located her errant pupil. But first, she'd get a piece of his mind.

≫⋙✦⋘≪

EFFIE WAS ON the mail coach. She'd packed only one bag and held it firmly on her lap as they rocked out of London at a speed that made her stomach churn. She'd not been able to shake the feeling, from the arrival of Sophie's letter, that something was terribly amiss.

They hit a particularly nasty rut in the road. The coach swayed, all of its occupants bumping against one another. And then it began to slow.

"We are stopping?" Effie asked.

"Never been on the mail coach 'afore?" the woman next to her asked, her gaze roaming over Effie's finely stitched traveling dress.

"No," Effie admitted.

"Stop every ten miles or so to change horses. They're fast, but like to make your head spin with all the stops and starts," the woman stated, then cackled revealing an utter lack of teeth.

"Oh," Effie said. "Will we get out at each location, then?" She hadn't planned for such. Surely they would not be unsavory locations.

"You can get out, but I wouldn't go far. Won't wait for you if you wander off," the woman replied. "Most just make use of facilities and then hop back on quick like."

"Right," Effie said.

Still, when the coach rolled to a stop in the inn yard and the occupants disembarked, Effie was in their number. She remained outside in the inn yard, walking, stretching her legs and waiting for some indication that the coach was ready to board again. Still, the center of the yard was terribly muddy and so she stuck to the outer edges where the earth was slightly more firmly packed and less likely to soil her skirts.

"You wouldn't have to worry about the mud if you were at home, in Mayfair, where you belong."

Effie thought at first it was a product of her own mind. She longed for his presence so, missed the bite of his wit and the sharp repartee that was so much a part of who he was, that hearing his voice in her head seemed far more logical than the possibility of him actually being there. But he didn't sound bored or slightly amused. He sounded angry, and that was her first clue that Highcliff was, in fact, right there with her.

Spinning around, she faced him, noting one dark brow arched in challenge and his jaw clenched with quiet fury. "Oh, I'm sorry, are you speaking to me again? I seem to recall our last exchange where you said I'd never set eyes on you again."

He stepped forward then, his eyes glittering with anger. "Well that was before you decided to be suicidally stupid. Do you have any idea what could happen to you? A woman traveling alone?"

"I'm not alone. There are other passengers aboard the mail coach. And once I retrieve Sophie, she and I will be traveling together, which is more than proper," Effie stated. "And forgive me for saying so, but I do not see that it is of any particular concern to you. You've made your lack of *regard* perfectly clear."

"My lack of regard? Is it a lack of regard that had me haring after you when you've clearly no sense at all as it pertains to your own safety?" he snapped at her. "If you're referring to our last meeting, it was the depth of my regard for you which prompted my refusal! Not the lack."

Effie started to answer, but then she glanced around her. The other occupants of the mail coach, even the driver and the outriders, had all gathered round and were watching the exchange with rapt attention. "You are making a scene."

"I'll make a bigger one still if you attempt to get back into that coach," he warned.

"Then what would you have me do?"

"I'll hire a coach and escort you back to London myself," he stated.

"And Sophie? I cannot, my lord. I must go after her," Effie was adamant. She would not allow one of her students, a girl she had brought up, to simply be abandoned to whatever fate the world had in store for her.

His eyes darkened. "My lord? When have you ever addressed me so?"

"When you made the choice for us both that we should be little better than strangers to one another," Effie answered. "I do not answer to you. I will not be cowed or bullied by you either."

"I will go to your father," he threatened.

It wasn't an idle threat. He would and they both knew it. And at present, her relationship with her father was strained enough that it might prompt him to break with her entirely. "So be it. I live by my own conscience and, at present, it demands I find my charge and see her to safety," Effie answered.

"Dammit, Effie! You can't go running off to Southampton by yourself!"

"What I do, and whom I do it with, are not your affair, Lord Highcliff. Now, please, the coach has a schedule to keep and I will not be the reason it is delayed," she stated imperiously and moved to sail past him. But he reached out, one hand snaking about her upper arm to halt her progress.

"No."

She turned her head then, her stare glacial. "No?"

"No," he stated just as emphatically as before.

A small smile tugged at the corner of Effie's lips. Then she brought her booted foot up and kicked out sharply, catching the side of his knee, sending him sinking to the ground. Then she wheeled round, smacked the heel of her hand into his nose, and while he knelt there in the dirt, bleeding, she walked away.

Her triumph was short-lived. She hadn't even made it halfway across the inn yard before he barreled into her, sweeping her up and over his shoulder like a sack of flour. She kicked and flailed to no avail, as he limped, with great purpose, toward the stables.

"Help me!" Effie called out to the woman who'd been seated beside her on the coach.

"A man like that wants to cart you off, Miss, the best help I can give you is to stay out of his way," the woman answered with a cheeky grin, which she followed by a low whistle. "Wish I had one what could cart me off like that!"

"Don't encourage h—oww!" Effie's protest was interrupted by the sharp sting of a hard slap on her bottom. "What do you think you're doing?"

"What someone ought to have done a long time ago," he stated. "You've had your head for entirely too long. It's time, Euphemia Darrow, that someone else took the reins."

Chapter Twenty

HENRY RETURNED TO his uncle's townhome to find the house in an uproar. Philippa was sobbing uncontrollably, his Aunt Cecile was wringing her hands, his uncle was blustering about it being "the right thing", while Horatia and Mr. William Carlton simply sat there, smug and superior. One person was very conspicuously absent. A feeling of dread crept through him. Something was terribly, terribly amiss.

"Where is Miss Upchurch?" Henry demanded.

"They sent her away!" Philippa cried out, the last going up in a high-pitched wail.

"What?" That couldn't be possible. Surely, she was mistaken. "Tell me that isn't true, Uncle!"

"It most certainly is true," the duke stated emphatically. "I will not harbor a thief in my home! I will not. You ought to be ashamed of yourself, Henry, for being taken in by the girl and bringing her into our midst! Look at the disappointment you've caused your dear cousin! Not to mention the upset that poor Horatia suffered when she discovered she had been robbed."

"I fear we may have been hasty," Cecile stated. "I am so terribly disappointed, but we might not have sent her away in such a manner. Surely we could have sent her back to London by carriage instead of just turning her out into the street?"

"I'm certain she has funds enough to see herself back to London as we have not yet managed a complete inventory of the house," the duke stated baldly. "No doubt, she has been pilfering from here and yon since she first set foot inside the door."

He couldn't fathom what he was hearing, not at first. Henry simply stared at the tragically farcical scene before him, as well as its many players, before the reality of it and its many implications began to sink in. "Do you even hear yourself?" he demanded.

"Perfectly well," his uncle snapped. "Do not dare defend her to me!"

"Miss Upchurch has been all that was kind and gracious. She has taken to Philippa and Philippa to her as if they were bosom friends. And Mr. William Carlton, who incidentally does, in fact, have some ties to the Darrow School in London from whence Miss Upchurch came, is in this house less than twenty-four hours and suddenly you are willing to brand her a thief? To what end?"

"It was a very valuable necklace!" Horatia protested.

"Yes, and Aunt Cecile has dozens of very valuable necklaces... most of which would never have been missed had Miss Upchurch decided to avail herself of one," Henry pointed out. "But, no, she elected to steal from someone who arrived here with a limited number of items and would know the count of every one of them. Not only do you believe her a thief, you apparently also believe her to be a stupid one."

The duke blustered, "Well, that's... she's turned your head, Henry. Pretty young girl like that. But you don't... that is to say, you aren't thinking quite clearly!"

"I'm thinking more clearly than all of you. So was Miss Upchurch! If you had been, you'd have done a bit more research on the man you entrusted with the care of your daughter!"

"What does that mean?" Cecile interjected. "What are you implying, Henry?"

"Dr. Blake, this physician you've obtained? He isn't Dr. Blake at all. His name, prior to reinventing himself here in Southampton, was Dr. Albert Evans of Salisbury. He married one of his patients there—a young woman suffering from megrims. While under his care, her condition continually worsened until she suffered a terrible accident and died. Conveniently enough for him, her death happened to coincide with the point in time when her family cut them off and refused to continue supporting his extravagant tastes!"

Cecile's face paled. "Dr. Blake is a fraud?"

"Indeed, he is," Henry stated. "And were it not for Miss Upchurch urging me to look into the matter, we'd have never known."

"He hinted that he had romantic feelings for me... and that when I was older, he might become more than my physician," Philippa offered, still tearful but slightly more calm. "I discussed all of that with Miss Upchurch this morning on our way to the bathing place. She told me what she did, about switching the elixirs after the two of you discovered he'd been giving me laudanum."

"Laudanum?" the duke bellowed. "I forbade him to give you that horrid substance! He swore to me on his life that he would not. He called it a foul poison."

"Clearly Dr. Blake, or Dr. Evans, as it were, has quite a gift for lying," Henry stated. "And he's not the only one, is he, Mr. Carlton?"

"I've no notion what you mean," Mr. Carlton denied quickly. "Just because the girl was right about this Dr. Blake, doesn't mean she isn't also capable of being a thief and a liar herself!"

"When did this necklace disappear?" Henry asked.

"Last night or perhaps this morning," Horatia said. "It was in the box on my dresser last night when I went to bed, and this morning it was gone. A maid said she saw your Miss Upchurch slinking about in the corridors last night. Why else would she have been if not to steal?"

"Because she was switching the drugged tonic with one that would not be harmful to me," Philippa answered. "I tried to tell you that, but no one will listen to me!"

"Henry?" Cecile asked. "Is this true?"

"It is. I met her in the kitchen immediately after she had switched out the bottles," he replied. "And furthermore, she had no need to steal from you, Aunt Horatia. Last night, I proposed to Miss Upchurch and she accepted. We elected to say nothing until we had the matter with Philippa and Dr. Blake more settled, but there you have it. She'd not have risked everything for your necklace when, as her husband, I could happily buy her dozens of them!" With every word his voice had grown louder until he was practically shouting.

"You can't mean to marry her," Horatia sneered. "She is beneath you!"

"And Mr. Carlton is beneath you, is he not?" Henry snapped.

"But, Henry—she is illegitimate," Horatia protested.

"As am I," Cecile stated. "You appear to have conveniently edited your memory, Horatia, of where I came from. Henry, do you love her?"

"Against all reason, yes, I do. She is kinder and lovelier than anyone I have ever known. She also does not simply expect that I should take care of everything for her and for everyone else, though I find myself quite pleased when the opportunity presents itself to rescue her," he admitted. "I know we are not of long acquaintance, but it doesn't seem to matter. Not in the least. I have to find her."

"She said she'd go to the coaching inn... the same one where she found you after discovering Lady Parkhurst had died," Philippa informed him.

"Henry, I forbid it," his uncle stated.

"Then I shall not return here. We will obtain a special license and be married as soon as possible before retreating to Haverton Abbey. I do hope you will put an end to Dr. Blake's nefarious schemes. I would hope, that after all I have done over the years, you would trust my judgment that much," Henry replied. And he meant it. If it meant being with Sophie, he would break with his family if they forced his hand. That, more than anything else, told him just how deep his feelings for her had grown in a very short time.

"Do not be hasty," Cecile warned her husband. "Henry is family… and his judgment has always been sound. I think perhaps it is time for Mr. Carlton to explain his connection to the Darrow School and why Miss Upchurch thought him so familiar at their meeting yesterday."

"Miss Upchurch was mistaken," Mr. Carlton said firmly.

Despite his vehemence, it was obvious that he was lying. The man had begun to perspire and his eyes shifted about nervously. Even the duke seemed to have honed in on the fact, despite his own assertions of Sophie's guilt.

"The truth, Carlton," Henry demanded. "Or I will beat it out of you."

"That will not be necessary!" Horatia said. "I placed the necklace in Miss Upchurch's room… at William's suggestion. He was convinced that she was an opportunist out to ruin you, Henry."

"No. That's what he convinced you to believe," Henry replied. "Tell the truth, man, or I will beat it out of you."

Carlton sneered. "You aren't even married to her yet and, already, she has you brawling like a common criminal!"

There was no thought. No planning or even consideration of consequences occurred. Henry's fist came back and then flew forward of its own accord, sending Carlton sprawling to the tile floor as blood poured from his obviously broken nose. While the result was satisfying, the degree of violence had not appeased his temper. Stepping forward, he grasped Carlton's shirt front and hoisted him up against the wall. Holding him there, he drew his fist back again. "I want the truth, Carlton. Not part. Not the pieces of it which cast you in a favorable light! You will tell us what you know or I will beat you until you do!"

"Miss Sophie Upchurch is my daughter," Carlton shouted, the

words coming out in a rush, all but tripping over one another.

"Your daughter?" Horatia gasped, sinking to the floor. "Your daughter? How could you lie to me about such a thing, William? How?"

"I have been supporting her anonymously at that school for years. I deliver the funds in person because I never wanted bank notes to be traced back to me or to have any record of my payments to Miss Darrow. It was a youthful indiscretion and a terrible mistake on my part. I have paid dearly for it since. And you will, too, Marchwood. Blood tells, and her mother was the worst sort of fraud!" Carlton explained, his voice taking on a wheedling note as he pleaded for sympathy. "When I saw her here, I thought... I thought my every chance at happiness would be ruined. That she was here because she knew the truth and would demand even more from me!"

"And hers? What about her happiness?" Cecile demanded. "Did you ever give any thought at all to the woman who is your child? Who even now has been cast from this house like a common criminal because you plotted against her? Oh, we have much to beg her forgiveness for!"

"Go after her, Henry," Philippa urged. "Please bring her back safely."

"I shall. And I think it best if Mr. Carlton is not here when I do," Henry replied, abruptly releasing Carlton so that he fell to the floor like a sack of stones. He landed with a thud and a whimper.

"That," Horatia said, "Is something we are all in agreement upon."

Chapter Twenty-One

S OPHIE WASN'T ENTIRELY certain where she was. She'd run as far and fast as she could until she reached the edges of the city. From there, she'd slipped down streets that were unfamiliar to her in an attempt to simply disappear. Dirty and disheveled, with her hair a mess and her dress torn and stained, she could only begin to imagine what she must look like. To say that people on the street looked at her askance was to put it mildly.

Still, with every step forward, she was looking over her shoulder for Dr. Blake. She knew that he would come for her. Men who would go to such depraved lengths would not simply give up, after all. And having wounded him, especially having damaged his handsome face, that would not be something he'd forgive easily.

"You lost, dearie?"

Sophie turned in the direction of the speaker and found a toothless woman, dirty and unkempt, but not old.

The woman cackled. "Aye, lost!"

"Can you help me? I need to find my way to Portland Street. Please," Sophie implored her.

The woman's laughter grew louder, drawing the gaze of others on the street. "Portland Street? What you want there? It ain't for the likes of you and me, girlie! Now, pretty as you are, there's work to be had here. Jem at the Whiteheart will give you a room to work out of if you want. He'll take a cut of it all, though."

Realizing that the woman was attempting to direct her to an inn that doubled as a bawdy house, though she was hardly supposed to know about such things, Sophie shook her head and quickly walked away. The woman was still cackling behind her. She needed to think. She needed to clear her head. And then the most miraculous thing happened.

Church bells rang out in the distance, giving her some semblance of a direction. Whether it was St. Michael's Church or St. John's, she could find her way back to the inn from either of those. But then realization dawned. She could not go to the inn because Dr. Blake knew to look for her there. She had told him she was returning to London and that was where the public coach would depart. *But she could go to Lady Hemsley.* Surely she would help her, Sophie thought. After all, she had been such an ally in discerning the truth about the physician and his diabolical schemes.

Sophie began walking in the general direction from whence she'd heard the bells and prayed fervently that she would not encounter any more difficulties. But a commotion behind her had her glancing back. Perhaps it was her own nerves, perhaps it was the harsh reality of having already been abducted once that day, but she was not especially trusting of her surroundings. It seemed her instincts were sound.

The woman who'd recommended going to the Whiteheart Inn for "work" was talking to a man and that man was watching her. When he took a step in her direction, Sophie took off running once more. She didn't care that she was creating a scene. She didn't care that people were looking askance at her. Her hesitance to make a scene was the very thing that had landed her in Dr. Blake's carriage, after all. It was not a mistake she would make again.

By the time she reached a point in the city high enough that would allow her to see the church's steeple in the distance, she was winded and exhausted. Every bump and bruise she'd incurred when leaping from that carriage had her battered body screaming for rest and relief. But there was none to be had and she knew it. Not yet, at any rate.

She trudged on, despite the pain and exhaustion. If she could get close enough to the church to get her bearings, she could find her way to Lady Hemsley and beg her assistance. Keeping that thought in mind, Sophie placed one foot in front of the other and fought back her tears. She wasn't about to give up, not when she had come so far.

>>><<<

HENRY HADN'T PANICKED. He'd been furious. He'd also been deeply hurt by his family's actions. Appalled at their snobbery, at their willingness to trust anyone over the woman he loved, it was a slight he wouldn't easily forgive or forget. But knowing that Sophie had remained coolheaded, that she'd instructed Philippa where she would await him, he had maintained some semblance of calmness himself.

The woman he loved. Henry's steps faltered. He was attracted to Sophie. He wanted Sophie. Sophie was a woman of virtue and marriage was the only honorable option for him to indulge his desire for her. Certainly, he admired her intelligence and her spirit. But love? Was it even possible to love someone after so short a time? The answer came like the crack of thunder. Yes. Yes, it was. He loved her. Whether one day, one year or one hundred years, it would stand true. And if he didn't find her and see her to safety, he might never get the chance to tell her so.

Quickening his steps, Henry hurried toward his destination. But as he entered the taproom of the Duke of Wellington Inn and he scanned each table, he saw no sign of her. The last shred of calmness that he'd managed to call upon had fled. Stepping deeper into the room, the innkeeper smiled at him and threw up his hand in greeting.

"Your lordship! Tis a fine day to see you here. A pint for you, sir?"

"The young woman I met in here a few days ago, have you seen her?" Henry asked.

"Pretty little thing... had just been robbed?" the innkeeper queried.

"Yes, that's her. She was supposed to be waiting for me here."

The innkeeper shook his head. "No young ladies have been in her today, my lord. We had two elderly women, sisters, what came in and caught the coach to Bath, but that's been all. If I see her—"

"If you see her, get her into a room and I will stand the cost of it. She's had a very difficult time. And you will send word to me at once. I will also check in periodically."

"Aye, my lord. Good enough."

Henry turned, strode out of the inn and back onto the bustling street. If not there at the Duke of Wellington, then where? She knew very little of Southampton. She'd accompanied him to an apothecary and Lady Hemsley's. Her only other outing had been for a sea bathing session with Philippa, and she's been in a closed carriage then. She wouldn't have followed the route taken in the carriage. It would have made no sense, he reasoned. Going purely on instinct, Henry retraced his steps to the only places in Southampton that he was aware of Sophie visiting. With a brisk stride, he made his way toward the apothecary's shop. Perhaps she had sought sanctuary there or even found more damning evidence against the doctor.

The moment Henry entered the small store, he knew that Sophie wasn't present. He also knew, beyond the shadow of any doubt, that something horrible had happened. There was a coppery scent to the air that could only be blood and a great deal of it. *Murder.* Someone had been murdered.

Stepping deeper into the space in spite of being consumed with the urge to simply flee, Henry walked past the shop area and into the corridor of small workrooms beyond. It was in that first room, the door to it standing wide, that he found the kindly man who had been of so much help to them. He lay prone on the floor, a large pool of congealed blood spilled out around his head. His skin was discolored already and a large bowl lay in pieces next to him. It wasn't much of a stretch to imagine that it was the murder weapon. Bits of porcelain littered the dead man's hair and there were smears of blood on some of the shards. Thick and heavy as the porcelain was, he'd have to have been struck with it several times before it broke in all likelihood.

Exiting the room, Henry backed out of the building and found a boy on the street. He tossed him a coin. "Fetch the constable. Bring him here and tell him there has been a murder, but do not go inside. Understand?"

"Yes, my lord," the boy said, bobbing his head before taking off a run.

Henry paced impatiently. He wanted to continue his search for Sophie but knew that if he left, it would not look at all the thing. He would need to speak with the constable himself. It would only raise more questions if he did not and that was not something he wished to deal with.

It was several minutes before the boy came rushing back with a constable in tow.

"What have we got here, sir?" the constable asked.

"The apothecary is inside. It appears he was struck over the head."

"And you know for certain he's dead?" the constable asked.

"There is evidence of death," Henry stated flatly. "I did not check for a heartbeat. Given that I felt safe in making the assumption."

"And your business here, sir?" the constable asked. "Did you know the man?"

"I met him a few days ago. He'd prepared a tonic for my cousin," Henry replied. He bristled at the constable's tone, feeling the weight of accusation in it.

The constable eyed him suspiciously. "And is that why you were here? You needed more of this tonic?"

"No," Henry said. "I am looking for the young woman who accompanied me here the other day. I had hoped to chance upon her here but, alas, that was not to be. If it is all the same to you, Constable, I'd prefer to continue on with my day and that task. I am Lord Henry Meredith, Viscount Marchwood. You can locate me easily enough if you have further questions."

"I'm certain I will, my lord," the man sneered. "Not that it does any good. Peers don't go to prison for murdering shopkeepers, do they?"

"And murderers generally do not summon the constabulary themselves, do they?" Henry snapped back at him. "Good day to you, Constable."

"You'll be seeing me, your lordship," the constable stated, clearly not believing that Henry was innocent of any wrongdoing.

Henry didn't respond. He was too busy sorting through the implications of the apothecary's murder. Could Dr. Blake/Evans have been involved? Had he and Sophie, albeit inadvertently, brought violence and tragedy to that poor man's door? He prayed that wasn't the case, that it was instead a simple robbery that had taken an awful turn. But if the murder of the apothecary showed him one thing for certain, it was that Southampton could be a very dangerous city and Sophie was alone. She might well also be the target of someone who clearly had no compunction about taking a life. He had to find her.

Chapter Twenty-Two

SOPHIE SAW THE carriage before the driver or the occupant saw her. Having already been abducted once that day and narrowly avoiding it a second time at the hand of some unscrupulous procuress, she was, perhaps, hypervigilant. But it had saved her. Cowering in the darkened gap between two buildings, much too narrow a space to even be considered an alley, she watched the street. The space was littered with crates and other things, offering her some concealment, at least.

As Dr. Blake's carriage rumbled past, she could see his face as he peered out the window, scanning the streets for any sight of her. It was heavily bandaged but blood had begun to seep through. There was a cold fury about him and Sophie had little doubt that her fate, if she fell into his hands, would be sealed. She wouldn't escape from him a second time. And she would likely not be handed over unscathed to the woman he'd mentioned. He would have his pound of flesh.

"What are you doing out here, girl? You'll not be working this alley! Tis not the sinful streets of London you're on!"

Sophie turned to see that a woman had emerged from one of the buildings that had a door set into the narrow-not-quite-an-alley. It had been recessed so deeply she hadn't seen it yet. "I'm not—that is to say, I have had very trying day, Madam, but I assure you my appearance at present is not indicative of my degree of virtue. I am hiding here to avoid a wicked man who would abduct me and do me grave harm."

The aging housekeeper gave her a skeptical once-over but, ultimately, the woman's hard gaze softened into one that seemed almost sympathetic. "You speak well enough, I'll give you that. And what are you doing here on this street then? Is there somewhere in particular you're trying to get to?"

There was the faintest hint of a brogue in the woman's voice, as if she'd once lived in Scotland, but years on English soil had eroded it to a mere vestige of one. There was, despite her initially harsh words, a kindness about the woman. She wasn't soft by any stretch of the imagination. That was for certain, but she wasn't without mercy either.

"I'm trying to reach Lady Hemsley... the man who would abduct me, he is known to her. His wickedness is known to her. She will help me," Sophie stated. How desperately she hoped that was true! If Lady Hemsley turned her away, there was nowhere left for her to go.

"Wait here," the woman said. "I've a notion of how you might go about unnoticed. That hair of yours will never do. It could be spotted from the next county shining like that.... especially with it standing on end."

The woman retreated down the alley and disappeared once more inside the building. She had moved quickly and quietly, far more cat-like than her steel gray hair and apparent age should have permitted. Minutes later, the woman returned. She held a bundle of cloth in her arms.

"Now, here's a shawl. It's long enough to cover most of your dress so the dirt and stains won't be so obvious. And there's a bonnet there, none too pretty, but big enough to shield your face from view and showy enough that none will think you're trying to hide," the woman offered. "Lady Hemsley is just around the corner from here. It ought to see you to rights. Will this wicked, wicked man know that is your destination?"

Sophie hadn't considered that. But he'd been on this street, only a short distance from Lady Hemsley's, after all, so she had to concede the possibility that those who he considered enemies might be working together. "I do not know."

"Right, then. If you go to the house that backs up to hers, on St. Anne's Street, the house with the dark blue door—there's only one— go to the kitchen entrance and tell them you must speak to Mrs. Tipton. She's the housekeeper there and a friend. You tell her that Agnes sent you to her. The back garden butts up against Lady Hemsley's and she can get you in that way, assuming Lady Hemsley's servants will grant you entrance. I've no friends in a house that fine, so I cannot guarantee it. The finer the house the more persnickety the help."

"I've been warned of that," Sophie stated. Effie had been telling her just that thing, albeit more diplomatically phrased, for years. Donning her disguise, Sophie noted that the items were particularly fine. "I couldn't possibly accept these. They're far too fine."

"They were destined for a charity bin, girl. The mistress has died and no one in this house has use for such fripperies," the housekeeper stated.

"What is your name, Madam?"

"My name is Agnes Ferguson, and you, girl? What is your name?"

"Sophie Upchurch," she replied.

"Well, Miss Upchurch, happy I am to have been able to help you. Get on with you now. You'll need to be quick or you'll catch the servants at their dinner hour and then no one will be inclined to help you."

Impulsively, Sophie hugged the woman, great tears in her eyes. "You've been so kind. Thank you."

Leaving the stunned housekeeper behind her, Sophie bustled onto the street and walked the opposite direction the carriage had been heading. There was a cross street only a few buildings down that was so narrow only pedestrians and the narrowest of carts could traverse it. That would get her over to St. Anne's Street and to the house with the dark blue door.

⤜⤜⤜⤛⤛⤛

HENRY STOOD IN the entryway of Lady Hemsley's home as the butler looked at him somewhat askance. It was past time for callers, he knew. "I did not bring my calling cards because this is not truly a social occasion. It is imperative that I see Lady Hemsley, at once. It is a most urgent matter."

"I will inquire if Lady Hemsley is at home for visitors," the butler replied, clearly nonplussed by Henry's disheveled appearance, the late hour of his call and the fact that it all appeared to be quite havey-cavey.

The truth was, Henry thought, if someone had shown up on his Aunt Cecile's doorstep in such a manner, their welcome would have been just as uncertain. There was no small amount of bitterness that followed that thought as another one came swiftly in its wake. It appeared that the welcome issued by his family was always uncertain and very easily rescindable. He couldn't imagine how hurt Sophie must have been, how utterly dismayed she must have been to have people who had seemed her allies turn on her so quickly. It was shameful, what they had done to her, what his absence had permitted them to do to her. If he'd only returned home before hying off to Salisbury in pursuit of information about the doctor, then he could have put a stop to it.

A moment later, the butler returned. "Lady Hemsley is in the drawing room. She will see you." He sounded less than pleased about it.

With a heavy sigh, Henry moved past the man and in the direction indicated. When he entered the drawing room he noted two things, Lady Hemsley dressed for dinner even when dining alone. *Dressed for*

181

dinner. The woman was positively dripping in jewels. They were piled about her neck and stacked on her wrists so thickly it was a wonder she could move.

"I will not be judged by you, young man. I like my jewels, Marchwood," she said with a raised eyebrow, as if daring him to challenge her. "Why should I not indulge myself?"

"Why, indeed, Lady Hemsley. Sadly, magnificent as they are, I'm not here to discuss your jewels. I've come with terrible news. There was a misunderstanding in my uncle's home and Sophie was turned out into the street through no fault or wrongdoing of her own."

Lady Hemsley blinked. "Sophie? Not Miss Upchurch? You are forgetting to pretend your indifference, Marchwood. Or is there some reason why you now openly speak so familiarly of her?"

"Miss Upchurch and I are secretly betrothed," he said. "But I fear it will not matter if I do not find her. I had hoped she would come to you for aid since the only other person she has met in Southampton has now been murdered."

"Murdered?" the elderly woman parroted. "Heavens! Sit down, Marchwood, and tell me all of it."

He'd thought mentioning that would get her on board. She loved nothing better than to know something before anyone else did, after all. "The apothecary who identified laudanum as the primary ingredient in Philippa's elixir has been murdered. I discovered his body today... bashed over the head with a large basin or vessel and left to die alone. I do not know that it has anything to do with Dr. Blake, besides my own suspicion. But if he took upon himself to ask questions..."

"And Dr. Blake... did you learn anything in Salisbury?" she demanded.

"I did. His name, when practicing there, was Dr. Albert Evans. He married a young patient of his who suffered similar attacks and ailments as Philippa. Then the young woman died under somewhat mysterious circumstances—mysterious and convenient as her death coincided with her family refusing to support the doctor financially anymore," he summed up.

Lady Hemsley shouted a triumphant, "A-ha! I knew it!"

"How did you know?"

She smirked. "It was to do with Lady Parkhurst's estate, you see? She named the doctor as her executor and the irascible little man whom he allowed to oversee everything was someone he hired from Salisbury. I thought it quite strange that he would bring someone from there rather than London. If you're going to hire out from Salisbury, why not just hire from here? He denies ever having been to London, but I have my doubts based on his clothing and his manner of speech. What do you think?"

"I've never heard the man speak. I could not say."

"We should summon him here and confront him!"

"Absolutely not," Henry stated firmly. "We will do nothing more until I have located Miss Upchurch and assured myself of her safety. If she arrives—"

Henry never finished the request. A commotion in the corridor drew his eyes. It sounded as if the entire house was suddenly in an uproar. He rose quickly, turning toward the door.

Behind him, Lady Hemsley gasped. "What on earth is happening? I must apologize, Marchwood. My household is normally more well-ordered."

The doors to the drawing room parted then and the butler stepped inside, quite flustered if his appearance was any indication. "There is a young woman here, my lady, demanding entrance and 'sanctuary'. She came to the garden door in the kitchen." The last was uttered with a sneer of disapproval.

Lady Hemsley let out an annoyed sigh. "Well, show her in! Good heavens. I've half a mind to dismiss you for being so foolish!"

Henry was so intensely relieved that it took his breath. It could only be Sophie. Who else?

And moments later, when the door opened and she stepped inside, disheveled and a bit worse for wear, but whole and very much alive, he'd never known such a feeling of joy. "Oh, thank God. Thank God."

He didn't care that Lady Hemsley was there. He didn't care that it was completely improper. Henry simply closed the distance between them and swept her into his arms, holding her close. She did not resist. Instead, she pressed her face to his chest and he felt the first tremors and heard a soft sob escape her. Whatever had occurred that day, it had left her shaken and terrified.

"I was so afraid," she whispered. "Dr. Blake—"

"What about him?" Henry asked.

"He met me on the street and he insisted on escorting me to the Duke of Wellington Inn. I couldn't refuse without making a scene," she said, easing back from him. "Oh, Henry, it was horrible. He was making terrible threats about... well, he intimated that there was a particular sort of business that would pay him handsomely for a girl like me."

"That villain!" Lady Hemsley exclaimed. "How in heaven's name did you get away?"

"His medical bag," Sophie explained. "It was on the seat, and so I bumped into it, knocking it over. When the instruments spilled out, I managed to get one of the scalpels. I've done him terrible injury and I know he is livid beyond imagining. He was looking for me after. I saw his carriage. That is why I came through the gardens."

"The apothecary—" Henry began.

"I know he's dead. Dr. Blake told me he killed him or perhaps had him killed. That bit is unclear. He also told me about a girl he'd married in Salisbury. He killed her, as well. Dosing her in secret with laudanum, just as he's done with Philippa. And he admitted to killing Lady Parkhurst. He was afraid that having a companion to nose into things would cause problems, so he began slipping her arsenic." The words all tumbled out of her, a long list of crimes with each more horrifying than the last.

"I know," Henry said. "Well, I knew he'd married the girl and done away with her. The how was a bit of a mystery, however. And his name, when he practiced in Salisbury, was Dr. Evans. Dr. Albert Evans. And, of course, there were suspicions about Lady Parkhurst but nothing confirmed."

"Then his bride in Salisbury was not his first victim," Sophie replied. "Or at least I have reason to believe otherwise!"

"Well do not leave us hanging, Miss Upchurch," Lady Hemsley said. "Tell us what you know!"

Sophie shook her head as if to clear it. "It was a scandalous story in London two or three years back, I think. There was a Dr. Evan Alberts who married a young widow in London. But she discovered his plot. He'd been poisoning her not with laudanum but with Paris Green. It was in the *Times*. They ran articles about it every week. Lurid and horrible. Everyone was talking about it. That plot could well have been borrowed from a gothic novel, and those were all that the girls in school were reading at that time. In secret, we thought. Not really secret. Effie knew. She simply let us feel like we were getting away with it. Regardless, the story in the paper was so ghastly that, as young girls often are, we were fascinated with it. How horrid we were!"

Lady Hemsley cleared her throat loudly. "While I appreciate your relief, Marchwood, at seeing Miss Upchurch safe, I do believe you can let go of her now."

Henry realized he was still holding Sophie to him, completely uncaring of where they were. Reluctantly, he dropped his arms and stepped back, but still clasped her hand in his, unwilling to break contact entirely. "I vaguely recall the incident but did not make the connection. The other physician I spoke with in Salisbury told me that our not so very good doctor had married an aging widow in London first. It is possible that it wasn't him, though I confess it unlikely. Given the similarity in name and method, it's a very good chance that he's the culprit."

"Right now, the only witnesses you have to this man's misdeeds here in Southampton are dead. The apothecary cannot help you. Lady Parkhurst is gone, as well," Lady Hemsley pointed out. "And, I do not mean to offend, Miss Upchurch, but it is your word against Dr. Blake's... or Dr. Evans' or Dr. Alberts' and what Marchwood has is nothing more than hearsay. Frankly, it will not hold much sway."

"I know that what you say is true, Lady Hemsley. I am not offended by that. My lack of rank and my obscure parentage make me, at least in the eyes of society—and by virtue of being female, I am, in the eyes of the law—less believable." Sophie's response was matter of fact.

The injustice of what she'd just said struck Henry very deeply. He'd never considered himself a reformer, but with what he'd observed from Sophie and with the way decisions were made for Philippa without ever considering her own desires, he was starting to see that changes should be made.

"A long term solution to such social problems is not yet available, but a shorter term solution is," Lady Hemsley replied. "If you marry—"

"When," Henry corrected. "And the sooner the better."

"When you marry, that will change things in terms of your word against the doctor's. A companion has much to gain. A viscountess would not! But given what you recalled about those news articles, perhaps the best option would be to go to London immediately and seek out this widow. If she can provide sworn testimony against the doctor, or better yet, identify him to local authorities, he can be arrested for his crimes and tried."

And executed or at the very least transported far from their shores.

"We will leave within the hour. The moon is full so we can travel through the night," Henry stated. "Lady Hemsley, would you be so kind as to permit Miss Upchurch to stay with you until I make the necessary arrangements for our journey?"

"Of course. We will go in and have some dinner and wait for your return," Lady Hemsley stated as she rose to her feet. "And I will have my maid see about getting you something more suitable to wear, my dear. I will be quite pleased to play a role in your elopement. Why, I haven't had this sort of excitement in a very long time!"

Chapter Twenty-Three

TWO HOURS LATER, under the cover of darkness, they had departed Lady Hemsley's and were making for London. In the carriage, Sophie sat on one seat in her borrowed finery, while Henry sat across from her. Despite the fact that she was still draped in the shawl granted to her from Agnes, the helpful housekeeper she'd encountered in that narrow alley, Sophie could not shake the chill. Perhaps it was simply the numerous shocks of the day all catching up to her, but she shivered there, unable to warm herself.

"You're cold?" Henry asked. Immediately, he moved across the carriage to sit beside her. "You're not ill after all you've been through today, are you?"

"Just very tired, I think," Sophie admitted. "Henry, what will happen when we are wed? Your family will likely cut you off. They will certainly never permit me to darken their door again! They were so furious. Your uncle—I've never seen anyone so cold."

He shook his head as he tightened his arms about her, pulling her close to him. "No, they will not do so. With everything else that has happened, I didn't have a chance to tell you. Horatia admitted that she planted the necklace in your room."

Sophie blinked at that. "Lady Horatia did it?"

"At Mr. Carlton's urging," he pointed out. "You were quite right about him. There are other things you should know about him and

I'm not certain how you will react to them."

"I know that he must be the father of one of Effie's students," Sophie reminded him. "But why he thought that made me such a threat to him—"

"It made you a threat to him, Sophie, because he is your father. Now that I think about it, there were similarities that, over time, would have become apparent to everyone, I believe."

Sophie blinked in the dimness of the carriage. "That's not possible. I was left as a foundling there!"

"I think it likely that he is the person who left you. I don't know the particulars. I left before asking those questions because I thought it more important to locate you. I'm sorry I can't tell you more."

Sophie took a deep, shuddering breath. "Well, it isn't your story to tell, is it? It's his. And from the sounds of things, we wouldn't be able to trust it at any rate. Ultimately it only makes it worse, doesn't it?"

"What do you mean?"

"I mean," Sophie mused, "that it was bad enough for him to make a target of me the way that he did when I was simply some unfortunate girl who might expose his secret shame. But I'm not just a stranger to him who happened to see him at a place that would mar his reputation, am I? I'm his flesh and blood, and he was still ready to see me carted off—transported or worse—because preserving his reputation and fulfilling his ambitions are all that matters. He's cold, ruthless and unfeeling. Not so very different from the doctor, is he?"

Henry's arms tightened about her further, pulling her in closer. It was a gesture of comfort, and one that she greatly appreciated. She had never thought to know who her parents were. But she'd certainly never expected to be betrayed to such a degree by one of them if identified.

After a few minutes of quiet, both of them thinking about all that had transpired, Sophie asked very softly, "What will your aunt do?"

"I know not and I care not," he said. "My fury at her is boundless.

It was bad enough what they did to you, the way they all turned on you. But for her to have played an active role in framing you rather than just being duped as the others were? It's unforgivable."

"They don't know me, Henry. Not really. I'd see your aunt and uncle at dinner and maybe share a few pleasantries with them. Your Aunt Horatia, well, we had just met. They do not know who I am. For that matter, you don't either," she said. "Is it any wonder they sought to protect you? And now we're rushing in to an elopement, the very thing they feared, and I am terrified that you will regret it later."

"Sophie, the only thing I will ever regret is that I didn't propose the very moment I met you," he stated solemnly. "There is nothing that could make me want anything but to be with you. It sounds utterly mad to say it, but I love you. I think I loved you the very moment I laid eyes on you."

Sophie leaned against him then, placing her head against his chest. She could feel his heart beating, steady and strong. She was also aware of the heat of him, of the strength in the corded muscles. And in that moment, it wasn't simply comfort that she sought. The memory of their kiss was still vivid in her mind, along with those remembered sensations. "If it's madness, then we are mad together, at least. I love you. I loved you instantly, I think. That was why your initial deception was so difficult to forgive. When I thought you just Mr. Henry Meredith, I could hope for a future with you. Your title just seemed to put you out of reach for me. All the fantasies I had about being courted and proposed to by this handsome man I met on my journey... they were simply gone and I was angry."

"I will never be out of your reach. And I do not mean to ever let you be far from mine. I do not want to be ever separated from you again," he admitted.

It was the most natural thing in the world to slide her hand upward along the front of his shirt, to curve it around his neck as she lifted her face up to his and catch the smoldering gaze he directed at her. "Will you kiss me, Henry?"

"It is not a wise decision," he stated. It wasn't a refusal, simply a statement. "We are alone in this carriage with no chaperone. I have no way of knowing if our request for a special license will be granted. If not, it could be weeks until we can wed."

"I do not care," she said. "It is enough for me to know that we will be wed."

He closed his eyes, as if wrestling with the choice, or possibly his own conscience. "Desire, Sophie, is a tricky thing. A kiss will soon not be enough… every touch brings with it a world of temptation, a need to push those boundaries and go a bit further. Eventually, there is a point of no return."

"As I've no wish to return, I do not view that as an impediment." It was a bold response and she couldn't say who was more surprised.

"Sophie—" Her name was uttered on a soft groan. But then he swooped in, his lips capturing hers and there was no more talking.

It was as she'd remembered, and yet so much more. Safe in the circle of his arms after so much danger and uncertainty, Sophie could only give herself up to that moment, savoring the play of his lips over hers. She was acutely aware of every point of contact. The rasp of his whiskers against her skin. The heat of him. The firmness of his body where it pressed against hers. The taste of him as his tongue swept boldly into her mouth.

The unfettered sensuality of it and the impossible intimacy with them cocooned in the dim interior of the coach, completely alone, had every sensation heightened. Clinging to him, holding on to the thing that felt real and solid in a world that seemed to be growing more ephemeral by the moment, Sophie let herself be swept away by it. Counter to everything she had been taught, to every caution that had been instilled in her over the years, she simply allowed herself to be carried away by it. And it was glorious.

HENRY WAS STRUGGLING for control. He was positively consumed with his need to hold her, to touch her, to take liberties that he knew she would grant him. That was the most damnable part of it all. He had to think of what was right for them both, regardless of what they both wanted. Whatever impassioned response she might have to his kisses, she was entirely innocent. There was no doubt in his mind on that score. And allowing things to progress too far in the confines of a moving carriage would mark him as the worst sort of cad.

And yet even as he thought it, one hand was sliding over the fabric of her borrowed dress coming to rest on her ribs, just beneath her breast. The tip of his thumb grazed the underside of it. She gasped and shivered in his embrace, but only pressed closer to him. All thoughts of what he ought to do, of what was right, fled in the face of a kind of hunger he had never known. Lust was not unfamiliar to him. Libidinous urges were simply part of being a man, of being human, and he'd slaked them as opportunity and desire permitted. But this was something else. It was deeper and more primal, more demanding and insistent.

"Sophie, if we do not stop..." he breathed against the curve of her cheek.

"Do not stop. Please," she implored him. "I know what happens between a man and a woman, Henry. In theory, at least. I am innocent, but not ignorant."

"That will not happen... not careening down the road in a darkened carriage," he vowed. "But there are things we can do. There are ways for me to give you pleasure without necessarily eradicating your innocence entirely."

"Show me," she urged.

Chapter Twenty-Four

E FFIE SAT IN the corner of the hired carriage, her arms crossed over her chest, glaring at Highcliff and wishing him to perdition. He'd held her over his shoulder like he was some sort of dock worker and she was a sack of grain while he'd procured transportation for them. Now, hours later when it was almost dark outside, she had yet to say a word to him.

"You can give me the silent treatment for as long as you like," he said companionably while shrugging his shoulders. "Frankly, I prefer it when you're not speaking."

Effie would not be baited into talking to him. It did bother him. Her silence made him uncomfortable. It was a tactic she'd learned from observing him, after all. *Let the silence stretch until someone else feels compelled to fill it.*

After a moment, he sighed heavily. "I will not apologize. I am not in the wrong. First, a woman cannot travel alone. Secondly, a woman who is young and beautiful can especially not travel alone. And finally, a woman who is young, beautiful and could be a target for ransom? Really, Effie, I gave you credit for more intelligence than your recent behavior suggests."

Her jaws ached from the effort it took to hold her tongue, but hold it she did. Highcliff would not goad her. He would not win. He might be stronger, as evidenced by the fact that she was in that coach at all, but stronger in body and stronger in will were entirely different matters.

"You haven't asked where we're headed," he mused aloud.

There was no sound but the creaking of the carriage and the pounding of the horses' hooves.

Another sigh. "Fine," he said, throwing his hands up in frustration. "We're going to Southampton. I ought to cart you back to London. But if there is one undeniable truth, your pupils create danger out of thin air. I've never in my life encountered any group of women quite so prone to finding themselves in dire jeopardy. Was that part of your curriculum? How to locate and attract the attention of villains? Of course, they also manage to land wealthy and titled husbands. I suppose you're doing something right."

She wanted to slap the smugness right out of him, but he'd finally done it. He'd finally irritated her to the point she could no longer hold her tongue. "You may think that bit of flesh between your thighs entitles you to say and do as you please, Highcliff, but I've yet to meet a man of any real moral fiber or fortitude so you need not bother to take the moral high horse and act as though you are somehow better than the young women who are my students simply because they've married and you've eluded such a fate."

"It isn't about morality," he said. "I simply have a far better understanding of the misery of marriage than most. Funny though that you would bring them up to aspire to independence and they would all so readily sacrifice it in the face of a title."

Now she knew he was being intentionally provoking. To intimate that her girls were fortune hunters or social climbers—he wanted a response, he'd get one. "I've yet to encounter one man who has the same amount of courage, bravery and resourcefulness as even one of my girls much less the lot of them. As to the charge of their jockeying for social position, were the children not punished for the sins of the father, most of them would outrank their husbands! I'll thank you to never utter another word about them or me so long as we both occupy this earth. I will submit to your will at this moment, because it happens to coincide with mine. I need to find Sophie. As for you, and whatever it is that you think exists between us, it does not. You are not my husband. You made it quite clear you had no wish to be my lover. And by your own admission, we are not friends. Therefore you have no say in what I do, when I do it, where I do it, or whom I choose to do it with."

"Isn't that precisely what led to that situation so many years ago when I was forced to rescue you? You doing as you pleased?" he challenged.

"Is that what it's called? A rescue? As I recall it," Effie stated, "I had the situation well in hand and my assailant writhing in agony on the ground before you'd even shown your face."

"If you are so capable, how was I able to get you into this carriage?"

"Because I chose to let you," she said. "Because I understood something about you, Highcliff, that you don't even know about yourself. You are incapable of not playing the hero. I knew that you would go after Sophie. My reasons for not asking for your help were never because I didn't think you'd grant it. I didn't ask for your help because I do not need it. I'm perfectly capable on my own. And also because your presence is a complication I'd rather not have to deal with. In short, you're little better than a nuisance and a predictable one at that."

His jaw had tightened with anger. "If I'm such a bloody nuisance, why did you try so very hard to get me into your bed?"

Effie smiled coolly. "Because even the most brilliant of women will occasionally make poor choices. I've since seen the error of my ways."

"We locate Miss Upchurch, we get her safely home," he said, "And then we never have to set eyes on one another again."

"It cannot happen soon enough for my part," Effie answered.

"At least we agree on something," he offered. "And for what it's worth, I never said I didn't want to be in your bed. I said I would not. You of all people, Effie, should understand the risks associated with such a scheme. It's one thing to be a bastard. It's another thing entirely to beget one."

"There are ways to mitigate such risks," she stated firmly. "I've done a great deal of research on the matter."

"Research?" He appeared utterly scandalized. "Please tell me you have not marched into a bookshop in London and asked for texts on how to prevent reproduction!"

"Not at all," she waved her hand dismissively. "I asked the Hound if he might arrange for me to meet with a woman who could provide instruction for me that I might pass on to my girls."

"When?" Highcliff glowered. "When did you do this?"

"A few months back," Effie answered. "It was what gave me the courage required to make my request of you. Little good it did. And no, I have not begun instructing my girls in the manner yet. I encourage them to talk to me about whatever is on their mind and I shall impart the knowledge to them as they require it."

"Why the devil would you do that?"

She blinked at him. "You mean even the playing field? Why on earth would I give women knowledge which we both know gives them power over their own bodies and their own lives instead of leaving them entirely at the mercy of men who would abandon them at the drop of a hat? I can't begin to imagine why I would do such a thing," she finished sarcastically. "You accused me of living in a fantasy world. I promise you, Highcliff, no one is more attuned to the realities of being a woman in this world than I am. Did I not open my heart and my home to countless young girls who are the product of this way of the world that has been accepted for so long? Do not ever preach to me on such. I knew the risks. I informed myself of how to mitigate them. You said no, Highcliff, not for any noble reasons but of your own cowardice. You are afraid to feel. You are afraid to have any deep connection with any person, but especially with a woman who already knows your darkest secrets!"

IT HADN'T BEEN his intent to touch her. But she'd goaded him. She'd pushed him like no other person ever had. And so he found himself up off the carriage seat and looming over her as he braced his hands on the back of the seat she occupied. She was caged there between his arms, but she didn't cower or give any hint of fear. Her shoulders squared and her chin inched upward as she met his gaze with a raised brow and an air of challenge.

"You never know when to quit, do you, Effie?" The accusation was both bitter and amused. "You must always push just past the boundaries until you make a man want to throttle you!"

"Is that what you want? To throttle me?"

No. No. That wasn't what he wanted. But what he wanted would ruin them both. Not their reputations. He didn't give a damn one way or another for that. No, it would ruin them to their souls. It would lay bare every tortured emotion they both had and leave them no armor, no protection from the world or one another.

The carriage hit a rut in the road. He caught himself, but in so doing came even closer to her in the process. Close enough that a stray tendril of her hair caught on his whiskers, close enough that their breaths mingled and he could smell the rose-scented soap she favored. She exhaled again, a shuddering sigh that told the truth of what his nearness had done to her, but her breath fanned over his lips like the sweetest of caresses.

"Damn it all," he muttered. "Damn it all and damn you."

He simply took her mouth in that moment. It wasn't gentle or seductive. It was passionate and angry, hard and claiming. He kissed her with all the ferocity that was born out of wanting her in vain for nearly two decades. He kissed her as if he meant to consume her. And God help him, she kissed him back with equal fervor.

It was a mistake, but like so many mistakes, once made, there was no return. It was irrevocable. It might be the last time he ever kissed her, so he meant to make it count for something. Moving swiftly, he turned so that he was on the seat and pulled her across his lap. Her hands pressed flat against his chest and he paused, just for a second. Did she mean to push away from him? Had she come to her senses long before he did? But no. She simply leaned in to him after she'd gotten her balance, slid her hands up his chest and tangled them in his hair. It wasn't gentle. She pulled. She bit. It was a little angry, a little vindictive. He didn't care. It was better than the alternative of not having her sprawled across him with the taste of her lips on his. He'd been denying himself and denying her for far too long.

"What are we doing?" she asked.

"The inevitable," he answered. "The inevitable."

Chapter Twenty-Five

THE CARRIAGE WHEEL disintegrated. One minute, Sophie was on Henry's lap. He was kissing her and touching her in ways that made her head spin. And the next, they were both sprawled on the floor of the carriage as it listed to one side and the horses whinnied in protest.

"I'll kill him. No. I won't. But I will sack him this time," Henry murmured.

"What are you muttering about?" Sophie asked as she pushed herself up from the carriage floor and dusted off her hands.

"My coachman who does not listen. Ever."

Sophie watched as Henry forced open the door and leapt down from the coach. She could hear him shouting to the driver and then could hear the driver's shouted return. It was harder to make out as he spoke with a heavy Scot's burr. But it sounded as he if said something about it being the other wheel.

A moment later, Henry returned. "There's an inn not far ahead. I'll secure a room for us... I don't want you alone there. I have no notion of how safe it is as I've never been to that inn before. It's not a stop on the regular coaching route. Under the circumstances, I think it best if I simply say you are my wife. I know you dislike lying—"

"Under the circumstances, I do not think we have a choice," Sophie replied. "I have no wish to be alone. I do not know that the doctor is in pursuit, but given what we know about him, I think it likely. It's fine, Henry."

"Right," he said. He quickly gathered their things and then helped her down. "I'm going to send someone back to assist Burton with the carriage. The road is wide enough and we are far enough to the side that it should pose no threat to anyone."

They walked in silence for a few moments, the bustling of the inn ahead becoming more apparent as they drew near.

"If we're sharing—"

"I don't want you to—"

They both stopped, as they'd been talking over one another. It was Henry who said. "It is imperative that I say this to you now, Sophie. I do not wish you to feel obligated to continue what we had begun in the carriage just because we will be sharing a room. I am content to sleep on the floor."

Sophie looked away, biting her lip as she considered how best to proceed. "I was actually going to suggest that having a room, shared under the guise of being man and wife, presents an opportunity to go beyond what we were doing in the carriage. Does it not? Had that not been your primary objection? That in light of my innocence, that was not an appropriate locale for our activities?"

He stopped walking. He simply stood stock-still in the middle of the road and stared at her. "You confound me at every turn. I am trying, Sophie, against every baser urge I have, to be a gentleman. To do the honorable thing."

Sophie laughed. "You don't understand, do you? You have been honorable. You are honorable. Everything about you, even when you were lying about your name, was honorable. It's not something you have to aspire to. It's simply who you are. That is why I love you, and that is why it matters not to me if we have been wed prior to or after... well, after."

"There's a carriage approaching. It isn't Dr. Blake as it's coming from the wrong direction, but we should get out of the way," Henry said. It was clear he was done with the discussion, but his decision remained a mystery.

Sophie sighed. "It was much easier when it was just the two of us locked inside that small space and pretending that the rest of the world didn't matter, wasn't it?"

"That it was," he agreed.

"Sophie!"

They both looked up at the shout of her name. The approaching carriage was one she recognized. It belonged to Lord Highcliff and the woman shouting her name from the window was none other than Effie herself.

"Well that decision has been taken out of your hands, it seems," Sophie suggested.

"Regrettably so," Henry offered. "I was painfully close to being seduced by you, Miss Upchurch."

Sophie grinned as Effie's carriage rolled into the inn yard ahead of them.

>>>><<<<

IT HAD BEEN sheer luck that had allowed Effie to see Sophie in the distance. The moonlight had shone on the girl's red-gold hair as their carriage had rounded a bend. And of course, sprawled across High-cliff's lap, she'd had an excellent view through the window at that precise moment. She'd scrambled off his lap so quickly that he was still sputtering and had promptly hung her head out the window and shrieked like a fishwife.

"It's Miss Upchurch," she tossed over her shoulder. "We've found her."

"So I gathered," Highcliff said. Without any embarrassment or even a hint of shame, he proceeded to adjust himself behind the fall of his breeches.

Effie's gaze was drawn immediately, following each movement and wondering precisely what would have happened had she not seen her charge. It wasn't a great stretch of the imagination to think that her curiosity about the act itself and about the man before her would have both been satisfied. "I suppose it is for the best... before we did something regrettable."

"I have regrets, Effie," he said. "And not a damned one of them has to do with what we did not do in this carriage."

Dry mouthed and with hands that shook ever so slightly, Effie straightened her clothing and tidied her hair. "And tomorrow? Will that change?"

He met her gaze steadily. "No, Effie. It will not change. If I were a better man—but I'm not. I'm not a better man. I cannot and will not be one. So I might as well have what I want and damn the consequences."

She had no notion of what he meant by that, but she'd take it. Because as much as it pained her to admit it, she'd take any part of him she could have. Even if it was only temporary. "Then we are to be lovers."

"Yes. But understand me, Effie. There will be no happy ending. We will be lovers, but we will never be more than that. I'll have no wife... I'll have no children. This cursed line will end with me. If that isn't enough for you—"

"Stop trying to irritate me so I'll let you off the hook," Effie interrupted him. "I know where you stand on the matter. If and when that isn't enough for me, I shall let you know."

"Then let us go and discover what sort of catastrophes have befallen your Miss Upchurch," Highcliff offered in companionable agreement. "The sooner her issues are addressed, the sooner we can resume our earlier activities."

Chapter Twenty-Six

OVER A POT of tea and a plate of roast duck with cheese and bread, Henry listened as Sophie told as much of the sordid tale as possible to Miss Darrow and Lord Highcliff. The indolent rogue he'd witnessed at parties and balls in London was a far cry from the watchful man who sat with them at that table. Henry had to wonder how much of the Highcliff he had observed was simply a facade and how much was genuine.

"Did you know that Mr. Carlton was my father, Effie?" Sophie asked softly.

Pulling his attention from Lord Highcliff, Henry watched the exchange, noting Sophie's sadness and Effie's regret.

"I had considered it a strong possibility. But he never said, and I was given to believe that asking would be unwelcome," Effie replied. "I was more concerned that he continue to provide for you than that he confirm my suspicions. Perhaps that was wrong of me."

"No," Sophie said. "It wasn't. If you didn't offer these men the promise of discretion about their indiscretions, who knows were girls like me would wind up?"

Effie huffed out a sigh. "Precisely. You have always been remarkably insightful about how things work, Sophie. I am just sorry that so many things have gone wrong for you. It's my fault. I should never have let you go when I did."

"I think you do her a disservice, Miss Darrow. Sophie—forgive me, Miss Upchurch," Henry corrected, "has done remarkably well in the face of significant obstacles. Not the least of which was my own family, taken in by Mr. Carlton. Frankly, the strange confluence of events could not have been predicted by anyone."

"The puppy is right," Highcliff said. "Poisoners posing as doctors, fortune hunters, social climbers, framers and likely blackmailers, too."

"Who has been blackmailed?" Sophie asked. "And don't call him puppy. It's quite rude."

Henry grinned. "It's all right, Miss Upchurch. When one is the age Lord Highcliff is, all younger men are referred to as puppies."

Miss Darrow choked on her tea. Highcliff frowned. Sophie offered up a sunny smile and Henry, for the first time since that morning, started to feel as if things were turning around. They had allies. They had other people to help them figure out what was happening and to get the necessary assistance for Philippa and put a stop to Blake's plans.

"The way I see it, we have a multifaceted issue," Highcliff began. "We need to find this woman who was married to Blake first, when he was calling himself Alberts so that he may be arrested for his crimes. We need to get a physician for your cousin who can determine what sort of illness she is facing and whether or not this man and his quackery have done her lasting harm. We need to get Miss Upchurch to safety... and we need to get the two of you wed as you have clearly been quite compromised."

"With all due respect," Henry stated, "that is why we were heading to London. We needed to obtain a special license if possible and marry at once. But not entirely because of Sophie's reputation or even because of Dr. Blake. Sophie and I wish to be married. We're very much in love."

"You're practically strangers," Highcliff protested.

"But they aren't," Effie said softly. "I saw this with Willa. I saw it with Lilly. I saw it with Calliope. Sometimes, when something is right, it doesn't take very long to see it or to embrace it. I wish you both every happiness."

"Excuse us for a moment," Highcliff said. He rose, grasping Effie's elbow and taking her with him. They retreated to a corner of the room where they proceeded to speak in hushed but obviously heated whispers.

"Does she know?" Henry asked.

"Know what?" Sophie asked.

"Does she know that he's hopelessly in love with her?" Henry shook his head. "No woman can make a man that angry unless he's well and truly sunk."

Sophie settled back against the banquette, close enough that beneath the tables their thighs touched. "I have a better question. Do you think he knows?"

"That she's in love with him?" Henry asked.

Sophie laughed. "No. That he's in love with her. I somehow doubt that Lord Highcliff allows himself much time for soul searching."

A few moments later, Highcliff and Miss Darrow returned to the table. Highcliff began speaking decisively. "Miss Darrow and Miss Upchurch will return to London. Normally I'd suggest staying until tomorrow and traveling in the light, but time is of the essence so you'll leave within the hour. The moon is full, and should afford you enough light to travel safely. You will use my carriage and I will secure a mount for myself. They will enlist the aid of Lord Deveril and Viscount Seaburn to obtain a special license and to locate Dr. Alberts' former wife, respectively. While they are doing that, you, Marchwood, will return to Southampton and keep watch over your cousin and track the good doctor's whereabouts. I will head to Bath. I have an acquaintance there, a man who is a very skilled physician, Dr. Nicholas Warner. I shall see if I cannot entice him to Southampton to see to Lady Philippa. Are there any other outstanding issues that have yet to be addressed?"

"I think that should do," Henry agreed. Yes, indeed. The insouciant Highcliff he'd seen in London had been naught but an act. The man before him was military and damned good at it.

>>><<<

HIS EARS HAD perked up at the mention of the doctor and Southampton. He'd been on his way to Salisbury on behalf of Miss Ruby. He was her debt collector, after all, and the doctor in question was her debtor. And the people gathered there posed a threat to the repayment of that debt.

Considering his options, he sized up the men in the group, thinking they'd be the biggest threat. Still, he was only one man and they were splitting into three. He'd need to hire out to get the job done. They all knew the truth about Alberts or Blake or whatever he was calling himself. If he went to prison, Miss Ruby would never see a sovereign and he was in deep. Which meant they all had to be eliminated.

Leaving the taproom, he made his way outside to the stables. There was always a game of chance or two happening out there. Men who'd lost their last guinea could often be persuaded to do just about anything.

"If it ain't the Hammer himself," one man said as he approached the group.

Taking them in, he smiled, revealing two gold incisors and a mouth full of large and abnormally sharp teeth. He knew several in that clutch of gamesters and they were all prime to do what was needed.

"Aye, boys. I got work," he said. "Who's a taker?"

One man grinned and rubbed a grubby hand over his chest. "Does it involve them two birds what went in earlier? One's a bit long in the tooth, but with a face like hers, don't matter too much, do it?"

"They're yours, Fred. Heading for London within the hour. You get on up the road and lay a trap. If you follow the brook, you should be able to get to the bridge before they do," he offered.

The man called Fred rose with a grin and held out his hand. The Hammer reached into his pocket and pulled out a coin. "Do it right, end 'em proper, and there'll be more than that to come your way."

Obtaining the services of one more man to follow the pup back to Southampton, he decided to follow the other gent himself. He was the biggest threat, after all, and it ought to be handled right.

Chapter Twenty-Seven

THE CARRIAGE ROLLED along the road at a good pace, despite the late hour. In the dim interior, Sophie thought how very different it was to be headed in that direction with Effie.

"So you and Viscount Marchwood have an arrangement," Effie said. "And he's very explicit that he means marriage. Are you prepared for that, Sophie, and all that it entails?"

"Effie, most of the girls in the school have spent a significant amount of time on the streets. Suffice it to say, I probably have gleaned more knowledge from one single eavesdropped conversation than most young women will ever have, much less prior to their wedding night," Sophie said.

"I don't mean that," Effie said. "I mean, have you given any thought to what it means to be the wife of a peer? You'll have responsibilities you've never dreamed of. I think perhaps the first thing we need to do is have you talk to Willa. Not Lilly. Good lord. She's a terrible example. But then so is Lord Seaburn. Indeed, Willa. Calliope has her hands full with that horde of children."

"You think I can't do it," Sophie mused, somewhat hurt at what she saw as her mentor's lack of faith.

"I think you are very young and the notion of running a household of any sort, much less one so exalted as that of a viscount, is something you have not been prepared for. I want you to be prepared for that.

I'm not trying to dissuade you, Sophie. I want you to succeed at this. And I want all of those who had the audacity to think you less than they are because of your birth and station; I want them to eat crow perfectly served on the finest of china... at your table," Effie stated fiercely.

Sophie considered that. In the aftermath of her abduction at the hands of Dr. Blake, of narrowly avoiding a truly terrible fate time and time again as she made her way back to Lady Hemsley's, the snobbery of the Duke and Duchess of Thornhill, their easy acceptance of any narrative that painted her a villain, had been all but forgotten. "I don't care. They may be as elitist as they wish. They are Henry's family and I will not hold grudges that would complicate his life."

"Then I will hold one for you," Effie said.

Sophie surveyed her teacher and mentor carefully. "We've addressed the fact that I am quite thoroughly compromised from traveling alone with Henry. What about your traveling alone with Lord Highcliff?"

"I am older, Sophie. I am well recognized as a spinster. The rules are different for me," Effie denied.

"Is that why your bodice is misbuttoned and you have a bite mark on your neck?"

Immediately, Effie was reaching for her reticule and the small mirror she carried with her there.

"I lied," Sophie said. "Not about the misbuttoned bodice but about the bite mark. Still, you seemed quite concerned about the possibility. What exactly were you and Lord Highcliff doing in the carriage?"

"Things that are not your concern," Effie fired back.

"Effie, you are the only family I have. Of course, it's my concern. You haven't been yourself for months and I am not the only one who noted that it was about the time you had your falling out with him. I do not wish to see you hurt."

Effie looked away for a moment, her hands clenching and unclenching on the reticule to the point that the small accessory was horribly crumpled. "I will be hurt. I know that. But it hurts already, you see? Wondering about what might have been is its own kind of torment. So, Highcliff and I have reached an understanding, one that will allow me to satisfy my curiosity. But I harbor no illusions. Neither of us do. Happy endings are not for us. They are for you and your Viscount Marchwood. For Lilly and Valentine. For Willa and Lord Deveril. For Calliope and her earl. But not for me. And that's fine. I have work to do still. There are girls out there who need me. A husband would only get in the way of that."

Sophie noted that she said it almost as if she believed it. But for the tiny quivering of her voice at the end, it had been quite convincing. She started to comment on that, but there was a loud and thunderous crack that rent the air. Immediately the carriage lurched terribly.

"Not again!" she cried out.

"Halt!"

The voice outside was rough and commanding. It was also unknown to them.

"This is getting ridiculous!" Effie stated.

"Now are we to be robbed at gunpoint on top of everything else?" Sophie mused. If it weren't so terrifying, she might have laughed.

"Not today, we are not," Effie said. With little effort and more than a hint of familiarity with the process, she kicked the decorative panel at the front of the carriage seat where she was perched. The panel moved sideways and inside was a treasure trove of weaponry. "Blades or pistols?"

"Both," Sophie answered. "Definitely both."

HENRY BECAME AWARE that he was being followed midway between Landford and West Wellow. He was still an hour or so from his uncle's home in Southampton proper. Every slight shift in the horse's gait, there was an answering shift in echoing hoofbeats behind him. Whoever it was was staying well enough back to avoid being seen, but on a still summer night, sound carried and had given them away. It begged the questions of who and why?

Had someone overheard their plan at the inn? Did the doctor have associates throughout all of Hampshire? If so, were there others in pursuit of Sophie and Miss Darrow? Henry patted the pocket of his coat, feeling the weight of the pistol and shot that Highcliff had passed to him before his departure. There was only one way to find out the answers to those questions.

After rounding a bend in the road, Henry slowed the horse ever so slightly. He eased out of the saddle and slid to the ground. The soft earth at the roadside cushioned his footfalls. The horse walked on. It would go to the next coaching inn up the way, expecting hay or oats. Concealing himself behind a large tree, he pulled the pistol from the pocket of his coat and waited for his pursuer to show himself.

It was not a long wait. Moments later, a man in a large hat, pulled low to conceal his face, rounded that bend. He was on horseback but clearly not at home there. His seat marked him for a city dweller. No man raised in the countryside would sit a horse like that.

When the man looked up, he noted the riderless horse ahead of him and let out a curse. "Bloody 'ell."

London it was, Henry thought. Stepping out from the trees, just behind the man, Henry raised the pistol and leveled it at him. "Dismount. Now."

The man glanced back over his shoulder. Henry could see that he meant to run, but he didn't try to stop him. If the man did spur the horse, he'd fall off it within a matter of seconds. No sooner had the thought occurred than the would-be brigand kicked the horse. It shot forward and the villain simply rolled off the back of it to land in the dirt with a thud.

"On your feet," Henry demanded. "Who sent you?"

"Call 'im the 'ammer," the man said grudgingly.

"Does he work for Dr. Blake?"

The man clamored to his feet, dusting off his clothes as he did so. "Don't know no doctor. The 'ammer works for Miss Ruby out of Brighton."

It didn't matter what strata of society one was in. Everyone knew who Miss Ruby was. Moneylender, madam, queen of the criminal underground along the southern coast of Britain, she was notorious. "What does Miss Ruby want with us?"

"Don't know. The 'ammer runs for 'er and collects for 'er between Brighton and Salisbury."

The memory of Sophie's tearful confession about her abduction and narrow escape from Dr. Blake came rushing back. She'd told him Blake was going to turn her over to a woman who would likely use her in a brothel. Just the thought of it made his blood run cold. But it wasn't any stretch of the imagination to think the woman in question was Miss Ruby. If Blake had exhausted the moneylenders in Southampton, he might have had to go further afield to borrow funds. Or he might have been willing to turn Sophie over to her in lieu of a portion of his debt.

"Did he send anyone after the women?"

The man clammed up, not saying a word.

Henry raised the pistol and pulled back the hammer.

"Go ahead. Kill me. If I talk, I'm good as dead anyway," the man spat out.

"Oh, I've no wish to kill you. But I am going to shoot you. The real question is how much agony do you wish to suffer? Now, I can shoot you in the leg and leave you by the roadside. It'll hurt but you'll live. Or I can shoot you in the gut and drag you into the woods to slowly bleed out unless someone happens to find your worthless carcass first. So talk and suffer a flesh wound that will leave you limping for a few days, or keep your silence and die alone with your guts spilling about you."

"Aye. 'e sent another bloke after the women and 'e went after the other gent 'imself," the man finally offered. "Now, either shoot me or piss off."

It was a first for him, shooting another human being. But he couldn't afford to be followed. So Henry did just that. He aimed the pistol, fired and watched the man crumple to the ground clutching his thigh. "Sorry," Henry offered. "If I send help it will only bring the magistrates down on you. There's an inn two miles up the road. You can hobble there, but it'll take you a while."

Then Henry simply left him sitting in the road, bleeding and cursing as he made his way toward that inn so he could acquire another mount. He needed to reach Sophie and Miss Darrow. The doctor would simply have to wait. And Lord Highcliff, well, for the time being he was on his own.

Chapter Twenty-Eight

SITTING ON THE bench seat of the carriage, a pistol tucked beside her and covered by the folds of her skirt, Sophie attempted to look helpless. Leaning to the side, she peered out the window and saw the man approaching, pistol drawn. The driver of the coach was lying on the roadway, shot presumably.

Ducking her head back inside, Sophie looked at Effie and pointed toward the door she'd just been looking out of. "He's coming up on this side. He should be near enough that you can slip out the other door without him seeing you."

They'd decided by mutual agreement that Sophie, by virtue of her youth, appeared to be the more helpless of the two. Effie nodded her agreement and crept toward the opposite door. She took a breath, pushed it open and then hopped down. They'd formulated the plan quickly and they could only pray that it would work.

Alone, Sophie placed her hand on the seat beside her, her fingertips resting on the butt of the pistol and waited.

Though it was only seconds, it seemed to take a lifetime for the door to be thrown open and a large, unkempt man to appear there.

"What we got here? There's s'posed to be two of you," he said as he lumbered himself into the carriage doorway.

Sophie, at that precise moment, raised her pistol. "There are two of us."

Behind him, there was a click. He glanced away from Sophie for just a second, just long enough to see that Effie had managed to slip up behind him and had her own pistol trained on him, as well.

"I'm a good shot," Effie said. "Better than most men. But at this distance, I don't have to be good. I can't miss."

The man's head swiveled once more, turning his gaze toward Sophie. She could see instantly that he meant to attack, that he thought her the weaker of the two. Without hesitation, she raised the pistol, pulled back the hammer.

"Do not," she urged. "Do. Not."

Apparently, she sounded convincing enough. He stopped his forward movement and raised his hands.

"Out of the coach. Back out. Slowly," she insisted.

"Can't back out! I'll crack me head open!"

"That is not my concern," Sophie stated. "I think I may prefer you with a cracked head."

"No call to be mean," the man said and appeared to be genuinely wounded by her statement.

"Other than the fact you shot our coachman and held us up on the roadside? None. None at all," Sophie stated baldly. "Out of the coach. I will not ask again."

The man managed to lower himself to his belly and half-crawl out until he could stand. Effie had backed away a few feet, out of arm's reach but still close enough that he couldn't risk her taking a shot. Sophie exited the carriage carefully, never taking her eyes or her pistol off him.

"What do we do with him now?" Effie asked. Their planning session had been quite abbreviated and beyond subduing him, nothing had been decided.

Sophie gestured to a tree near the roadside. "Walk to that tree."

The man did so, grumbling all the while.

Once they reached it, Sophie said, "Now sit down with your back to it." When he'd done so, Sophie added to Effie, "Take your petticoat off and we shall use it tie his hands."

Effie complied without being missish. She slipped off her petticoat from beneath her skirts and tore several strips from the fabric. Stepping close enough, she tossed one of the fabric scraps into his lap. "Tie that about your right wrist. Tightly and securely."

He complied, grumbling all the while.

Something about the man's attack bothered Sophie. It registered rather suddenly and with her brows knit from her frown, she demanded to know, "How did you know there would be two of us?" That statement had been niggling at her. It wasn't simply chance or opportunity that he'd halted their coach, she realized. He'd been looking for them specifically.

"Followed you from the inn yon," he stated. "Was supposed to stop you all getting to London."

"On whose orders?" Effie demanded, tossing him a second scrap. "Tie that around your left wrist. Again, tightly and securely."

The man glowered at her but did as he'd been bade, while explaining, "Twas the Hammer. Works for Miss Ruby out of Brighton. She runs all the bawdy houses and moneylenders. I reckon you've got on her bad side."

They hadn't. But Dr. Blake had. They'd been overheard at the inn. The realization made Sophie's stomach turn. "Tie his hands together now, Effie. We have bigger issues to deal with."

"Have others been sent after Lord Highcliff and Viscount March-wood?" Effie demanded, clearly catching on to what was afoot. She used additional scraps from her now destroyed petticoat to be certain the bindings were quite secure and the knots impossible to reach. He might free one, but he'd never free all of them.

"Don't know their names. Didn't ask. Don't matter to me no—ow! Och, you've tied it too tight! Me hands will fall off!"

Effie had retrieved her pistol and once more had it leveled at him.

"That is not my concern. The gentlemen who were with us at the inn... have others of your ilk been sent after them?"

"Another fellow went after the young one. The Hammer himself went after the older bloke. Figured him to be the bigger threat," the man admitted.

Effie brought the butt of the pistol down on the man's head, leaving him slumped over. "Knots aren't my specialty," she admitted. "I don't know how long his bonds will hold or if someone will come looking for him and free him. What should we do, Sophie? I can't drive a carriage and those horses aren't meant to be ridden! Even if they were, you've never ridden astride and certainly not bareback. I'm not even sure that I could manage it without breaking my neck."

The realization that, while their would-be abductor or attacker was subdued, they were still stranded hit Sophie like a leaden weight. "I don't know, Effie. I think I've exhausted my resourcefulness for the day. I'm literally at my wit's end."

And then came the sound of hoofbeats, distant but growing stronger with each passing second.

"Hide," Effie said.

"What?"

"Hide," Effie repeated. "We do not know if the person approaching is friend or foe. Hide."

And Sophie did just that. She was too exhausted to question, too exhausted to manage even a protest. But she kept her pistol primed and watched from the bushes where she'd concealed herself in the event that Effie found herself in need of assistance.

THE DISABLED CARRIAGE up ahead had Henry's heart beating like a drum in his chest. Racing toward it, his pulse skittered when he recognized it. Nondescript though it was, there was a scuff along the back of it that told the truth. It provided confirmation that it was, in fact, the carriage Sophie and Miss Darrow had been bound for London in. The realization left him feeling quite ill. As he drew nearer still, he noted the fallen form on the road.

Uncaring of whether or not he was making a target of himself, he called out. "Sophie? Miss Darrow? Are you here?"

"We're here."

The softly called reply had come from a grouping of trees at the roadside. Hearing Miss Darrow's voice had been a relief. But he still hadn't seen Sophie. "You are unharmed?"

"We are both unharmed," Effie said. "Sophie, come out. It's Viscount Marchwood. He is safe."

Sophie emerged from the woods then and Henry didn't think twice. He simply ran toward her and swept her into his arms. "Thank heavens. I was so afraid. How on earth did you find us? And what happened to the brigand that was sent after you? The man who waylaid us said someone had been sent after you, as well!"

"I shot him," Henry admitted. "Wounded only, of course. I didn't kill the man."

"Neither did we," Miss Darrow stated. "He's tied up in the tress just over there. I hope those are actions we do not come to regret."

Deciding to let that slip by without comment, Henry continued, "While I held him at gunpoint—I do believe that he and the man sent after you were far more willing than capable criminals—I questioned him about everything else. He told me another fellow had set out in pursuit of you. I know it was not part of our plan, but I had to be certain you were well. Both of you."

"We are," Sophie admitted. "But I'm ever so glad to see you and to know that you are well, also. I was terrified and then we don't know how to drive the carriage—"

"I'll be revising the curriculum," Miss Darrow interjected. "That will never happen again."

"It is my fondest wish, Miss Darrow, that no other young woman, much less your pupils, should ever have to undergo the sort of difficulties that Sophie has faced over the last several days," Henry stated firmly.

"We can't think about that now. What's next, Effie?" Sophie asked. "Where do we go from here?"

"The two of you will take the carriage to London," Effie said. "Take the coachman, get him treatment, and continue on as planned. Have Lord Deveril obtain the special license. He owes Highcliff a favor—or several—and he will be going on his behalf. Also, have Viscount Seaburn locate the doctor's first wife. He has the resources to do so quickly. I'll take Viscount Marchwood's mount and seek Highcliff. If he's unharmed, we shall obtain the services of the new physician and then leave Bath for Southampton."

"Where did those pistols come from?" Henry asked, noting that both women had seemed to handle the weapons with no small amount of both familiarity and skill. Recalling Sophie's statement regarding Miss Darrow's somewhat unorthodox curriculum, it was little wonder.

"They were in the coach," Sophie said. "Behind a hidden panel. Which, of course, begs the question why Lord Highcliff would have a hidden panel in a carriage that looks like half the other carriages in London."

"Highcliff is a man of many secrets," Miss Darrow replied. "And most of them are kept in service to the Crown. That is all I know and all that you need to know in the matter. Now, we must all make haste for there is not much time. I'm afraid you will not have much of a honeymoon as you will need to leave immediately after you have been married to return to Southampton yourselves."

Henry bristled. "You cannot mean to go running alone through the countryside after him! Miss Darrow, the danger—"

"Henry, do not. If the situations were reversed, I would come after you," Sophie said. "Effie is more than capable. And Highcliff may need her. She would never forgive herself if something happened to him."

With that, Effie nodded, pocketed her pistol, took Sophie's and deposited it in her other pocket, and left them.

Henry sighed, watched her go, and then muttered a curse. "Saints preserve us all from headstrong women."

"That headstrong woman is the most capable person I know," Sophie mused. "And if Highcliff requires rescuing, he will be rescued. That is what you do when you love someone, after all. Now, let's tend to the coachman. I've no notion yet how serious his injuries may be, but he hasn't moved since he was struck down."

Chapter Twenty-Nine

HOURS LATER, JUST past dawn, Sophie and Henry had left the injured coachman in the care of Highcliff's butler. The man had suffered a knock to the head when the relatively minor pistol wound had propelled him from his perch. Henry had driven the coach with remarkable aplomb, Sophie thought, as they walked hand in hand through the deserted streets of Mayfair. It was much too early for the quality to be up and about. Servants tended not to use the main thoroughfares as they could cut through the mews to save precious time.

It seemed the entire world was asleep, everything dampened beneath a light blanket of fog. They stopped in front of the elegant doorway of the townhouse belonging to Lord Deveril. It was early. Very early. In terms of paying a call, though it was hardly that, it was so far beyond the pale no words existed to describe such a breach of etiquette. The entire household would be scandalized by their arrival, but there was nothing for it. They needed a special license and they needed to marry as soon as possible. Lord Deveril, as a proxy of Lord Highcliff, would call in a favor to obtain one for them. While he was doing that, they would go to Viscount Seaburn just as Effie had instructed.

The butler answered the door after they knocked, sniffing with displeasure. "May I help you?"

"I am Miss Sophie Upchurch here to see Lord and Lady Deveril. And before you slam the door in our faces, know that I attended the Darrow School with Lady Deveril and we are here at the behest of Miss Euphemia Darrow and Lord Highcliff."

She'd uttered it all in a tone far more imperious than she would normally have used. But looking bedraggled and worse for wear after running hither and yon through the countryside, a bit of imperiousness was called for. She doubted very seriously he would admit them otherwise.

The butler sighed wearily. "Please do come in. I shall send someone to fetch the lord and lady of the house. You may wait in the drawing room just there."

Ushered into the well-appointed drawing room, Sophie settled herself on the settee and noted Henry's smirk. "What?"

"You're going to be very good at terrifying servants, my bride to be."

Sophie frowned at that. "Is that something I must aspire to as a viscountess? Terrifying the servants?"

"My servants, on occasion," Henry admitted. "I've been a very lax taskmaster, I'm afraid. I never enforce my will. I never follow through on anything. I've just sort of let it all go... I think because I was so exhausted from managing everything for my uncle."

"But why would you sacrifice your own household for his? Why should he expect you to?"

Henry couldn't answer that question immediately. It required careful consideration. "I think I have blamed him for burdening me with responsibility, but I have also never protested the weight of it. I let my own interests go because I would rather suffer the discomfort than see him disappointed. He raised me, you know? He and Cecile. Oh, I was a boy when my mother died and at school when my father passed. But they were not attentive parents... ever. I have a tremendous amount of gratitude to them both."

"They didn't do those things, they didn't raise you and love you so you would respond with gratitude. They're your family and they can't help but you love because you're wonderful. Because you're kind and good and honest and all the things a gentleman should aspire to be. You do not have to do anything but simply be who you are to be worthy of them," Sophie insisted.

"I've never stood up to them. I've never refused them anything." He shrugged and a slight smile curved his lips. "Because none of it mattered until you."

"Are we mad?" Sophie mused. "We hardly know one another. From the moment I've entered your life, it's been nothing but chaos. Plots and criminals and murder... murders, as it stands. More than one. And more likely to be uncovered still."

"We are mad," he agreed. "But I wouldn't have it any other way. I'll withstand all the chaos this world can throw at me, so long as I have you by my side. Also, Dr. Blake and his crimes are really something we deposited at your doorstep. I think perhaps we should be apologizing to you!"

"Well this is touching. Do you know what time it is?"

Sophie looked up to see Lord Deveril standing in the doorway. He was dressed, but not with his usual panache. His cravat was looped about his neck, hanging loose. His coat was nowhere to be seen and his waistcoat was misbuttoned. Close on his heels was Willa. Her hair was tied back hastily with a ribbon and she wore a simple day dress. Both were somewhat bleary eyed and Willa had a telltale bit of whisker burn on her neck.

Willa smacked at his arm and moved to stand before them. "What's happened to Effie? Really, Douglas! Do not be rude! Clearly they need our assistance."

"Couldn't they have needed our assistance at ten in the morning instead of before the blasted sun is fully up?" Deveril snapped, crossing to the door once more. Opening it, he bellowed into the corridor. "We need coffee. Lots of it."

"Effie is in pursuit of Lord Highcliff now, somewhere on the road to Bath. Where, specifically, I cannot say. But he is being followed by a criminal called the Hammer who works for a—well, I'm not precisely certain what she is," Sophie admitted.

"The Hammer," Henry interjected, "is an enforcer for Miss Ruby, the notorious mastermind of all criminal activity of note that takes place south of London."

"How the devil did Highcliff run afoul of her?" Deveril demanded, clearly wide awake now.

"Well, it was actually us... or me," Sophie admitted. "There is a physician in Southampton, Dr. Blake, who is a fraud, a charlatan, a confidence man—whatever you choose to call him. And Henry and I have both run afoul of him."

Willa blinked at her. "My word, Sophie, you certainly know how to embroil yourself in a ridiculously thickened plot!"

"I'm aware, Willa," Sophie admitted balefully. "Quite well aware, in fact. And now we are here, at Effie's insistence, because we require assistance in several ways."

"First," Henry said, "We need to obtain a special license. Highcliff stated you'd be able to procure one for us."

Deveril glowered at him. "I'm beginning to understand why Highcliff hates those words. But go on."

"Secondly, we must seek out Viscount Seaburn so that he can locate a woman, a Mrs. Alberts, who was poisoned by her physician husband a few years ago but miraculously survived," Henry continued.

"Why do you need to find this woman?" Willa asked.

"Because the doctor she was married to, who attempted to murder her after borrowing heavily against the annuity she'd received from her first husband, is the same doctor Sophie told you about now practicing medicine in Southampton under the name of Dr. Richard

Blake… and he is currently treating my cousin, Lady Philippa Mere-dith, daughter of my uncle, the Duke of Thornhill. The doctor has also murdered a local apothecary who was assisting us, and he abducted Sophie yesterday but she managed to escape. During that abduction he also revealed to her that he had poisoned another young woman he had married in Salisbury while calling himself Dr. Albert Evans. And he admitted to poisoning Lady Parkhurst who was to be Sophie's employer because he didn't want a paid companion nosing about."

"How on earth did you get pulled into all of this, Sophie?" Willa asked in dismay.

"It is a very long story. Suffice it to say, the doctor will be hoisted on his own petard. Without my position with Lady Parkhurst, I was in need of rescuing and Henry was there—ready to rescue me. And then once I met Philippa, I knew something was terribly wrong. As we began to look into her treatment and this doctor, everything else sort of fell into place."

"Which does not explain," Deveril pointed out, "why Miss Darrow is hying off into the countryside after Highcliff or what the hell Miss Ruby, a key figure in the criminal underworld of this county, is doing involved in any of this. Any insights on that, Marchwood?"

Henry nodded and explained, "Unfortunately, the doctor owes a great deal of money to Miss Ruby and her underlings. No doubt, she would prefer that we not see him sent to prison as it might hamper his ability to repay her. One of her underlings, by sheer circumstance, happened to be at the inn where we met up with Miss Darrow and Lord Highcliff last night. He overheard our plan and made arrange-ments to have us all… well—"

"Killed," Sophie interjected. "No point in prettying it up now. We were to be murdered to protect Dr. Blake so that he will be able to marry Philippa and pay his debts."

Willa and Lord Deveril blinked. Finally, it was Willa who spoke, directing her comment to Sophie. "You've only been gone from

London for four days."

"I've been very busy," Sophie answered. "They were very eventful days."

"I should think they would have to be," Lord Deveril deadpanned.

Willa, unable to tolerate the chaos any longer, took charge. "Douglas, go to the archbishop. Beg, borrow and steal if need be, but get them that special license. I shall get Sophie outfitted in something more appropriate for her nuptials and have Lilly and Val meet us here. You and I shall accompany the couple to the church to act as their witnesses while Val does whatever it is that Valentine does."

"Right," Deveril leaned in and planted a kiss on his wife's cheek. "I'm off. The lot of you," he leveled a warning glance at Sophie and Henry, "stay out of trouble."

⋙⋘

TWO HOURS LATER, bathed and dressed in borrowed clothes from Lord Deveril that were only slightly ill-fitting, Henry stood next to Lord Deveril and the cleric. Across from them, waiting expectantly, were Lady Deveril and her half-sister, Viscountess Seaburn. From the moment they'd deposited Lord Highcliff's coachman at the former's townhouse, it had been a flurry of activity. Apparently, Viscount Seaburn was very good at whatever it was he did because he'd already located the former wife of Dr. Alberts and had made arrangements to escort her to Southampton to make her claims, backed by several peers of the realm, to the authorities there. They would leave the following morning in a caravan of coaches. He did not, by any stretch of the imagination, presume it would go off without a hitch. There was still ample time and unlimited opportunities for things to go awry.

But what he wanted more than anything was to see Sophie. Lady Deveril had spirited her away from him after their debriefing and he had not seen or spoken to her since. He'd made a brief stop at a jeweler to obtain a ring for her.

As rings went, it wasn't overly ornate or ostentatious. He'd elected to go with small and delicate, the thin gold band topped with a filigreed setting set with one diamond and one sapphire along with a few minuscule pearls.

The church doors opened and Sophie stepped inside. At first, he could not see her at all. He could only make out the silhouette of her in the church doorway. But then the doors were closed, the light dimming and he could see her fully. Her hair was done up in an elaborate style with curls piled high atop her head and others left to cascade over her ears and along the curve of her neck. She wore a muslin dress, the embroidery done in shades of deep blue and gold, with blue slippers on her feet and a gold and blue paisley shawl draped over her arms. In a word, she was stunning. If he were to wax poetic, he'd say she was the most ravishing creature to have ever graced his vision. But he didn't say either of those things. He simply looked at her, drinking his fill, while thanking whatever strange fate had aligned to bring them together.

"You have the license?" the cleric asked. There was a note of disapproval in his tone that was difficult to miss.

"We are not unknown to him," Lord Deveril whispered with a smirk. "We've scandalized the poor man with numerous hasty weddings."

Henry bit back a grin as he recognized it would not be well received. "We do, sir."

"Very well. We may proceed."

At that, Sophie began walking down the aisle, escorted by Viscount Seaburn. The closer she came, the more his heart hammered. There was no fear, no nerves. Just the overwhelming anticipation of being able to make her his wife. After all, despite the briefness of their courtship, and the fact that it hadn't really been a courtship at all, they'd been through more and seen more of one another's measure than most couples ever would. They knew one another in the face of danger and catastrophe—something most people never experienced until well after they were wed, if ever.

When she reached him, Seaburn placed her hand on his arm and, together, they faced the cleric who appeared to not be amused by any of them.

"Dearly beloved," he began, sounding both bored and annoyed, "We are gathered here today in front of God and this congregation, who will be very generous to this church in light of the inconvenience their impatience has created, to join this man and woman in holy matrimony."

"Can he do that?" Sophie whispered.

"Do what?" Henry asked.

"Just add things to the service. Will it be legal, if he does?"

"So long as we both say I do, and sign the registry, it's legal," he whispered back.

The cleric cleared his throat loudly, gifting them both with a dark and threatening look. At their silence, he continued. "This honorable estate, instituted by God in the time of man's innocence..." And from that point forward, every word was unintelligible. Uttered at a speed and volume, rather like someone skimming through a text to find the pertinent part, which rendered it completely incomprehensible.

"Ah, here we go," he said. "Are there any impediments to declare."

There was not a sound in the church. Everyone present had been stunned to silence.

"All right, with no impediments... wilt thou have this woman to be thy wedded wife, live together under God's ordinance and all that?"

Henry blinked at him for a moment. It was only an elbow to the ribs from Deveril that cleared his stunned stupor.

"Just say yes, Marchwood."

"Yes," Henry said. Then more enthusiastically. "Yes."

The cleric rolled his eyes. "Wilt thou have this man to be thy lawfully wedded husband, live together in God's ordinance… I'd mention obey but the lot of you preclude such a sentiment."

Sophie's lips were pursed in a mixture of amusement and disapproval, but she managed to utter, "Yes. I will."

"There's more," the cleric said, waving his hand over the book of common prayer he was reading from. "But there is no one to give you away as I understand it?"

"I have no guardians," she said. "But I am of the age of consent."

"Fine," he said, clearly uninterested in the details. "Then I pronounce you husband and wife. We shall sign the registry and be done."

Moments later, they were all standing together outside the church. "That was the strangest wedding I've ever attended," Lilly stated. "And my own was somewhat unusual."

"Doesn't matter if it's strange," Deveril pointed out. "Only if it's binding. The man might be eccentric, temperamental and unpleasant but he is a cleric."

"We don't have a wedding breakfast, but I'm certain if you wish it, we can whip something up," Willa offered.

Deveril shook his head. "They don't want a breakfast."

"But they must have a wedding breakfast!" Lilly insisted, linking arms with her half-sister.

Seaburn stepped in, claiming his wife's other arm. "They have twenty hours before we have to depart for Southampton, Lilly. Do you really think they want to spend it with us?"

"Oh," she said. "Well, in such succinct terms, I think we will forgo the wedding breakfast and plan to have a celebration at a later date."

And then the foursome separated, Lord and Lady Deveril in one direction, Viscount and Lady Seaburn in another. He and Sophie were alone outside the church.

"Where shall we go?" She asked.

"I do have a house in London but it is not… the servants were not told we were coming to town and it will not be ready. So Mivart's?"

"I've never stayed in a hotel before. I suppose it's a day for firsts, isn't it?"

His blood heated at the slightly risqué double entendre. "You're very bold for a new bride, Viscountess Marchwood."

She grinned. "I like the sound of that... not because it's a title. But because it's your title. Are we really married, do you think?"

"We'd better be," he stated as he hailed a hack. "Or that cleric will not be receiving his sizable donation. Do you want another wedding? Later, when things are not so harried? Traditional with orange blossoms and the whole of it?"

She shook her head as he helped her into the hack that had just halted in front of them. "No, so long as it is a legal ceremony and no one can challenge it—though I can't imagine anyone would—I think the slightly hurried and eccentric version of the service rather suits us."

"That it does," he conceded with amusement. "That it does."

Chapter Thirty

THEY HAD NOT lingered checking into the hotel. Instead, they'd been ushered to their room with the promise of a meal to be sent up. Since all of Sophie's clothing was lost somewhere in Dr. Blake's carriage, Willa and Lilly had put together a valise for her packed with necessities. Henry was sending a boy to fetch things from his London townhouse that would be delivered later.

In short, there were no tasks to be seen to. There were, beyond the delivery of a tray of food, no interruptions that could be foreseen. They were alone. Completely and entirely alone. And newly married. And while Sophie understood, in theory, and was even quite eager for what was about to occur, it would be a lie to say she didn't have some trepidation. It was the unknown, after all.

To distract herself from her own treacherous thoughts, Sophie took in her surroundings. The small sitting room boasted a fireplace, a settee in the center and a table flanked by two wing chairs that were positioned in front of the room's lone window. For reading she supposed, as it would give the best light and could also serve as a writing desk. There was a door behind her, ornate and heavy. It would lead to the bedchamber. Her mouth went dry and her palms began to sweat.

"Sit down," Henry instructed.

"What?"

"You look like you're about to swoon and while I am quite anxious to have you in my arms, that is not the way I would prefer," he teased gently. "Sit down."

"Am I so very obvious?" Sophie asked.

At that moment, a servant knocked then entered with the tray of food requested. It was placed on the table and then he quickly removed himself, leaving them alone once more.

"You are not the only one to have nerves," he said.

"You're nervous? What on earth could you possibly be nervous about? I refuse to believe you have any maidenly sensibilities," she replied teasingly.

He nodded and then crossed the room to sit by her. Taking her hand in his, he said, "Of course, I am. They always say you should begin as you mean to go on. I want this to be more than enjoyable for you, Sophie. I want it to be perfect. So, yes, I am nervous."

"It will be perfect, Henry. Because it's you... it's us," she said.

"But this is completely unknown to you."

"Well it's not entirely unknown. Simply unexperienced," she said. "There is a difference."

"So there is," he agreed. "I don't want you to feel pressured or to think that because we were married this morning that you must do anything you do not wish—"

"I do wish to!" she stated, her tone expressing all the frustration she felt. "The problem is I simply don't know how to begin."

"I can certainly help with that," he said, bringing one hand up to gently cup her cheek. His thumb lightly stroked the arc of her cheekbone, causing her to shiver. "With a kiss."

Sophie didn't have time to ask any further questions. He'd leaned in and captured her lips before she could even form the words. And suddenly, everything was right with the world again. When he kissed her, she could forget everything else. The world shrunk down until nothing existed but the two of them.

It was gentle at first, just his lips moving gently over hers. But, as before, it became more insistent. Then her lips parted beneath his and the sensual glide of his tongue over her lower lip caused the breath to rush from her body. How could a thing feel so wicked and so glorious at the same time?

It was the most natural thing in the world, like a well-practiced dance. Sophie found herself reclining on the settee, pressed back beneath the weight of his body as he rendered her senseless with that kiss. And when his mouth moved from hers to press soft kisses along her jaw, along the delicate column of her throat, and then over the arc of her collarbone, she made no sound of protest. Instead, she allowed her hands to roam over the breadth of this shoulders, into the crisp brown hair that curled against his collar and always seemed to gleam with sun-streaked gold.

And then her clothing seemed to simply disappear. She wasn't entirely certain how it happened as that gown had been far more difficult to get her into than it apparently was to get her out of. But the bib front had been freed and there was an alarming amount of bare flesh visible above her stays and the very low chemise the gown had required.

"You're very good at that," she muttered thoughtfully.

"I'm very motivated," he replied. A little desperately, he added, "Don't talk. Don't think. Not now."

Sophie giggled. She hadn't meant to. But he sounded so terribly distressed it was impossible not to be slightly amused. "I'm trying. Really. I am trying."

And then she felt his breath ruffling over her skin and realized that he was laughing with her. "What a pair we are," he finally managed.

"I don't need to be seduced, Henry. And I don't need to be ca-joled," she said, suddenly serious. "So I think the first order of business should be to find the bed and begin in earnest."

He rose from the settee and looked down at her. "You're wrong,

Sophie. Not about finding our bed. But you do need to be seduced. Every woman, on her wedding night—or day as it is—should be seduced. Regardless of their degree or lack of experience."

Sophie started to rise, but she never made it that far. He simply swept her into his arms, carrying her toward their waiting bedchamber. It was such a primal thing, to be carried that way; to have that undeniable evidence of his strength, of his care and gentleness with her. Leaning in, Sophie pressed a kiss to his cheek. Then she allowed her own lips to wander over the slightly whisker-roughened skin of his jaw, his neck. And she felt the shiver that rippled through him. It was a heady thing to realize that she could do that to him—that she didn't simply have to be the passive party and could do some seducing of her own.

He opened the door and swept her into the bedchamber. As he did so, Sophie carefully untied his cravat, unwinding the cloth from his neck as he moved them toward the waiting bed.

"Dammit, Sophie," he muttered breathlessly.

"I think bridegrooms deserve a bit of seduction, too. Don't you?"

He placed her on her feet next to the bed. When he did so, her gown fell away, crumpling into a pool of fabric at her feet. "Yes. We do. But you may consider me thoroughly seduced." He kissed her cheek. "Enchanted." Another kiss landed upon her neck. "Enamored." His lips moved over the curve of her shoulder. "Enrapt." And then he pressed his lips to the curve of her breast just above her nipple which was only barely contained by the fabric of her stays. "Enticed."

"Don't. Don't think. Not now," she said, throwing his earlier words back at him. Her fingers dove into his hair, holding him to her. Then he was tugging at the laces of her stays, the garment falling away and only her chemise and petticoat remained. Each one was made short work of, disposed of readily and then she was nude but for her stockings and garters. And she didn't even care. Because in all the time he'd been removing her clothing, his mouth had never stopped moving. His tongue had traced a burning path on her skin, punctuated by the slight scrape of his teeth with the most tender love bites. She was breathless with it already and yet she knew they had only just begun.

Impatient for more, Sophie reached for the buttons of his waist-coat, slipping them free with hands that trembled. Even as she did so, he was shrugging out of his coat. When he'd managed to divest himself of both garments, he eased back from her just long enough to pull his shirt free from his breeches and slip it over his head. He tossed it carelessly into the growing pile of their clothing.

Sophie was utterly transfixed. Of course, she'd seen men shirtless before. But they'd been dockworkers or prizefighters at fairs. This was Henry. *Her husband.* The man she, against all reason and sense, had fallen hopelessly in love with almost at first sight.

Tentatively, Sophie reached out to touch him. She placed her hand flat on his chest, testing the texture of his skin, of the dark hair that dusted his chest before thinning to a slim line that disappeared into his trousers. Then his hand came up to cover hers. He shifted it slightly, pressing it directly over his heart. She could feel it thumping there, strong and steady.

He stepped closer and she stepped back, but not in fear—in invita-tion. When the backs of her knees brushed the edge of the bed, she sank down on it, easing back until she could lie across it and beckoned him to come with her. Then they were lying back in a tangle of limbs. And when he placed his mouth to her breast, he didn't simply kiss the delicate skin there. He took the taut peak into his mouth and Sophie felt it like a shockwave throughout her body. It was the most exquisite sensation. Everywhere he touched, everywhere he kissed, it seemed she came alive. Then he slid one hand over her thigh, dipping between them. Instinctively, she wanted to shield that part of herself from him.

"Let me touch you," he whispered against her ear. "Trust me."

And she did. She trusted him implicitly. Sophie parted her thighs for him. At the first brush of his fingertips over the curls shielding her sex from him, she shuddered. Her hands clutched at his shoulders. It wasn't fear. But the nerves she'd shaken off earlier were threatening to return. And then he touched her directly, parting that tender flesh and caressing her in a way that robbed her of breath. Her lips parted on a silent cry and she closed her eyes. Surely, nothing was supposed to feel like that?

"Just wait," he teased. "There's infinitely more."

THERE WAS NOTHING more beautiful than seeing the woman he loved in the full throes of passion. Except perhaps the joy of seeing her spent from pleasure. He was determined that would happen before ever seeking his own release. He hadn't been simply placating her when telling her that he was nervous, too. While he had experience on his side, it was very different with her. The stakes were higher, after all.

Moving carefully, watching and cataloguing her every response, he learned just what she liked. He memorized which touches would make her sigh, which would make her cry out, those that would make her gasp and shudder. Everything was committed to memory and with every second of exploration, he pushed her closer to that precipice.

When at last she fell, when she let out a broken sob and he could feel the ripples of her pleasure, only then did he lever himself over her fully. She welcomed him, wrapping her arms about him and clinging to him.

Henry didn't make promises about not hurting her. He prayed that was true and that he wouldn't, but he couldn't know. There was an element of that which was simply beyond his ken and beyond his control.

But Sophie, as with everything else, surprised him. Rather than being shy and reticent, she slipped her hand between them and began to unbutton his trousers. Her fingers brushed his rigid shaft and he hissed out a breath.

"Did I do something wrong?" she asked.

"No," he said. "It's right. So very, very right. But if you do it again… well, this will be embarrassingly abbreviated."

Apparently she interpreted that as a challenge, because she pressed the palm of her hand against him. "Did you mean that?"

"Minx," he murmured, as he grasped her wrist and pulled her hand away. "Be patient. It will be worth it."

She wrapped her arms about him again, her hands roaming over his back, her nails lightly scoring his skin in a way that was sure to drive him made with lust. But Henry remained focused. There were tasks to be seen to, pleasurable as they might be. Shifting slightly, he managed to push his trousers out of the way. With no barriers left between them, he cupped her face gently and kissed her.

Pulling back, she said, "I know this is the part they warn us all about. It's fine."

Guiding himself to her entrance, Henry prayed for strength. He prayed for the ability to control his own urges. And then, he thrust through the fragile barrier of her innocence.

In theory, he claimed her. In reality, they claimed one another. She might as well have marked him visibly for all that she owned him body and soul in that moment.

For all that it cost him to deny his own raging need, he moved slowly. Gently. Easing his way and hers. When she found the rhythm, moving with him, it was beyond glorious. And when she began to cry out softly, when she clung to him as she arched beneath him, it was all that he could stand. Pleasure claimed them both.

Collapsing breathlessly onto the bed, he held her close and wished they had far more than a few short hours in that chamber.

"When things are settled," he promised, albeit raggedly, "I will take you on a proper honeymoon. I will show you the world."

She smiled at him. "You already have."

Chapter Thirty-One

I T WAS THE sensation of being watched that had awakened Effie. When her eyes popped open, she found herself staring into a pair of pitch black eyes. That they belonged to a small gray squirrel was both cause for relief and concern—concern because she really didn't want a rodent scampering over her and relief because she wasn't fit to face another human.

Effie moved to sit up and the squirrel scurried away with its hazelnut prize. Brushing her hair back from her face, she stared around at their makeshift campsite in confusion. Highcliff was gone, though she did not think he had gone far. The man was not going to abandon her to her fate when he'd inserted himself into the current predicament, after all. Still, she worried. When she'd caught up to him in the wee hours, the Hammer had beaten her there.

She'd screamed a warning at Highcliff prompting him to turn just as The Hammer had fired his pistol. That warning had saved his life. The pistol ball had grazed his shoulder instead of hitting him squarely in the chest.

Rubbing her hands over her face, Effie tried not to think of what happened next. But it was no use. They'd been locked in battle and despite his superior size, Highcliff had been losing. The other man, having no honor, had thrown dust in Highcliff's eyes and while he'd been blinded, had garroted him.

The weight of the pistol in her hand, the reverberation in her arm when she'd fired it—those phantom sensations were still present. And in her mind's eye, she could clearly see the look of shock on The Hammer's face as he'd slumped to the ground, blood dripping from his mouth.

The snapping of a branch pulled her from those thoughts. Brushing her hair back from her face in some attempt to tidy her appearance, she glanced up to see Highcliff emerging from the woods carrying a cloth-wrapped parcel. "What is all that?"

"We aren't far from a village," he explained. "So we have a bit of bread and cheese along with a bottle of cider."

It sounded like the purest heaven. Her stomach didn't grumble so much as roar with hunger. Highcliff's lips quirked into a smile as he sat down near her.

"Hungry?" he asked.

"Just give me a hunk of that bread," she said.

Obediently, he opened the makeshift sack and pulled out a small-ish loaf of dense bread. Splitting it evenly, he handed her half and then reached in for the cheese, breaking it into two pieces as well. The bottle of ale was then set between them to share.

There were no linens, no china, no silver cutlery polished until it shone. It was reminiscent of their youth, of two adolescent children running about the countryside and sneaking items from their respective kitchens for impromptu picnics by the lake that overlapped the property line of their family estates. How many afternoons had been spent that way? As many as could be managed, she thought.

"That past is gone, Effie," he said. "You are not that girl and I am not that boy. Do not get sentimental and maudlin on me now."

"I'm not," she insisted. "And perhaps we are both different people. But the young and hopeful versions of ourselves are at least worth a thought now and then, an acknowledgment that they once existed."

They made short work of the meal, as it was. Reaching for the bottle of cider for another swig, Effie's hand encountered his, their fingers brushing. Immediately she pulled back.

"Go ahead," he urged.

Effie lifted the bottle, took a hearty drink, but was mindful to save some for him. When she returned the bottle to its previous spot, he picked it up. And as she watched, he carefully turned it so that the part which had touched her lips would also touch his. It was a small gesture, but one that made her pulse quicken. When he raised it to his lips, he looked at her as he took a long sip.

"What happens now?" she asked.

"We go to Bath, get Dr. Warner, and return to Southampton," he insisted.

"I meant with us," she said. "It was one thing for you to refuse me, Highcliff, when I thought it was because you didn't want me. But you do. Don't you?"

"Now is not the time for this conversation, Effie," he insisted.

"We are entirely alone with no prying eyes or ears about. When will be better? When we are returned to London and the walls have once more been erected?" she demanded.

He sighed. Sitting across from her, he drew his knees up and rested his arms on them. His coat and waistcoat had long since been discarded and he wore only his bloodstained shirt and breeches with riding boots. His dark hair was disheveled and the morning light filtered through the trees to highlight strands of silver weaving through it. She could see fine lines about his eyes and deeper grooves beginning to bracket his mouth, a mouth that smiled far too infrequently. The life he lived—his self-enforced loneliness—was taking a toll on him.

"I do want you," he admitted. "I've wanted you from the moment I met you—when I didn't even understand what that meant. But I'm not the man for you, Effie. There are things about me that you do not know."

"I know that you were not sired by the man the world knows as your father," she insisted.

"If only that were the whole of it," he said with a laugh. "I will not burden you with the darkness that stains my soul. I have that much honor, at least. But we shall continue what had begun in that carriage. My honor is rather conveniently flexible in that way. I only pray you do not regret it."

Effie ducked her head, to hide both her relief and her tears. "I'd much rather reach the end of my life regretting something I had done than something I had not."

"There is too much at stake and our time is too limited now for all that I have in mind for you," he promised. "This will not be the polite lovemaking that women are given to expect from marriage, Effie. Whatever your expectations are, you should cast them aside now."

Her heart pounded and she felt heat rush through her at that statement which was equal parts promise and threat. "I never expected anything... so you need not worry for me on that score."

Highcliff reached into the pocket of the coat discarded at his side. From it, he withdrew a small parcel and passed it to her.

"What's this?"

"I know you like to be tidy," he quipped.

Effie unwrapped the bundle and found a brush and hairpins. "Where did you get this?"

"There was a millinery shop in the village. Alas, I did not procure new clothing for you. Only the brush," he said.

Effie clutched the wood-handled brush tightly. "Thank you."

"It's a small thing," he said. "Hardly worthy of gratitude."

But it was. Because it was thoughtful. Because it was him. Saying so would only create discord between them, so instead, Effie loosened what was left of her chignon from the previous day. Carefully and with precision, she began to work the brush through her hair, freeing each snarl. And she felt his gaze upon her the whole while.

DR. RICHARD BLAKE paused outside the residence of the Duke of Thornhill and took a deep breath. He placed one hand to his face, checking the heavy bandage there. It covered his left eye and much of his forehead. Certain that the bandage was secure, he knocked.

The door was opened almost immediately. The butler, beyond a raised eyebrow, said nothing. The man merely stepped aside and permitted him to enter the foyer.

"I've come to see Lady Philippa," he said.

"I've been instructed, Doctor, to show you to his grace's study," the butler stated impassively.

A muscle ticked in his jaw as it clenched and unclenched. The motion caused the stitches below his eye to pull painfully. "Certainly," he agreed, his voice modulated to be both pleasant and agreeable despite his inner turmoil.

Following the butler down the corridor, he felt the servants staring at him. Was it the heavy bandage on his face and curiosity about what lay beneath it? Or was there more? Had his secrets been discovered? He would find out soon enough.

The butler knocked on the door of the duke's study, and upon being bade enter, stepped inside and announced, "Dr. Richard Blake, your grace, at your request."

"Show him in," the duke stated. His tone was impossible to read. It sounded brusque and clipped, but that was the case every time they'd ever had cause to speak.

The butler stepped back and allowed him to enter. The room was a masculine sanctuary. Dark wood and rich leather, with wine velvet draperies at the windows. But the drapes were pulled back and the windows open wide to let in the light.

"Your grace," he said, and bowed.

"What the devil happened to your face?"

It was a question he'd expected and he had a story ready. "Foot-pads. I paid a call at the docks... a ship's captain was quite ill. As I was returning home, I was set upon and robbed. Shameful that the criminal element is taking over so much in Southampton these days."

The duke narrowed his eyes. "It is, indeed. Shameful, Dr. Blake... or should I call you Dr. Evans?"

He'd suspected that his false identity was blown, that they knew he wasn't who he said he was. He hadn't suspected that they'd managed to unearth who he had been previously. "Call the authorities then," he challenged. "I've done nothing illegal. I am a doctor by training. I have documentation of my identity. You hired me to treat your daughter and I have."

"Poisoned her!" the duke thundered. "Drugging her with vile, wretched concoctions full of laudanum."

"Which is also not illegal," he pointed out.

"Well, legal or not, you are finished in Southampton. You are done here and you will never see my daughter again," the duke stated.

"There are other wealthy young women who suffer mysterious illnesses," he said smugly.

It was the duke's turn to be smug. "Aye, there are. But you're not as handsome as you once were, are you? Footpads! What happened to you really?"

"It's not your concern," he answered, and then simply turned to walk away. He needed to get out of Southampton before the news made its way about town. If Miss Ruby discovered he was no longer serving his wealthy clientele, she'd be eager to collect and he was disastrously short of the funds he owed her.

Exiting the duke's home before he could be tossed out of it, he made his way several blocks east, to his own fine but certainly less luxurious home and let himself in. There were only a handful of servants that remained. The butler had long since departed for lack of payment. The cook only stayed because he paid her with opium—the same opium that he owed Miss Ruby for.

No sooner had he crossed the threshold than he recognized that something was very, very wrong. The house was completely quiet. Not even the sound of rattling pots and pans or the grumbling of the cook could be heard. He stepped deeper into the entryway and the door closed softly behind him, not by his own action.

Turning, he found himself face to face with a large, beefy and very familiar man. If the behemoth had a name, it had never been shared with him. But where he was, Miss Ruby was. She had come to collect and brought her inner circle of henchmen with her.

He didn't feign ignorance. It wouldn't do him any good. Instead, he simply asked her trusted guard, "Where is she?"

"I'm in 'ere, Doctor."

The voice had come from his rarely used drawing room. Crossing the scarred wooden floors of the entry hall, he entered that room and found her perched on a settee, a small and fluffy white dog beside her. She wore a wig, as she always did. It was bright red and done up in a style that had been popular twenty years earlier. Large, ornate and bedecked with feathers and jewels, it was hardly appropriate for morning. It was hardly appropriate at all. Her dress was equally dated in style but certainly new in construction. The dark green silk was heavily embroidered and indecently low cut, as her corseted bosom all but spilled over the top. Powdered and rouged, she looked exactly what she was—an aged tart.

"You're looking well, Miss Ruby," he said.

"You're looking poor," she said. "And I don't mean your 'ealth. Where is this wealthy bride you promised? Where is my money?"

"In another month—"

The decorative vase on the table beside the settee came hurtling past his head. The small lap dog situated beside her yipped and then cowered.

Immediately contrite, Miss Ruby picked up the small creature.

"Oh, mummy is sorry, Jezebel. I didn't mean to scare my lil' girl. There, there, luv. There, there."

She'd just hurled things at him like a madwoman and cooed to that dog as if it were actually an infant. "I can get you the money, but it requires a degree of patience."

"I got many things, *Doctor*. Patience ain't ever been one of 'em," she snapped. "I gave money in good faith that it would be returned to me in a timely fashion. I gave opium to you in quantities that could make me a fortune in the dens in London. And you... you promised to pay for it. Time and time again, I've let it slide. I've been generous to a fault, I 'ave! But no more. There's no more extensions. There's no more *lenience*. You've got until the end of the week. You'll put that money in my 'and or you'll find out what 'appens to them what cross me."

He nodded. Begging would do nothing. Mercy was a foreign concept to the likes of her. And to him, if he were honest. "I'll get it for you."

"You do that, Doctor. By the way, your cook 'ad a bit of an accident. She's in the cellar... shame about that."

Why on earth had they killed the woman?

When they'd gone, he went to the cellar first. And then he understood why they'd killed her. She wasn't simply dead. She'd had her throat cut and had been strung up like a slaughtered animal. It was a message. She'd been his warning. The next carcass strung up would be his.

Chapter Thirty-Two

SOPHIE AWOKE WITH a jolt. She'd been dreaming of soft beds, downy pillows and the gentle patter of rain against a window. The only part of her dream that had any bearing on reality was the rain. It pelted the carriage, but far from gently.

"How long have I been asleep?" she asked, placing her hand on Henry's chest and pushing herself up to sitting.

Henry checked his pocket watch. "About five hours."

She'd slept on him for five hours. How uncomfortable he must have been! Yet, he'd not complained once or even shifted about to disturb her. He'd simply held her there and allowed her to rest.

They'd hired a coach and four which traveled at an astonishing speed of more than ten miles per hour. By her calculations, given that she'd been awake for the first two hours or so of their journey, they would be reaching Southampton at any time. "Oh, I must look a fright."

"You look, as always, astonishingly beautiful," he said. "But your hair is rather mussed and I fear one of the buttons from my waistcoat will be permanently imprinted on your cheek."

Reaching up, Sophie found the divot in the fleshy part of her cheek and massaged it gently. "Do not tease me so. I was very tired."

His eyes darkened. "As I am responsible for your state of exhaustion, I will not tease you at all. But you will have to forgive my masculine pride as I gloat about it."

"Have you had any rest at all?" she demanded, ignoring his gloating altogether.

"Some. Enough. I had a word with Deveril. He and Lady Deveril arrived at the last coaching inn just as we were preparing to depart," he said. "We should all arrive en masse. Mrs. Alberts is with the viscount and viscountess in their coach and they are a bit ahead of us, I think. Apparently Mrs. Alberts is quite eager to see her former husband brought to justice."

Sophie shuddered. "I can imagine. He lulled her into marriage with nothing but lies and deception. Then he tried to murder her. He left her all but penniless as I understand it and she lives in constant fear of his return."

"Not for very much longer. We will put an end to this. I swear it. Neither you, nor she, will have to live in fear of this man."

"And Philippa? What will become of her?"

He looked away. "I hope that she will recover when not being regularly dosed with whatever poison he was giving her and that she will once again become the bright and cheerful girl I've always known. And I hope that my family will have made some sort of peace with our union so that both of you may enjoy your friendship again."

There was every possibility they would not. It was a complicated situation, one where they would have to confront their own prejudice and their own wrongdoing. There was a very real possibility that by choosing her, Henry might well have to break with his family entirely. Her heart ached for that.

"I'm sorry," she said.

"Whatever for?"

Sophie huffed out a breath, heavy with regret and no small amount of guilt. "I'm sorry that I may have come between you and your family permanently."

He leaned toward her and captured her hand "You've nothing to be sorry for. Sophie, you have done nothing wrong. From the moment you entered my life, you've done nothing but try to help my family by seeing through the charade this *doctor* created. You've likely saved Philippa's life. At the very least, you saved her fortune and spared her endless misery. And for your trouble, you've been falsely accused by your own father, cast out into the street, abducted and, by your own wits alone, rescued yourself. If anyone needs to beg forgiveness, it is I… and the whole of my family."

"But they are your family, Henry. They are the people who know you best and you love so dearly—"

"Do they know me best? I do not believe that they do," he said. "I believe that they know I can be counted on to manage estates, to fix problems, to take on the tasks they themselves want no part of—they love me. I know that. I don't question it. But I can't be what they need me to be for them anymore. I need to be my own man. I've made my choice."

"Your choice?"

"I choose you, Sophie. Every day. Every moment of every day. Whatever else may be presented to me, I will always choose you."

Overwhelmed by that declaration even more than by their hasty and somewhat irregular marriage ceremony, Sophie simply launched herself at him. Sprawling over his lap in a most improper and inelegant manner, she kissed him with an unseemly amount of enthusiasm. In fact, she rained kisses upon him—his lips, his cheeks, the strong line of his jaw, the firm jut of his chin. And between those kisses, she managed to utter, "I love you. I love you more than I can ever say. And I probably do not deserve you—"

"You deserve to be happy… and to be loved," he said, tucking an errant strand of her hair behind her ear. "I can handle the latter, but the former—that, Sophie, is entirely up to you. I can only promise that I shall endeavor to never give you cause to be unhappy."

They held on to one another, snuggled close together in the confines of the carriage, until it began to slow in the congested traffic of Southampton. And when it finally halted in front of the home of the Duke of Thornhill, Sophie's little cocoon of happiness and peace seemed to burst. She didn't want to confront the million and one possibilities that awaited them through those doors. The unknown response of others was a threat to the perfect moment of peace they had captured.

⫸⫷

HENRY COULD FEEL the tension in her as they disembarked from the carriage. He knew what she was thinking. If nothing else, Sophie's face would always be an open book, showing clearly what was in her heart and her mind. There were reassurances he could offer, but he knew that they were empty. Until they faced the aftermath of her banishment and their subsequent marriage, there would be nothing for it.

Disembarking from the vehicle, he helped her down. Placing her hand on his arm, he walked toward the door to his uncle's home and ignored his own surging emotions. They were his family. He didn't want to be put into a position of making a choice, because there was no choice.

The door had opened before they'd even cleared the steps. The butler stepped back insistently, holding it wide for them. Henry could only hope that was an indication of their welcome.

As they entered, it would appear there had been no need to worry. Philippa, apparently more than happy to shake off the restrictions placed on her by the fraudulent doctor, launched herself at Sophie, wrapping her in her arms as she hugged her fiercely.

"I was so very worried for you!" Philippa exclaimed.

"I'm well. As you can see, all is well."

"Dr. Blake was here yesterday morning… Sophie, his face—"

"I didn't have a choice. He lulled me into his carriage and—he

249

made terrible threats. I knew my only means of escape was getting hold of one of the instruments from his medical bag," Sophie explained.

"He told some story about being set upon by footpads near the docks, but father didn't believe him."

"Where is your father?" Henry asked.

"He is in the drawing room with mother and Aunt Horatia," Philippa answered. "Mr. Carlton has left. Aunt Horatia has ended their betrothal and he has taken rooms at a local inn. Do you wish to see him, Sophie?"

"No," Sophie replied. "I've no wish to see him. I have seen him. Once per quarter for as long as I can recall and, in that time, he has never deigned to acknowledge our kinship. I think I shall continue to honor his wishes on that regard. It's a kinship I've no wish to claim either."

"Philippa, why don't you and Sophie go out to the terrace. I shall go speak with my aunt and uncle alone first," Henry offered.

Sophie shook her head. "No. I think we should face it together… but Philippa, it may be very distressing."

"Oddly enough, since I've left off with taking any of the elixirs provided by Dr. Blake, if that is even his name, I find that my megrims have not returned. Perhaps they will in time but, for now, I am more well than I have been in ages," the young girl said.

Henry nodded his agreement and they moved together toward the drawing room. A footman opened the door and they stepped into the room with its bright furnishings and sun-drenched windows. Despite the cheerful setting, the expressions of the people gathered there were tense and dour. Henry faced the trio with Sophie on his arm and Philippa standing behind them.

Cecile was the first to break the silence. "Henry—"

"Before you speak," Henry said, "I have something to say. You should all be aware that Sophie and I were married yesterday morning by special license while in London."

Silence stretched. He felt Sophie's hand clench on his arm. The tension emanating from her was palpable.

"Congratulations," Cecile finally managed to utter. "I am certain you will be very happy together. I am sorry we—well, I am sorry that such a special day could not be shared with family. But I'm certain when other matters are more settled, a celebration of your wonderful news will be just the thing that we all require."

His uncle rose. "I owe you an apology. Both of you."

Henry blinked at that. "Pardon?"

"You heard me, Boy. I owe you an apology for taking advantage of your good nature and leaving most of the estate business to you. I've been doing it for years and when faced with the prospect of having to run my own estates after mucking things up with you, I realized that I no longer knew how. It was a hard lesson," his uncle admitted. "But I owe my deepest regrets and apologies to you, Miss Up—Viscountess Marchwood. I allowed myself to be taken in by someone when I should have trusted those to whose judgement I had already been deferring for years."

At that point, both the duke and duchess turned to look rather deliberately on Lady Horatia. Under their expectant gazes, Lady Horatia bowed her head. "I've no right to ask your forgiveness, Viscountess Marchwood. My behavior was reprehensible and beyond immoral. I am deeply ashamed of my actions and my motives. Any man who would suggest such underhanded tactics should have been immediately suspect." As if realizing that the man she'd just referred to was also the father of the woman she'd just apologized to, Lady Horatia looked up in horror. "I mean no insult to you."

"None is taken," Sophie stated. "He may be my father, but beyond recognizing his face, I do not know him. I think until I encountered him here that we had never spoken a word to one another. His sins are his own and cast no pall over me, now or ever. And I understand how easy it can be to be swayed when love is at stake… not only the love of him, but your belief that you were protecting all those you care for. It was a terrible misunderstanding and should be spoken of no more."

Cecile rose then and moved to embrace Sophie. "You are more gracious than we deserve. Now, what on earth are we to do about this charlatan who has been making my daughter so ill?"

"There is another woman who will see to his punishment," Henry explained. "Before he was Dr. Albert Evans in Salisbury or Dr. Richard Blake here, he was Dr. Evan Alberts in London. He married a widow there and borrowed heavily against her inheritance. When he could borrow no more, he attempted to get rid of her by poison— miraculously, she has survived. Friends have returned from London with her. They are to go to the local constabulary and initiate his arrest."

HE WAS IN a state of panic. Packing everything he could into a single bag, Richard Albert Evans, whose mother had been an actress by the name of Fiona Blake, needed to disappear. It was no longer a question of finding a new city or village in merry old England to start anew. There was a ship setting sail that evening, which would give him roughly twenty-four hours before he was expected to pay Miss Ruby the entire amount owed. As he had barely been able to scrape together the funds to pay his passage, that was clearly not in the cards.

With only a few possessions, he headed down the stairs. The body of his cook was still in the cellar and there it would stay. He hadn't the time, the means or the inclination to bury her. In all honesty, he hadn't liked her very much and her food had been terribly bland.

A last glance around at the house, the finest, certainly, that he had ever lived in, and he made for the door. Whether it was somewhere on the Continent or he made his way to America, he would reclaim his position. He would possess a fine home, a well-appointed coach, and perfectly tailored clothing. All that was being taken from him would be returned, he vowed. And then he opened the door and found himself face to face with several of the local constables.

"Dr. Evan Alberts?" the first one asked.

"Or should we call you Dr. Albert Evans? Dr. Richard Blake?"

"You're making a terrible mistake," he said.

Then just, beyond them on the street, a carriage door opened and a well turned out gentleman stepped out. Immediately, that gentleman turned back to the carriage and aided a woman draped in black to step down. She lifted her heavy veil and the shock of recognition was staggering. He'd known, of course, that she had lived. It had been in all of the news sheets, even those far from London. What he hadn't expected was that she would ever manage to locate him.

"Sarah, this is a mistake," he said, calling her name.

She looked up at him. Her gaze was unflinching and her expression quite hard as she stated, unequivocally, "That is him. That is the man I married under the name Dr. Evan Alberts. He poisoned me and left me for dead. He is an attempted murderer, a defrauder, a bigamist, apparently, and should be immediately placed under arrest."

The first constable sniffed the air. "Hold him here for a minute," he instructed before moving past the accused and into the man's abode.

The sound of doors opening and closing throughout the house echoed. And then the unmistakable squeak of the cellar door could be heard. Perhaps it was only his imagination, but he could even hear the stairs creaking under the constable's boots. And then, moments later, the man returned, his face ashen and a fine sheen of perspiration on his skin.

"We've got him for more than attempted murder," the constable declared to his compatriot. "There's a body in the cellar. Strung up and with her throat cut... the murder weapon was still beside her."

He hadn't even looked to see what they'd done her in with, but it didn't require a great deal of intelligence to realize it was something that would further implicate him. A glance over his shoulder confirmed that the constable was holding up a bloodied scalpel.

"I didn't kill her," he denied hotly.

The constable smirked as he removed a pair of manacles from a loop at his belt. "Says every guilty man I've ever met."

And that was the moment that Dr. Richard Albert Evans knew that there would be no fresh start on the Continent or in America. He was going to prison and he would likely hang. And any contents in the leased house that belonged to him would be forfeited to Miss Ruby as she held his markers. The bitch would get some payment after all.

Chapter Thirty-Three

WHILE VISCOUNT SEABURN and Henry had gone to Bath to locate Highcliff and Effie, Willa, Lord Deveril, along with Lilly and Mrs. Alberts were ensconced in suites or rooms at the Dolphin Hotel. It was Southampton's finest hotel, after all, and had hosted everyone from wealthy merchants to nobility and even royalty. But they were taking the waters with Sophie at the Long Rooms that morning, while Lady Hemsley gloated over her new gossip across the room. It had been four days since they arrived in Southampton and the fraudulent doctor had been arrested. In that time, Philippa's megrims had returned but had not left her nearly as debilitated as they had in the past.

"Where do you think they are?" Lilly asked.

"All I can say, with any certainty," Sophie stated again, "is that Lord Highcliff's destination had been Bath. He intended to seek out a physician of his acquaintance there, a Dr. Nicholas Warner. It isn't more than a day's ride."

Lilly rolled her eyes. "I know that, Sophie. You've already told me that. But do you think they've found him yet? Are they on their way back? I miss Valentine and I'm terribly worried about Effie and Highcliff. I feel responsible for all of this."

Willa sighed heavily and then took a drink of the rather unpleasant water. With a grimace, she added, "If anything, it's my fault. If we'd just had her kidnapped, none of this would have happened."

Sophie's ears perked at that. "You—what?"

"It was a briefly considered and then discarded plan," Lilly said, waving her hand dismissively.

And then the subject of their conversation entered the room. Wearing a recently purchased, or so it would seem, dress with a matching bonnet and shawl, Effie had never looked more fashionable. Directly behind her was Henry. Together, they crossed the room to where they were all gathered.

"Effie!" Lilly and Willa cried in unison.

Effie looked at them both, sniffed in disapproval and then stepped forward to embrace Sophie. "I'm very happy to see you safe... and wed," Effie replied.

"Where is Lord Highcliff?" Sophie asked.

Effie's smile shifted, tightened imperceptibly, but her gaze became positively glacial. "He has returned to London. But Dr. Nicholas Warner is here in Bath and currently at the home of the Duke and Duchess of Thornhill to attend Lady Philippa."

Sophie glanced at Lilly and Willa who appeared to be completely puzzled but not at all apologetic. To Effie, she added, "Let's take a turn."

Effie linked arms with her and they began walking around the large room full of people buzzing with gossip as they supposedly took the waters to improve their health.

"What has happened between you?" Sophie asked softly. "And do not think to put me off. When you believed him to be in danger, you never hesitated to go after him at great risk to yourself! Now, you are positively icy when speaking his name."

Effie's lips firmed. "There are things I cannot tell you. Not because I do not wish to but because I do not fully understand them myself. Highcliff and I have parted ways... and it will likely be forever. That is all I care to say on the matter, Sophie. I have other matters that I must see to. I will be returning to London tomorrow morning. I've obtained a room for us at the Dolphin Hotel until that time."

"Us?"

Effie's expression shifted once more, to one that was entirely unreadable. "I've acquired a new pupil. She is older than most of my students and will require a great deal of one-on-one tutelage. I mean to hire another teacher for the school and take her to the country myself for a time so that we might close the gap in her skills before depositing her in a classroom."

"Where did you acquire this student?"

Effie's steps faltered. "The workhouse... Walcot in Bath, to be precise. She is sixteen years old and her name is Delilah."

"So she is a charity case?"

"No," Effie answered sharply. "I know who her people are. They are aware of her new situation and will be billed accordingly."

Sophie had no notion of what was really going on. Effie seemed very strong and had great resolve, something she had occasionally lacked before, but she was not any happier than she had been. "Do not harden your heart to him so much that it embitters you. Your warmth, your kindness, your generosity and forgiving nature are aspirational for us all."

Effie's breath rushed out as she bit back a sob. "Some things, Sophie, are unforgivable. And he is guilty of the worst one for me. I will not say more on it. I must focus my energies elsewhere. I beg of you, do not make me say anything further."

Impulsively, Sophie hugged her. "I will always be here for you."

Effie hugged her back. "I know you will, darling girl. I know that you will."

AN HOUR LATER, Henry was escorting Sophie back to his uncle's home.

They'd taken the waters, seen and been seen by all as Lady Hemsley had requested. They had also stopped by the dressmaker for a fitting for the gown Sophie would wear when the ball Cecile was hosting in their honor could finally be held. He was patiently waiting for the questions.

"What was happening when you discovered Effie and Highcliff in Bath?"

They had found Highcliff on the road. He'd been traveling alone back to London. Effie, per his report, had acquired rooms for herself and a young woman she had taken in. They were to be found at the York Hotel in Bath. He'd then informed them that Dr. Nicholas Warner was escorting Effie and her new charge to Southampton. Then he'd simply ridden off. It had been terribly mysterious.

"I could not say. I have the distinct impression that there has been some sort of catastrophic falling out between Lord Highcliff and Miss Darrow, but the nature of it is unknown to me," he said.

"We need to find him," Sophie insisted. "We cannot leave things this way between them."

They had reached his uncle's home. There on the steps, Henry halted her progress until she turned to face him. "We cannot interfere. Too many people, I think, have interfered already. Miss Darrow and Lord Highcliff are headstrong individuals—each of them forces of nature in their own right, I think. They must find their own way from here, Sophie. If we do not allow them that, we will only muddy the waters further."

She shook her head sadly. "But they love each other."

He closed the distance between them, planting a frustratingly chaste kiss on her lips. "Perhaps they do. And if that is so, love will always find its way. We have but to let it. Now, I do not wish to discuss Lord Highcliff... or Miss Darrow... or my cousin, my aunts, my uncle, or anyone else. In fact, I've no wish to speak at all. What I want, more than anything in this world, is for you to go upstairs to our room and wait for me."

"What are you going to do?" she asked.

"I'm going to wait five minutes before joining you in a vain attempt to disguise the fact that I mean to completely ravish you," he whispered against her ear. "And the clock is ticking."

Sophie's eyes widened, but she immediately turned, scurried up the steps and hurried past the stunned butler. Henry followed, bade hello to his relatives and attempted to act like he had a small degree of patience as he made his way up the stairs in her wake.

When he entered their chamber only a moment behind her, she was struggling to reach the back buttons of her gown. "You said five minutes!"

He grinned. "I lied."

She tossed a baleful stare over her shoulder at him. "Very funny. Now that you're here, you might as well help me with this."

He stepped closer, brushed her hands aside and made quick work of the buttons. "That, my dear wife, was precisely my intent." He pressed a kiss to her shoulder just as he tugged the garment free. It pooled at her feet and he lifted her free of it, carrying her to the bed.

"Is it all really over?" she asked. "Everyone is safe, if not entirely happy?"

Henry shrugged out of his coat and waistcoat before joining her on the bed. "Yes. Everyone is safe. The villain has been apprehended and justice will be served. And we are happily married. It is truly done."

"Is it wrong to be so happy when those I love are not?" she asked as she looped her arms about his neck and pulled him to her.

He kissed her lips, quick and hard, before answering. "No. Those who love you want your happiness. And they are responsible for their own happiness, as well. Your only option is to lead by example. Show them how glorious it can be to share one's life with a person they love."

She reached for the hem of his shirt, tugging it free of his breeches until he could pull it off easily and toss it aside. "Then you should remind me of that... now, please."

He laughed. "I live to please, my darling viscountess."

And so he did.

Epilogue

Ten Months Later...

S OPHIE SMILED AS she looked up from her sewing. She could hear carriage wheels approaching. They were sequestered at Haverton Abbey, a small estate in Hampshire near Basingstoke. It was where she and Henry had chosen to make their home, as it allowed easy travel to Southampton and to London. Still, she was overjoyed to have company for the summer. She was even more overjoyed that it was Philippa. Under the care of Dr. Warner, she had made not a full recovery, but was much improved. The megrims that had left her completely debilitated before now happened less than once per month, which she insisted was a miracle.

For her part, Sophie was convinced the girl was right. She only hoped that Philippa would not be too disappointed when she heard the news. The plan for Philippa's debut that winter had included the lot of them going to London together. But that would be impossible.

Moments later, Philippa came rushing in. She was vibrant and lovely, her cheeks flushed with healthy color and a lovely smile curved her lips. "Sophie! It's been ages!"

"I saw you only three weeks past," Sophie insisted. "Henry and I came to visit and we attended the theater and an assembly."

Philippa shrugged. "So I exaggerated a bit! Still, it feels like it's been forever! Three weeks with Mama and Papa fussing over me at every turn. I continue to tell them daily that I am much recovered, but they will not stop worrying!"

Sophie chuckled. "They are your parents. I daresay that is part and parcel, my dear. Where is Henry?"

"Oh, we found the most adorable puppy!" Philippa exclaimed. "He rescued it from the roadside. Poor thing. He's talking to one of the servants about treatments for fleas, or some such thing."

Of course, he had rescued a dog. Another dog. It would have good company with the two cats, a parakeet, donkey and a sickly goat. He was forever bringing home a stray. But since that was precisely what he'd done with her, she could hardly complain. "Naturally. There is something I need to discuss with you, Philippa. I know we were supposed to head to town in the fall and stay there through the entire season, but I am afraid we have to alter our plan."

"You're not going to be there for my first season?"

"No," Sophie said. Leaning in, she all but whispered her explanation, "I'm terribly sorry. It's just that... well, it would be rather frowned upon for a woman in my condition to be out in society at such a time."

Philippa's eyes widened. "Oh, my gracious! Oh, does Henry know?"

Sophie laughed. "I'd hardly tell you first. He does know, but we haven't told everyone else yet. I thought to wait until we know things are going well."

Philippa nodded gravely. "I understand. Mama became that way. After so many were lost, she stopped announcing it to anyone but immediate family. But now, she has little Georgie and he is as hale and hardy as a lad could be. Oh, and loud! Heavens but he is loud!"

"I believe that is the propensity of babies," Henry said as he entered the room through the terrace doors. "They scream and scream to get what they want... it wasn't so long ago, dear cousin, that I was saying the same of you."

Philippa smiled. "I was never so rude. I refuse to believe it."

Sophie looked up at her husband. "Are you forgetting something?"

"Never," he replied and promptly leaned in to kiss her cheek. "And how is my lovely wife this afternoon?"

"Aware of the new four-legged creature you've brought home," she replied.

He simply grinned. "It's the sweetest thing, Sophie. You'll love it. Once it's been cleaned and divested of any vermin, I shall introduce you to your new pet."

"My pet? I do not recall saying that I wished to have a pet!" she protested.

"But of course you do! It's tiny and helpless and utterly adorable," he insisted with an impish grin.

"This is the last one. It's the last one or we'll have to find a larger estate," she relented, trying to suppress her laughter.

It was a daily occurrence, Sophie realized. There was not a day spent in Henry's company where she did not laugh. Perhaps their wedding had been irregular, and their courtship nonexistent as it was fraught with murderous plots and villains. But their marriage—that, they were doing perfectly.

"I love you," she said.

"And I love you."

"And I'm going to my room," Philippa said and rose, leaving them alone.

Henry wrinkled his nose. "We are a bit hard to tolerate, aren't we? Being excessively happy, affectionate and in love makes us very bothersome, apparently."

Sophie put her sewing aside and rose from the settee to drape herself across his lap where he sprawled on one of the chairs. "It's not such a burden... being left alone with you because others can't abide us."

His hand slid upward, cupping the back of her head and sending hair pins scattering to the floor. "I believe that was your diabolical plan all along. Are you trying to seduce me, Viscountess Marchwood?"

"Always."

Author's Note

EFFIE AND HIGHCLIFF

I know everyone wants their story. I want their story, too! It's why they keep creeping into all of my other books. There are three more books in the Hellion Club Series (as it was originally planned). I may extend this world slightly beyond the initial seven titles but that is up in the air at this time. The next book will be *When an Earl Loves a Governess*, then *The Duke's Magnificent Obsession*. There will be tidbits and snippets about Effie and Highcliff in each of those. And the final book of the original plan will be *The Governess Diaries*—where Effie and Highcliff will finally take center stage.

They are such strong, dynamic characters. But they both have such troubled pasts and tortured souls that I couldn't simply let them fall into a happily ever after. I needed to make them work for it so they (and hopefully all of us) will appreciate it so much more when it comes.

Thank you,
Chasity Bowlin

About the Author

Chasity Bowlin lives in central Kentucky with her husband and their menagerie of animals. She loves writing, loves traveling and enjoys incorporating tidbits of her actual vacations into her books. She is an avid Anglophile, loving all things British, but specifically all things Regency.

Growing up in Tennessee, spending as much time as possible with her doting grandparents, soap operas were a part of her daily existence, followed by back to back episodes of Scooby Doo. Her path to becoming a romance novelist was set when, rather than simply have her Barbie dolls cruise around in a pink convertible, they time traveled, hosted lavish dinner parties and one even had an evil twin locked in the attic.

Website: www.chasitybowlin.com

Made in the USA
Monee, IL
20 June 2022

98315717R00154